we are the gems.

dominique j. smiley

dedication.

To all the girls who just want to be seen.

You are seen and you are loved.

You matter.

chapters.

acknowledgments.

Thank you to all the people who gassed me up through your support of my various endeavors.

I love you.

We are the gems.

We are the light in the darkest of nights.

We are the twinkle in the caves riddled with gold.

We are the diamonds in the rough.

We are the treasure beneath the sea.

How do we know this?

Because you must search to find us.

one.

October 5th. The Night Everything Went Down. I never thought I would get caught up, and I would have never fathomed that it'd be for something I *didn't* do. Sure, I'd gotten into trouble many times, and sure, I might have had the hook up in high places that got me out of said trouble, but this time I didn't do it.

I couldn't even look at myself in the county jail bathroom mirror as I stalled waiting for my one phone call. My parents were asleep and so were Mackie and Rachel, so there was no way I was getting out of this without having to wake someone up.

"Let's go!" the officer called into the bathroom. I wiped away the sticky mixture of sweat and tears from my face and confronted my impending doom.

Eve's the name. I belong to the Johnson's, as in the Riverside Johnsons, as in "one of the most affluent Black families in Riverside" Johnsons. Despite being born in *that* family, I don't belong; I don't exactly go with their flow and stick to the status quo. They would completely disown me if it didn't look bad on them. They got better publicity dragging me along and claiming me as their work in progress child than they would kicking me out, so I guess we both benefitted.

Truth is, I was a troublemaker. I did what I wanted and didn't care what the consequences were. The therapist that my dad paid $200 a week to fake analyze my psyche and feel me up thought I was a narcissist who found joy in ruining my parents' legacy. I, the narcissist, had to agree. I did enjoy it and slept better at night knowing my family suffered when I was around.

To be honest though, there were days I wanted to do them all a favor and just leave. I always wondered what it would be like to just rough it on my own. I was pretty sure it was something I could handle

4

considering I had been running the streets since I was 14, but I could never bring myself to do it. I had guessed that one day soon I would get the courage to dip, but a thread of bad decisions landed me in the worst situation I had ever faced, and it looked like I was going to jail for it.

"Don't make me say it again... get out of there!" the now impatient officer demanded. I squinted once more at the mirror and studied my ragged appearance–smeared makeup, a ratty hair bun, a torn shirt, dirty pants, and a sad girl.

I saved the officer an uncomfortable trip into the foul-smelling ladies' room and exited with my hands up and a smirk plastered on my face.

"Do you need to go?" I asked him, pointing at the door I just walked out of. He looked right at it, and instead of laughing like I was doing, he yanked me by the arm and dragged me to his desk.

"You're not funny, and it's not the best time to be making jokes. Better yet, don't say anything at all," he growled. If I wasn't so used to men jostling me around, I would have been offended and caused an even bigger scene.

"You can't do this! Do you know who my father is?!" I kicked and screamed. It was a line that at least three other officers heard in the Riverside precinct at some point, and it was usually enough to get them to ease up.

"Nice try, but it won't work," he stated coldly. I sat back in the chair he slammed me in and sucked my teeth.

"It works every other time..."

I had been in the Riverside Police Department five times that past year alone. It was usually for getting caught smoking a little weed or disorderly conduct, although there was one time when they almost got me for prostituting. They couldn't book me for it though. All they caught me doing was asking a stranger for money. At any rate, I could weasel my way out of trouble with ease, but this time was different.

I took a deep breath and played it cool so I could at least get out of there. I knew going home would not be an option, so I would have to figure out who I could pay to pick me up in the middle of the night. All while planning my getaway, I noted the officer filling out forms, something that *never* happened to me.

"What's your name?" I politely asked the man.

"Officer Rickers," he responded.

I should have known he looked familiar. Aside from seeing him every time I got in trouble, Officer Rickers was the father of a girl I knew in elementary school, back when I cared about being a principled person. His daughter, Jessica, and I were in the same girl scout troop and we tied for the most merit badges. The last I heard, Jessica, her mom, and little sister packed up and moved away once they found some richer fella to latch on to. I looked at him with sorry eyes, though I more so felt sorry for myself.

"Look Officer Rickers, let's just forget about all of this. You and I both know that my parents will kill me anyway, so just let this go, yeah?" I suggested. I stood up and walked away as if I was off the hook when Rickers' hand gripped my shoulder.

"Oh no. You're in serious trouble this time, Eve, and there's no getting out of this one."

Appalled and a little scared, I snapped back, "Hold on, I told you it wasn't me! I had nothing to do with that!" He shook his head and shrugged.

"It doesn't matter, Eve. You were in the car so as far as it concerns the law, you were in on everything."

"But I swear, I had no idea this was going down! And besides, no one got hurt, and they didn't take anything! Please, just let me go! As a matter of fact, call my dad. I'd much rather him ream me out than this. Please!" I pleaded.

By that time, I had triggered the waterworks and the few officers on late night duty were all watching me put my acting skills to use.

"No can do. Daddy's orders."

Just as I was about to kick my begging up a notch, I stopped. Did he say *daddy's orders*? What did that mean?!

"Wait, what?" I asked. He didn't respond, but he kept plucking away at his keyboard and making random notes on his paper pad. I slammed my hand down on the desk and demanded his attention.

"What the hell are you talking about?!" I roared. He glared at me with hard eyes, but then they went soft. He let out a deep breath and instructed me to sit.

"I already spoke to your father. Had you not wasted time in that bathroom, you would have known that," he began. I stared at his mouth, waiting for the "but," and I knew that it would not be pretty.

"Okay... and?" I kept my voice calm and did everything in my power not to lose my cool, but the ticking time bomb in me was seconds away from exploding.

"He said he's not coming this time. He said you made your bed, so now you have to lie in it, and he instructed me to do what I have to do."

I *lost* it. *I made my bed, so I have to lie in it? Do what you have to do?*

"You're lying... my dad would never-"

"Do you see him here?" Rickers interrupted. I entertained the argument and looked around, but it wasn't funny. He *wasn't* there. The giant clock read *12:13 a.m.* and as I watched the secondhand slowly pass each number, actual tears left my eyes.

"This isn't real. I have to go home," I contended before getting up and making a literal run for the door. I almost made it past the five other officers in the room, but it only took two of them to take me down. One grabbed my arms, and the other grabbed my legs and they both hauled me back into a holding cell as I kicked and screamed for mercy.

I fought as hard as I could to break free, but the officers were much stronger and trained for this. Despite my efforts, I couldn't even move until they dropped me in the cell with one other girl awaiting bail.

The cell door shut behind me and once I heard that clank, I knew it was over. No amount of begging, pleading, or kissing butt was going to get me out of this. I screamed to the top of my lungs before dramatically dropping to my knees. I knew the other girl was looking at me like I was crazy, but I didn't care. I wanted-no-*needed* to be free or else I was going to go crazy on everybody and everything.

"This can't be happening," I cried. But it was, and in retrospect, I had no one to blame but myself.

•　　　•　　　•

"Babe, do me a favor? :) xx" Johnny texted. It was midday lunch period, and me and my girls, Mackie and Rachel, were hanging outside, eating our lunch, and gossiping about people as usual. I responded with, "depends on what it is... ;) xxx" and attended to the conversation in front of me.

"Word on the street is Mariah was pregnant again, but she got an abortion," Mackie claimed as she put her long, curly hair into a ponytail. Mackie was always with the mess and she never failed to keep me and Rachel entertained. Of our group, Mackie was the tomboy. She almost always had a t-shirt, jogging pants, and sneakers on, and she was ready for a fight. Despite her soft features, Mackie was the brawn.

Rachel was practically the polar opposite of Mackie-she was short, darker skinned, petite, and very ethereal. School and overachieving came naturally to her, so she was the brains of all our operations, and we looked to her to be the logical one. Since the third grade, I, the beauty, seemingly bridged the gap between the two of them and we were joined at the hip from then on.

Our nickname at Riverside Academy, our high school, was the

"shea butter babies," named after the Ari Lennox song, because our melanin was poppin' and we were the envy of most of the girls.

"Didn't she just have one like two months ago? It's like, girl, close them legs and get your life," Rachel added. We all shared a laugh at the expense of our sexually liberated classmate.

"I ain't even gon' hate though, the girl gets mad dudes," Mackie retorted. "Like that cutie Ramone. Funny thing is, he's been checking you out, Eve."

I snapped out of a fantasy about Johnny when I heard my name. "Huh?"

"I said Ramone likes you. He asked about you the other day," Mackie explained, now chowing down on her curly fries.

"Girl, I don't care nothing about Ramone. He's cute and all, but y'all know I got Johnny."

"Johnny? You still with him?" Rachel gasped.

"Yes, and I'm very happy with him, thank you."

"Ain't he like 23 or something?" Mackie chimed in.

"Twenty-five, and? He's a *man* that can handle me."

"Oh please, he's a bum," Mackie said. They both cracked up laughing, but this time at my expense. I didn't find any of it funny, so I excused myself from the table and roamed the halls. I checked my phone, hoping that a text from Johnny would change my attitude.

"Skip school and come with me... I got something for you xx."

My heart fluttered for him and so I obliged.

"Ohhh okay, come get me boo!" *Send.*

I *should* have ignored his text, marched back into the cafeteria, and went on about living like a normal teenager, but I was too much of a menace to high society to ignore trouble. Within minutes, Johnny was waiting at the back of the school in his old beat up Toyota Camry and in a flash, I was out the doors and we were on our way to a place I knew would be better than school.

"So, what we doing?" I asked.

"Nothing much. I just got a surprise for you," he said with a cute smirk. "Don't worry, you'll love it."

There was just something about Johnny that made me weak. He was so smooth, and he could rope me, or any person for that matter, into doing anything he wanted. He glanced at me with his sultry, mellow eyes and flashed his gorgeous and perfect smile at me, and I nearly melted in my seat as we zoomed out of the parking lot and off into the distance.

Johnny lived on the opposite side of town. We called it "Hoodside," because that's where us rich kids went to do "hood rat stuff with our friends," but older uppity people like my dad referred to it as "the urban decay of Riverside." It was definitely a "different" place to be, and anyone who grew up like me would never step foot there for any good reason, but I loved it. It was gritty, noisy, and real. Reputations ran "Hoodside", not money. You could do the same things those of us living in the lap of luxury were doing without the honestly earned money if you knew the right people, and that fascinated me.

We pulled up to his apartment, and I groaned. I knew right away what his surprise was, and even though I couldn't get enough of Johnny, I was hoping for something a little different.

"It's inside, come on," he said. Even though I knew where this was going, I rolled my eyes and entertained him. He grabbed my hand and led the way.

"All I know is this surprise better be good," I asserted.

"It is, you'll see." He covered my eyes with one hand, opened the door with the other and when we stepped into the living room, I was greeted with the faint sound of plastic baggies being opened and a smell so dank that there was no doubt the neighbors would notice.

I yanked his hand from in front of my eyes and gasped.

"Where did you get all of this?!" I exclaimed. I ran over to the dining table, where his boys, Merv and Big Rob, were bagging weed and pills. I was in substance heaven.

Weed was my poison, but I indulged in percs from time to time. I was a hot mess, but I knew it, and that was the difference between me and a lot of other people.

Big Rob handed me a joint and sparked it up for me. I kissed him on the cheek and made myself at home on the couch, where I freed my mind and elevated myself to the highest level of high I could get.

While I was enjoying my high, Johnny was in the backroom rummaging around for what I had hoped was my *actual* surprise. When he emerged, he had that irresistible smirk and his eyes stayed fixated on me as he strutted down the hallway like he was on a runway.

"Here, open it," he said, plopping down right beside me. I looked at him for a few moments as my high settled in, and once I could get my body to do what my brain wanted it to, I snatched the box from him.

"Whoa... now where did you get *this*?" I inquired, starry eyed. The necklace glistened in the sunlight from the window, and it looked real, but a quick trip to an appraiser would confirm that.

"I got it from work," he revealed. Johnny didn't have a job, and I knew that, but I continued to let him think he was impressing me with his lie of being a man making an honest living. He couldn't be making too honest of a living since he had his goons packing up drugs for a drop later that night, but I digress.

"I know it's nothing compared to what you're used to, but I just wanted to give you a little something to show you how much I love you."

"This is so nice, oh my God!" I gushed. Even though I had at least four other necklaces like it, it still meant everything to me. I put it on, stared into his eyes and we shared a deep, tender kiss that led us to his backroom where Merv and Big Rob soon joined us. I had never been with more than one guy at the same time until I met Johnny. It made me cringe, but Johnny said it made him and his boys happy. I loved him, so I did what made him happy.

After a crazy afternoon, I took a light nap, while the guys planned their mission for that night. I could hear bits and pieces of their little scheme, but none of it made sense to me, so I tuned them out. They always acted like they were about to go undercover or something; it was so dramatic but kind of cute. I came out of my sleep at around 7:30 and sighed at having to go home.

"I need to get out of here," I said sleepily as I stood there in just my undies and a t-shirt.

"No problem, baby, I'll take you after we do this thing," he said. The atmosphere in the room suddenly got weird. They were staring each other down as if they were communicating through the airwaves so I couldn't hear.

"What thing? And how long is it going to take?" I probed. By then, Merv and Big Rob were getting antsy and I could tell Johnny was also getting tense with all the questions.

"Just a thing, don't worry about it. Go get dressed. We're leaving soon." I didn't want to leave without more details, but since it appeared that they weren't going to spill, I just rolled my eyes and went back to the room to get dressed. All I knew was I needed to get home because I skipped a test in biology and my friends were blowing up my phone.

Once dressed, I walked back out to the living room where the guys sat waiting for me.

"All right, let's go," I said, leading the pack out the door, but not before getting one last glimpse of the apartment. I noticed that all the pills and ganja were gone, and the place was clear of any sign of drugs. *Please don't let this be a drop,* I thought to myself. I had no problem taking care of business with them, but *this* kind of business was over my head.

They say the freaks come out at night, but more than that came out in Hoodside–gangbangers, pimps, druggies, drug dealers–you name the illegal act, and the people behind it were out doing their dirt. Anyone living in or around Riverside would tell you that being on the streets of Hoodside after dark was a death sentence that you asked for.

Since I could tell that I annoyed Johnny and his subpar gang of clowns, I made sure not to do too much talking, but I can't say that I wasn't the least bit worried about what was about to happen. We started driving back into the part of town where the streetlights worked, and my nerves eased. I sat back and chilled for the rest of the ride, which only amounted to about 30 minutes.

The car stopped abruptly, and the guys got out with no words to me on what to do. I stayed in, but looked out the window and saw that we were in front of Riverside Credit Union, which stayed open until nine and notoriously held accounts for old people who didn't trust big banks to keep their money.

I rested my head on the window and ended up dozing off for less than 10 minutes when suddenly the doors opened and then slammed shut.

"Go! Get out of here!" I heard voices yell. I jolted out of my cat-like slumber with my heart beating faster than it ever had, and before I could say a word, the car was speeding off full throttle away from the building.

"Oh my God, what happened?" I asked.

"Did you get anything?" Johnny asked the guys.

"Hell nah, everything happened way too fast!" Big Rob stuttered. They were all wheezing, and Big Rob was sweating bullets.

"What happened?!" I chimed in again.

"Yo, how the hell did that go left? Johnny, I thought you said you cased the place, man?" questioned Merv.

"I did, bruh! I don't know what happened..."

They continued to argue back and forth about whose fault it was, all while ignoring my calls for explanations. Once they were all finished pointing fingers, I found my space to say my piece.

"Okay, I don't know what happened in there, but you need to take me home, *now!*" I demanded. Johnny was still putting the pedal to the metal as we darted through side streets at alarmingly high speeds.

"I can't, baby," Johnny retorted. My eyes grew wide, and I went into full panic mode.

"Why?! What did y'all do?!"

"Sit tight," he said before slamming on the gas, as if we could go any faster. We were going 85 mph in a 50 and one thing was for sure, if he didn't slow down, we were all going to be wrapped around a tree.

"Let me out! I swear to God, Johnny, if you don't let me go-"

"Fine!"

He caved, but just as he began slowing down, red and blue lights followed by a siren zoomed up towards us. Johnny hit the gas so hard that the force jerked us all over the car. The chase began and while looking back at the colorful lights that quickly multiplied, all I could think was that I was in trouble, though a small part of me believed that I could escape unscathed.

Despite the constant calls to pull over, Johnny kept driving, bobbing and weaving through very light traffic. I slumped in my seat while a million thoughts ran through my head at once. Even though I never cared what my parents thought of me, one thought kept popping up. *What are they going to do to me after this*? I did some outlandish things, but they weren't *that* crazy for a teenager. Whatever was happening here was on felon status, and since I was 17, I feared that the authorities would see me as an able-bodied and level-headed adult.

Johnny picked up a little more speed, and now the speedometer read 110. The cop cars trailed further and further back, but Johnny didn't let up until there were no lights in sight. He drove a little longer just to make sure, but then stopped the car in the middle of the gravel pits.

The gravel pits was not a place any normal person went unless they were trying to hide themselves, someone else, or something. The area got its name because of the bumpy gravel terrain and the freakishly deep holes that were sprawled throughout the area. When I was a kid, I used to hear jokes about how if you fell into one of those pits, you'd end up in China because of how deep some of them went.

Driving through the pits wasn't half bad during the day; the landscape on the horizon was vast and mountainous and was a constant reminder of how beautiful nature was when you left it alone. But at night, the pits turned into the scariest place to be. There were no lights aside from those shining from your car, and the nocturnal animals came out in droves to hunt. If you ever had the misfortune of getting stuck out there after dark, there was a 10 out of 10 chance you'd never be heard from again.

The pits were miles out of town, a little beyond the Riverside Police Department's jurisdiction, so it was always the go-to place for anyone up to suspicious activity.

As soon as the car stopped, the three of them got out, leaving me without so much as a word or instructions. I figured they were so into their own heads and consumed with whatever they did–or tried to do-that they forgot I was there, so I slipped out of the car and trailed them.

I walked with caution, since we were in the middle of nowhere, but then stopped as I frantically tried to refocus my vision. Somehow, I lost track of the guys and was now alone. The night sky was a beautiful, deep blue and millions of stars over my head shined bright. I would have panicked if they didn't offer some light. There was something serene and relaxing about being under the night sky alone. I looked up while breathing the fresh, cool air and imagined myself gliding in between the stars, drifting further away from Earth.

I was yanked from my beautiful dream when a muscular arm wrapped itself around my waist and a dirty hand covered my mouth.

"Shh!" the voice hushed as he muffled my screams. It was too dark to know for sure, but by the way he was holding me, it had to be Johnny.

"They're here. Don't make a sound." Johnny whispered. I stopped fighting and let him escort me to their "hiding spot" in a five-foot-deep pit that I could barely see out of. I figured we were about a half a mile away from where they parked the car, but I never paid much attention in math. We heard the faint slams of car doors and I snuggled under Johnny; I at least wanted to feel like he could protect me in this doomed situation.

The guys huddled around me and formed a shield that guarded our faces from the roaming beams that shined from the officers' flashlights. We all stood still and breathed in unison as 5-0 ambushed us.

"Here they are!" one yelled. Not even a second later, both Big Rob and Merv attempted to escape the pit with no luck; both runaways were intercepted by a hoard of other cops who we hadn't known tagged on to the chase earlier. While the other officers tackled and ushered the boys to their cars, the two officers who found all of us struggled to grab a hold of me and Johnny. Big Rob and Merv drew attention to themselves when they tried to dip, so Johnny wasted no time in scooping me up and tossing me out of the hole with him crawling out a second later.

Hand in hand, we zoomed from the site, but without guidance, we were running into an abyss. A couple moments later, a few cops caught on and began pursuing us in their cars. Our legs were no match for burning rubber tires, but we continued to run until police lights surrounded us and guns pointed our way. With our hands up, we surrendered and were dragged to separate cars.

The ride back into town seemed longer than the ride out, perhaps because I did a lot of thinking. I thought about how I could get my way out of this, who I was going to call to come get me, and how pissed my parents would be. My most pressing thought was *where do I go from here? How am I going to bounce back from this?* Considering there was a police chase and a federal crime involved, there was a strong possibility that I was going to get more than just a slap on the wrist this time.

I peeped into the window separating the front from the back seat and saw that time had escaped us. It was going onto 11 o'clock and the night had only just begun for us. I slumped in the seat, trying to get comfortable, but I ended lying flat on my stomach for the rest of the ride until we parked almost 30 minutes later. With a little jerking around and some wrestling, one officer got me out of the car while the other held the precinct doors.

"My father will just love to hear how you're handling his youngest daughter," I smart-mouthed.

"I'm scared. Really, I am," he snapped back. We walked through the all-too-familiar building, but this time I led the way. I crossed Charlie, an older man who worked as the head of the cleaning crew around the precinct.

"Back again, I see," he joked.

"Yeah, but I'll be out in an hour tops," I boasted back.

"See you then," Charlie waved. I winked back at him, knowing for sure I would be out of there in no time.

"You seem a little too confident there, Eve," the officer stated. I guess he didn't know, but I knew the police department like the back of my hand. Even without my dad's help, I could get out of anything.

Well, I *thought* wrong.

•   •   •

I didn't know it was possible to cry in your sleep. I surprised myself when I woke up in a salty puddle and had a sticky face, but I was even more shaken up when I realized that the horrible nightmare was real.

The girl there before me had since left, and I was there all alone. I thought I knew this place, but I had no idea.

Staring at the walls was all I could do; I didn't walk, didn't talk, and didn't cry. I just stared. Time stood still while my mind wandered in nothingness and I learned to appreciate the surrounding silence.

"Johnson," A voice called out to me. It took me a minute to realize the man standing at the cell door wasn't a mirage or a sick trick God was playing on me.

"Let's go," he demanded. I slowly turned my head towards the cell door to see who spoke and I didn't recognize him.

"No," I stated. What did I need to go with him for? So he could haul me away to a more intense location where they would question me and scare me into admitting something that was a lie? No thanks, I was fine in my little sad place.

He groaned. "Rickers wants to speak with you."

"If he wants to speak with me, he can come to me, but I'm not going with *you*." I felt his gaze burn a hole in my head, but I didn't flinch or admit that his stare made me uncomfortable. Instead, he turned around and walked back out. Minutes later, two other men accompanied him, one of them being Rickers.

Rickers opened the cell door wide and said, "Eve, let's go."

I stood up but didn't take a step forward.

"Where are we going?"

"To an interrogation room."

"Nah, I'm good," I responded, sitting back down. I could feel the level of annoyance they had for me, but I didn't care. They weren't getting anything from me; they were just going to have to let me go.

"Get her," Rickers said with a sigh. With that, the other two grabbed a hold of each of my arms and toted me to an interrogation room. I had a mind to make a scene, but I figured, what was the point? Whatever nonsense I tried to pull now was just going to add to the never-ending list of reasons they should lock me up for good.

They sat me down in the cold, dark room and left me alone. I learned from the movies that keeping a poker face and not saying a word was your best bet out of trouble. Soon, Rickers and a female detective waltzed into the room, both staring me down.

"Hello, Eve. I'm Detective Johnson." She introduced herself with a smirk and an arrogant air about her that I liked, but since I knew she was about to go in on me, I had to play it cool.

"Looks like we're cousins."

"Is that a joke?" I asked as I examined her pale-as-paper skin and blonde hair.

"Well it *was*, but..." she stared back at me hoping I would catch her feeble attempt at "relating" to me because of our last names. I had no intention of giving her the satisfaction of thinking it was humorous, because it wasn't.

"Okay then," she began. She sat down in the chair right across from me and took a load off. I could tell this was one of her first times at the rodeo, so I intended to make it one to remember.

"Seems like you got yourself into a bit of trouble here."

I shrugged. "It looks that way, don't it?"

"You want to tell me how you got mixed up in all of this?" she probed. I wished I could give her a straight-forward answer, but since even I had no clue, she would not get anything helpful out of me. So, I shrugged again.

"Oh, come on. There's no way you got in a car with those three grown men and didn't know their intention was to rob a bank."

Her accusation hit a small nerve considering I had no idea, and I hated being accused of something I had no part in, but what was I going to do? She and I'm sure all the cops in the department had already made it up in their minds I was in on everything, so I stated, "Well, I guess there's really no reason to speak with you now."

Based on the puzzled look on her face, I don't think she expected that response.

She asked, "What do you mean?"

So, I responded, "Well, you've *clearly* made it up in your mind that I'm guilty of this horribly planned robbery, so just send me to jail. And besides, even if I told you the truth, you wouldn't believe me..."

"Try me."

I stared at her in amazement as she sat with her fingers intertwined. So, I told her my side. All of it. By the end, Rickers was rubbing his temples trying to digest my claims while my "long-lost cousin" Johnson sat mortified. I did a good job of not snitching on anyone until that point. I had no real reason to tattle on anyone because every choice I made until then was my own, but *this*? No, *this* was not me and I refused to go down for it. I had hoped that my sob story would lighten whatever consequence Detective Johnson would throw at me.

"Wow," she began. "That was interesting..."

I shrugged and bowed my head but smiled to myself. She bought it and she was going to let me off and escort me out of here personally.

"Too bad I don't believe you," she stated. Rickers and I both shot her a look, confused as can be.

"Huh?" We both asked in unison.

"I know all about you, Eve. You've become quite the storyteller over the years."

"But I'm not lying, I-"

"You were trying to weasel your way out of a much-deserved punishment and it *almost* worked too. You're quite the actress." She pulled out a file with my name on it and began sifting through papers.

"I *would* have believed you if you hadn't already been busted for countless other infractions and misdemeanors, including petty theft, driving under the influence of drugs *and* alcohol, possession of drug paraphernalia, assaulting an officer, and prostitution."

"You forgot assault with a deadly weapon. The girl didn't die, but she had it coming..." I remarked with a dry tone. She smirked and collected the police reports I didn't know existed and stuffed them back in my file.

"And for the record, that officer threw me on the ground and my foot landed where the sun don't shine. All I did was walk up to that car. Y'all assumed I was selling myself."

With her arms crossed, Johnson sat back and just stared at me with a devious grin on her face.

"What?" I snapped at her.

"You are something else–not *quite* what I expected."

With that, she swiped the file from the table and walked out of the room, leaving Rickers and me alone. Every time I glanced over at Rickers, he was trying to keep calm, but it was clear he was disturbed.

"Wow," he said, sitting down in front of me.

"I shot myself in the foot, huh?" I responded stale faced.

"You think?" he shook his head.

"It doesn't even matter. The *one* time I tell the truth, it does nothing for me. I'm screwed either way." I slammed my head down on the table, and despite the throbbing pain in my forehead, I kept myself from screaming out in pain.

"Well, if it means anything, I believe you," he said to me. I didn't budge, but the one percent of me that was good wanted to walk around the table and hug him. The rest of me just knew I would get what I had deserved, so I prepared myself for the worst.

"You know what?" Rickers began. "I'll be back."

He scooted out the door and left me by myself to wallow in my misery and the thought that I might go to jail for the one thing I didn't do.

two.

*T*he Interrogation & Judgment Day. *How can I get out of this?* I thought to myself. Using my wit or asking dear old daddy for help wouldn't be enough this time, so I had to think of plan C.

Fake sick. Yeah, fake sick. They would have to take me to the hospital, and I can escape there.

Nah. They knew better than to leave a suspect unattended. They would probably have someone watching me closely anyway.

Plead insanity. You're halfway there.

Nah. If I claimed I was out of my mind, they would be able to prove that I was, in fact, sane.

Lie. Say they made you come. Say they made you do it.

Well, it wouldn't be a *complete* lie - they *did* make me go with them, and had I known we were on our way to rob a stupid credit union, I would have gotten a rain check, had my girls Rachel and Mackie come get me, and we could have had a nice night in doing girl stuff.

My mind instantly wandered.

Rachel and Mackie. If I go to jail, I might never see them again.

School. I mean, I hated school, but I would give anything to go to that prison instead of a real one.

My bed. The only place I felt safe... and I gave that up...

My head rose from the table as I had my first "come-to-Jesus" moment. *I messed up. I messed up bad.* Not only that, I burned the bridges between me and my family and re-burned the ones they tried to rebuild. I ruined my life, and for what? Quick fixes and temporary bliss? I did this to myself, and the only thing I could do was accept my fate.

Actual tears strolled down my face and for once I wasn't the least bit confused by them. I felt so bad for myself. I pitied my stupidity, and maybe I was just being a self-absorbed narcissist again, but for once, I was seeing clearer and not through a fog of weed smoke or blurred, drunken vision.

Just then, Rickers reappeared, looking chipper.

"Hey, you doing okay in here?"

I stared at him, hoping that my silence would speak volumes. He took the cue and proceeded.

"Well, I have some news. Detective Johnson ordered the surveillance tapes of the credit union." I stared blankly, waiting for the follow up.

"... so that means that if it's proven that you weren't a perpetrator of the actual robbery, you have a chance of walking out of here."

"I can tell you right now, you will not see me on those tapes, but what makes you so sure Johnson will let me go?" I rolled my eyes.

"Well, I'm not sure... but there's a chance."

"Look Rickers, I love your optimism, but my future doesn't look all that bright. There is *no* way I'm walking out of that door unless it's in handcuffs."

Defeated, he bowed his head and sighed. I laid my head back down on the cold metal table and began thinking about what nickname I'd have in prison and how many tattoos I'd get. In the very least, I hoped to get sent to a prison with food that at least *looked* edible and that I wouldn't get shanked on the first night.

"I remember the first time you walked in my house," Rickers began. "You and my Jessica were in 1st grade and as soon as you stepped in the door, you looked me up and down, smiled, and gave me an enormous hug. You didn't know me, and little did you know that I needed that hug so bad. It was around the time that me and my ex-wife were having problems. I'm sure you've heard the stories, so you know how that all turned out, but I cherished that hug."

I took in his words, trying to find the point of it all. I didn't want to shrug him off because he seemed to be having a moment, so I let him continue.

"You came over every week and played and slept over sometimes, but as you both grew older, you started coming over less and less and soon, not at all. Jessica got new friends, but I would always ask her about you. She would always say she didn't know or that you 'fell off the face of the Earth.' I asked myself *how does someone just disappear*, but it took me until today to realize that it is possible."

"I don't know what to say to that," I responded. He glanced at me.

"What happened to you? What happened to that sweet, innocent little girl?"

His question made me barf in my mouth and if I didn't have a good sense of what was appropriate and what wasn't, I would have reminded him that my life was not some white bread sitcom where everything turns out good in the end. Instead, I just kept it formal.

"Things change, Rickers... *people* change."

Silence ensued for a while, the both of us avoiding eye contact while desperately wanting to find resolutions. We were eyeing each other for a good 10 minutes before Detective Johnson opened the door and motioned for Rickers to follow her out. He left and once again, I was alone to wallow in my misery. I nestled my head into my sleeve and closed my eyes. I inhaled and exhaled, and with each breath, I pictured all the things I gave up when I hopped in that car with Johnny. A few whimpers and a couple ear-shattering screams later, I was out like a light.

I woke up hours later with my face plastered to the cold, hard metal table in a puddle of my drool. My head went on a slight trip while my eyes tried to readjust back to normal and when they did, I looked up at both Rickers and Johnson, who were both smirking.

"Good news. You will see a judge on Monday," Johnson revealed. I wasn't sure how that was good news, but I played along since they both seemed pleased with that outcome.

"Okay... so I can go home then," I said preparing myself to leave. Their smiles faded, and they both looked at each other.

"Not quite. You have to stay here until then."

"You're joking, right?" I asked calmly. I knew it was typical protocol, but considering it was early Saturday morning, I was not trying to spend my weekend locked up in the county jail. There was no doubt that the public would catch wind of my "involvement" in this ridiculous scheme, especially since my family was hosting a huge charity event later that night. The town knew I was trouble, but I always made it a point to show up at these events–and by "made it a point", I mean I was dragged, but I showed my face, so me not showing up this time would raise some eyebrows for sure.

"I'm afraid not," Johnson interjected. "You'll be fine, don't worry. You'll have a cell all to yourself and we'll even give you a plush blanket," she chuckled. It took everything in me not to lunge at her and take her out, but I held my composure because there was no way I would ever be free if I whooped a detective's ass.

"Fine," I huffed. "Since I have no choice, can I at least get my one phone call?"

●   ●   ●

The weekend dragged on and on. I regrettably wasted my one phone call on my dad, who didn't answer, so I was forced to speak to his voicemail box. I put on a show and included tears and pleas, but I doubted he got the message or cared because he never called back.

I didn't have to spend much time in my cell, thankfully. Rickers was on duty all weekend, so he let me out to watch TV in the office and ordered food for me. I did my best to get my phone back, but Rickers wouldn't budge on that, so I was without Instagram, memes, and YouTube for two days.

It was only hours leading up to my hearing, and dread set in. Rickers told me that Johnny and the guys were facing up to 15 years in jail for attempted armed robbery and possession of drugs with the intent to distribute, but because it was their first official offense, the judge may give them the minimum. My fate, on the other hand, was not as easy to determine. Because there was no evidence of me being present at the scene of the crime, they couldn't pin me for the robbery. At most, I'd be considered an accessory, but because I was also a minor, they'd probably send my case to juvenile court. I asked Rickers if there was a possibility that they would just let me off and he said, "Highly unlikely," so I braced myself for the worst.

"Ready?" Johnson asked of me.

"I don't exactly have a choice," I responded, sticking my hands out for her to cuff. When she placed the cuffs around my wrists and tightened them, I felt so little... and guilty.

Both Rickers and Johnson escorted me to the van, where there were two other people, a girl who looked my age and a homeless-looking man, also sitting in cuffs. Rickers helped me in and then hopped in the driver's seat, while Johnson propped her elbows on the driver's side window. She whispered something to Rickers, which prompted a somewhat awkward stare down and then a nod. He then rolled up his window and backed out of the lot as Johnson stared at us with a puzzling look on her face. I couldn't figure out what was going on in her head, but the only thing that came to mind when I looked at her was that she seemed deep in thought.

The drive to the courthouse seemed to drag just as slow and painful as the weekend did. There was a strong possibility that I wouldn't be coming out of the courthouse without being shackled and taken to a prison far away, and the closer we got to court, the more disparaging my situation seemed.

We stopped right in front of the steps, and my heart sank. I knew there wasn't a way to back out of the hearing, but my diabolical mind began thinking of ways that I could flee from this scene and skip town. As we all ascended the courthouse steps, I realized that there was no way out and that this was real.

This was my first time stepping foot in a courthouse, and much to my dismay, it was just how I imagined it; stuffed shirts and pencil skirts glided in packs through the halls laughing and schmoozing with each other while preparing for the cases they were about to prosecute or defend. I had hoped that I would get a lawyer with glasses because the ones with glasses were the most understanding people. He or she would look at my record, then look at me, and see the facade that is my life, have sympathy, and persuade the judge to do the same.

That very thought gave me an unnerving and unreasonable arrogance, and a smile that spread across my face. If I could play the "misunderstood young rebel" girl role well, there was no doubt everyone in the courtroom would eat it up and I would be gliding out of there a free bird. Once I was free, my next stop would be the house, so I could pack up my stuff and hit the road. I didn't know where I would go, but my family had given up on me and didn't want me there, so I couldn't stay.

The doors to Courtroom 3B opened, and all eyes turned to our small band of miscreants, with the other two leading the way. They looked like repeat offenders and didn't bat an eye, but I kind of liked the spotlight. They say all publicity is good publicity, so I soaked up what little attention I could get from normal people before I either jetted off into the wind or jetted off to prison. I trotted down the aisle with my head held high, while all gazes were on me. It boosted the air in my head, but I could feel certain stares piercing my confidence bubble and I couldn't help but find the threat and annihilate it.

I looked to my right and could not place the disturbance, but then I looked to my left and knew why my senses were going haywire. Despite somehow missing all my calls, my father, mother, my brother, Kobi, and my sister, Chelsie, all made it to my undoing. I stopped in the middle of the aisle, causing a domino effect and instantly snapped out of my enraged trance when a court defender walking behind me almost knocked me over.

"Keep it moving," he barked. Although my blood was already boiling from seeing my fake family waiting to see me off, I let the guy off with just a death stare. I knew I had to be good if I expected to make it out of this in one piece. My family sat in the third row, side by side, and it was amazing how uniformed they looked. Dad had a fresh, bare face and donned his three-piece suit he claimed he wore for good luck when he was closing real estate investment deals. Mom looked clean and oddly young in her bright red pantsuit, her hair falling to her shoulders. I had a love/hate relationship with Kobi and

Chelsie, but I was relieved to see them, especially Kobi. He was a lawyer, so I figured he was there to back me up. I had hoped that Chels and Kobi would have my back since I knew my parents were fed up with me, but when I saw that they all had the same annoyed and disappointed look on their faces, I knew I was there on my own.

There was no time wasted; as soon as the clock read 9 a.m., everyone stood up to greet our honorable judge, whose reputation preceded her. Judge Cynthia Basin was her name and putting thugs in jail was her game. She was known for her harsh sentencing, and anyone who she deemed incapable of rehabilitation, which mostly seemed to be Black and brown people, were often treated the worst. I didn't want to judge a book by its cover, but as soon as the 5'3" pale faced, brunette-haired dragon entered the room, I just knew it would be a long day.

One by one, each detainee faced the dragon judge and met their fate.

"Two years jail time, five years probation." -*slammed gavel hard*-

"After you serve your time, you must stay away from your children and remain at least 300 yards away from all schools." -*slammed gavel harder*-

"10 years minimum in a federal prison." -*slammed gavel really hard*-

I would have never guessed by looking at the crowd I was in that I was among actual murderers and pedophiles. I did my best to sit as far away from them as I could once I realized who I was being lumped with, but then I heard my name and I realized that the judge would still group me in with those guys anyway.

"Eve Johnson, put some pep in your step," the bailiff called out to me. I was frozen in my seat as all eyes fixated on me and I regretted delighting in the attention I got early that morning. Each step closer to the podium made me realize that there was little hope of getting out of this courtroom a free girl.

I stepped up to the podium, never taking my eyes off Judge Basin. Her gaze was intense, but I was determined to show her I had fight in me and that I was innocent.

Joining me at the podium was a young, white man, looking straight out of the 80s, wearing wire-framed glasses and a cheap suit that was too big for him.

"Who are you?" I whispered to him. I had hoped that my parents would have at least hired the family's attorney or that Kobi would step up and act as my counsel, but I probably ruined the chances of that happening.

"I am your representation," he murmured back. I looked him

once over and turned back to my parents who were stone-faced.

"A public defender?!" I screeched at them. My bite took Mom by surprise, but Dad remained emotionless. I looked into his eyes and all I saw were two middle fingers aimed right at me.

"Miss Johnson," Judge Basin called to me. "If you please..."

I continued my stare off with my father until she called my name again. This time there was impatience and the threat of a petty charge behind it, so I gave her my attention.

"Yes, your most honorable one?" I bowed. I heard a few snickers in the crowd behind me, but she was not entertained, so I straightened up and addressed her a second time.

"Yes ma'am?"

"That's better," she smirked. "Miss Johnson, I have reviewed your file and you've gotten yourself into a lot of trouble these past couple years. I will give you a courtesy I don't give other people." She looked down at my file and then looked back up at me.

"Do you want to explain yourself?"

YES. Yes, I do.

I nodded, took a deep breath, and began.

"Well it all started..."

So, I told her a smattering of truths and embellishments that would make me look like a naïve little rebel who just wanted attention from her fake ass family, but in much nicer, more appropriate terms. Since she had already seen my file, I had to make sure that what I was telling her was believable.

I looked at Judge Basin with remorseful eyes, hoping that she would show signs of compassion or empathy.

"Hmmm," she said with a soft voice. She closed her eyes and ingested my half-truth soup. She took her time tasting and swallowing every word I spoke, and when she finished savoring the taste, she stared at me and smiled.

"Now I'll begin sentencing." The switch up was so cold, I could sense everyone behind me shiver while in shock. If I didn't know any better, I would have thought she was patronizing me or something, like all she wanted to do was egg me on and make me think I had a fighting chance.

"Wait, hold on," I blurted out. The entire courtroom stared at me, including my inexperienced and badly dressed defender, and once again, it made me uncomfortable.

"You have something more to add, Miss Johnson?" she huffed. Her face alone told me she was not willing to entertain anything else I said, but the stubborn bull in me told me to speak up once more.

"Yeah, I do. I hardly think it's fair to send me off to some prison for a crime I didn't commit." She cut her eyes at me and gave me a confused look.

"Oh, honey. I know you are unfamiliar with the law, but in the eyes of it, you were a part of this crime. Even still, you had marijuana in your system, and you ran from the police. That insinuates guilt."

"But I'm not guilty! I'm *telling* you I'm not. I ran because I didn't think I had a choice."

"And what made you believe that you didn't have a choice?"

"Because if I surrendered, I'd still be looking at you." The room fell still for a few moments. Not so much as a cough could break the tension rising between Judge Dragon and me.

"I'm sorry you believe that, but surely if you would have-"

"No, I *know* that. And surely nothing. I could have given in, told the cops everything I knew and *still* would have been standing here because, like you said, in the eyes of the law I was still a part of this crime," I snarled. We continued the biggest showdown of the day, eye wrestling one another until one of us gave in.

"Miss Johnson, I will get to the point. The state is prepared to offer you a chance to make things right. Since you are a minor and it was concluded that you were not involved in the perpetration of the crime, you will not serve time in an adult prison," she began. I let out a relieved sigh but braced myself because I knew there was a caveat.

"But since you are considered an accessory to this federal offense, you had drugs in your system, and your file doesn't do your little story any justice, you will be required to serve at a juvenile detention center until your 18th birthday."

The muscles in my mouth began to spasm out of control until words poured out in word vomit. I said a lot of things–an awful lot of things–but the point I was trying to make was that I would not do any amount of time at any type of center.

"You're going to have to drag me out of here because I'm not going anywhere near a detention center," I stated. The bailiff murmured some code word into his walkie talkie and soon enough two officers appeared and dragged me right out of there.

"You can't be serious!" I yelled as the officers detained me. "You can't do this to me! I'm sorry, what don't you understand?! Please!"

"You don't have a choice in the matter, Miss Johnson. Don't do the crime if you can't do the time."

The sound of her gavel slamming before she welcomed her next case rang through the courtroom, and that was it. In one fluid motion, I was being swept out of the courtroom in cuffs. I tried to get one more look at my parents before the door closed on me for good, but when I did, I saw nothing; Mom and Dad both sat emotionless as they avoided watching their youngest daughter being herded out of the door by strangers. I blew it; the last bridge was burned and there was no salvaging it.

The sun kissed my skin, but I couldn't appreciate it. Fear and regret took over my blood and ran through my veins as I was hauled into the transport van to be taken back to the precinct and be processed out.

Weeps of sorrow and grief filled the van, and they all came from me. There was another girl who got sentenced right before me in the van too, and she was eyeballing me like I was making an unnecessary scene or something. She looked at me with pure disgust and agitation as I let the world know that I could not handle what I had coming to me.

"What do I have to do to get out of this?" I asked the driver. He looked back at me and then faced front without a word.

"You can save your cry baby tears because none of it matters anyway," the girl snarled at me. Her words prompted more tears and outrage before I exhausted myself of all emotion.

While throwing my fit, Rickers had made his way back into the van, this time in the passenger's seat, but he stalled the driver from driving off until I pulled it together.

"Eve..." he began.

"Don't say anything to me. I don't want to hear it," I pouted.

"No, I'm going to say what I need to, and you will listen," he asserted. I looked at his eyes through the rearview mirror and felt his power and sensed his seriousness.

"Eve, you're going to be fine. Truth is, you got the best deal you could."

I found that hard to accept considering the *best* deal would have been to let me go free, but like I kept hearing that day, the law saw me as an accomplice, and you can't argue with that. I scuffed and rolled my eyes, but then my heart sank when I realized just how long I would be away for.

"Seven months may seem like a long time, but time will come and go; you'll be out soon, as long as you do what you're supposed to do."

I glared at him. "Is that supposed to make me feel better?"

"Well it's *supposed* to..." he responded.

"Well, I have to say, you're doing a marvelous job of making things worse," I retorted.

"I should slap the shit out you," the girl spoke up.

I slowly turned around to look her in the eyes like I had nothing to lose, and said, "Excuse me?"

"You heard me. You just a privileged little shit and you deserve to get yo' ass whooped."

My heart was beating fast, but I wasn't going to let this irrelevant trash know that she scared me.

"Oh, and I bet you want to be the one to do it, huh?" I hissed.

"Trust me, if I wasn't risking getting more time by slamming your face into the window, you would be in the middle of getting yo' ass tagged right now."

"Girls, enough," Rickers imposed.

"I wish you would touch me. My father would-" I began. I couldn't finish because the realization set in–my father wasn't going to do anything if she beat my ass and that all of this was in fact *his* doing. He was trying to teach me a lesson, and it was a very hard pill to swallow.

"Yo' daddy ain't gon' do nothing to me. He don't even want nothing to do with you," the girl egged on.

"Tatiana, *enough*!" Rickers interjected again. She got the message loud and clear this time, and so did I. I kept my mouth shut for the rest of the ride back to the precinct and wrestled with the fact that I was no longer free, but under the watch and care of the system I tried so hard to play.

three.

The Transfer. Tatiana and I sat side by side, eyeballing each other and exchanging nonverbal insults while Rickers processed our transfer paperwork. She was a stockier girl and had a good half a foot on me height-wise, but the biggest thing that made her intimidating was her scowl. When she frowned, she looked like she could become rabid at any moment. However, when she spoke, it was hard to take her seriously. She had a higher-pitched voice and talked like she stopped going to school after fifth grade. We continued to judge each other quietly, and before I decided to ignore her like the irrelevant mess that she was, I noticed how dirty she looked. It was like she had been rolling around in dirt before getting caught for whatever she got caught for.

"So, what's your deal? Why you got so many sticks up yo' ass?" Tatiana picked on me.

"I have no deal, and I have as many sticks up my ass as your mom does," I responded.

That didn't sit well with her. She busted me upside my head so hard, I couldn't do anything else but feel the pain and shield myself as she wailed on me. I hit a soft spot, but as long as she dogged me, I would dog her. Rickers and the neighboring officer jumped up from their desks and broke us up. The other officer hauled Tatiana to another area, while Rickers calmed me down.

"You need to control your mouth," he insisted.

I shrugged, "She needs to control herself, period. She came at me first!"

"It doesn't matter. You responded, and it was below the belt," he went on.

"How?!"

So, apparently, Tatiana's mom was notorious for having "sticks" up her ass. She was just as known in five surrounding counties for causing trouble as I was, except they always picked her up disoriented, half naked, and with pockets full of crinkled up twenty-dollar bills.

"Well how was I supposed to know that?" I shrugged again. Rickers gave me a disapproving look and continued typing away. I watched him as he completed our paperwork.

"Could you be any more eager?" I asked. He was typing so quickly, I would have thought he didn't like my company. He glanced at me, confused.

"I'm not eager, I'm on a deadline. We have to get you girls out of here by one o'clock today." I read the clock–it read 12:30. I looked down at my hands that desperately needed a manicure and remembered that I had an appointment on Saturday that I missed because I was locked up. Then I thought of the many days, weeks, and months I would have to go without manicures, cable TV, and my own room and became even more disheartened.

"I will never survive this," I moaned.

"You'll be fine. It's not as bad as you think, and besides, at least you'll know someone," Rickers attested. I shot him a perplexed look.

"Know someone? Like who?!" Just then, Tatiana, who had a smile on her face, came marching out of another room with a grape soda in hand.

"Nope, uh-uh. No way! You're not talking about *her*, are you?!" I probed. Rickers and the other officer smirked at each other.

"That's right, princess. You're stuck with me for the next seven months," Tatiana jested while sticking her tongue out at me. I let out the loudest groan I could, while Tatiana cackled and Rickers finished processing us out.

"All done."

My eyes widened as I watched Rickers retrieve the documents sealing my fate as a juvenile delinquent from the printer. He handed the papers to the driver from earlier, who then looked at me and Tatiana and motioned for us to follow him.

My body did what it was told, but my mind was thinking of everything else. *What was I going to do in kid prison? How was I going to survive? Will I survive?*

Rickers did his best to persuade me that seven months wasn't a long time, but in troublemaker-finally-doing-the-time-she-deserves time, it was an eternity. I tried to keep the atmosphere lighthearted, though my insides were ready to burst due to my anxiety.

"So, what does a girl have to do to get those papers ripped up and get on the next train out of town, huh?" I nudged the driver. I examined his smudged name tag, which read Tom, and proceeded to butter him up.

"Tom, that's a great name-very wholesome. Is that short for Thomas?"

He glared at me. "No, it's short for get in the van."

I gulped and bowed my head as I inched my way towards the van that would take me and Tatiana the pest to our new home for the next several months. I had epiphanies and realizations all day, but none as real and anguishing as the thought of being trapped in a cement building with liars, cheats, scammers, and other future scum of society.

I don't belong there. It's not me, I thought. It wouldn't be fair to send me to a place that was better suited for an actual threat like Tatiana or any of the other girls I was about to meet. I hadn't realized I was quivering in my seat until Tatiana tapped me on the shoulder and pointed it out.

"Chill out, princess. Enjoy your time now because you ain't seen nothing yet."

I went into full-blown panic mode and was not afraid to show it. Tatiana sat behind me giggling at the scene I created, while Rickers and Tom tried to suppress me.

"I can't-I can't do it, Rickers. I will die in there!" I insisted. He did his best to calm me down, but he still couldn't handle me. Tom had long given up and was sitting in the front seat, smoking a cigarette. While I was getting more worked up, I could tell he was getting calmer.

"Listen here. Eve, is it?" Tom spoke. I stared at him for a moment and nodded.

"I don't know what or who you think you're dealing with. All that tantrum throwing may have worked in the past, but it won't work now and it sure enough won't work when you get to the center. They don't play there. It's best you get it together because if you pull this nonsense once you get in, your time will be worse than you can imagine."

I stared at him in utter horror as I digested his words, but a part of me still believed that I could get away with *some* stuff while in the "kid pen." Rickers, who had long taken his hands off of me, was relieved-not only because I was finally calm, but that it seemed as though I was finally getting it in my head that this was something I was just going to have to accept.

When you go around swinging your balls like yours are the biggest thinking you can protect yourself from getting them chopped off, the trouble you find can rise above your head. All I knew was that I was no longer Eve Johnson of the Riverside Johnsons-I was just Eve, a crap stain on the musty cloth of society.

I hung my head low as Rickers closed the van door. Tatiana, who hadn't uttered a single peep to me since Tom intervened, sat behind me quietly. For a moment, I wondered what she had even done to get sent to the center and how she was feeling, but I let the thought escape me because she wasn't important enough for me to care.

Tom stubbed out his cigarette, flicked it outside, and started the van. My eyes met Rickers' and it surprised me to see concern swirl in his eyes. He knew this wasn't for me, but he also knew it would help me. I didn't see it, but if he did, I guess it was worth accepting–even if it would take me a while.

I made sure not to look out the window as we drove out of the city. I knew I'd relive some of my best and worst moments while parading around the streets like I owned them. Oddly enough, the one time I caught a glimpse of the outside world I was about to leave for a while, the only thing in my line of vision was the "Thank You for Visiting Riverside" sign. I kind of chuckled at it because I knew that, even in the short time I would be away, Riverside was going to be so different when I got back–if I even went back.

Suddenly the sight of upper-middle-class suburban homes turned to tree-lined highways. I was heading somewhere between Pittsburgh and Cleveland and was about to settle into my new normal for the next seven months at the Bennings Detention Center for Young Women. According to Tatiana, it was newly renovated and housed some gruesome girls.

I'm not sure how I even dozed off, considering how anxious I was, but I did and when I woke up, the van was stopped in front of a gray automatic gate that slowly opened after Tom rang the buzzer. My heart palpitated and whatever was lingering in my stomach was ready to come up. I was losing control of my own bodily functions and just as I felt myself about to throw up, Tatiana patted my back.

"Oh, for cryin' out loud. Take deep breaths, princess. It ain't that deep," she told me. Her face was blank so I couldn't tell if she cared or if she was just tired of my antics. She was so cool and collected, and that made me calm but not unaware of the fact that I was about to be up against upward of 50 other girls who were in trouble for far worse than being in the wrong place at the wrong time with the wrong people.

I took deep breaths like Tatiana suggested and I latched onto the tranquility it brought me. It didn't ease every nerve, but it was helping me get in the right headspace for what lied ahead for me.

We had a longer drive up to the detention center after entering the gates, and it was only after I looked through the windshield, I realized that we had only passed one of a few gates.

"With all these gates, you would think they were trying to keep people in here or something," I joked. Tatiana giggled and Tom scuffed, still letting a smile show. The amount of initial security the place had seemed over the top and unnecessary considering who was being held there. It wasn't like there was a bunch of 250-pound men up in there causing riots every five minutes. Then I realized the gates might have been reactionary and not included in the initial plans for the place.

"You'd be surprised how many girls they have to chase after," Tom chimed in, looking back at Tatiana through the rearview mirror.

I looked at Tatiana, and she nodded and smiled to herself. I smiled to myself too as I imagined Tatiana jumping fence after fence, and I knew that she was one of the "many girls" who tried their hand at escaping.

We pulled into the second set of gates and the center was getting bigger. It was huge and did in fact look brand new, but just because the outside looked presentable didn't mean the inside was. I marveled at the bright, unweathered red brick structure and the nicely trimmed lawn, but snapped out of it when I remembered that I was there to serve time.

Somehow, time went twice as slow as we pulled up and when I found myself only a few hundred feet from the front door, time stood still. For a few moments, it was only me standing in front of the center and I was stuck in place.

"Here goes nothing," I said to myself as I snapped back into reality. All while I was daydreaming, my hands and ankles were cuffed together, and I was being escorted through the front door. I wanted so badly to imagine that I was on a vacation or something, but it became incredibly hard to imagine having a view of a beach from my room when I walked in and was met with harsh florescent lights and even harsher-looking correctional officers, COs for short, staring me down. I bowed my head, but with a firm *"eyes front"* from a small, but surprisingly loud female correctional officer, I kept my gaze straight ahead of me.

I had expected to be bombarded by a bunch of bitter chicks in orange jumpsuits who had been waiting to get fresh meat, but there wasn't anyone around. A couple guards quickly whisked me and Tatiana to the "welcoming chambers", as in the counselor's office, for in-processing. We passed a couple girls along the way, but they seemed to be busy scrapping with each other to even care that we existed.

The female guard placed us in a confined office space that made finding comfort an impossible mission, which was odd, considering it was supposed to be the one place us degenerates could find some peace. It was supposed to be a "safe place."

The first thing that caught my eyes was the chaotic mess of a desk. I tried to figure out how this so-called counselor got anything done with a desk that looked like it would eat up and spit out whatever you laid on it. The desk was muddled, from the coffee mug that looked like a first grader made it in art class, to the disarray of various writing utensils sprawled on the desk, to the stack of files that happened to have one with my name on it right at the very top. I got out of my seat to take a quick look but was stopped by Tatiana who shook her head and then pointed to the guard who was standing right outside the door, staring at us.

"I wouldn't if I were you. Bates over there is always ready to use his stun gun," she explained.

I looked over at CO Bates, a decent but harsh looking white man, who was looking annoyed and ready to zap the mess out of anyone who tested his patience. He looked like a tired, worn out, angry version of Captain America with a brunette buzz cut. I slowly sat back down and examined the rest of the room. Signs and posters spewing positive messages and affirmations decked every wall, and it almost made me cringe how try-hard it was. I couldn't imagine anyone falling for the false hopes those signs were trying to promote.

Just as my eyes finished its lackluster tour of the room, in walked a woman named Patricia. All I knew in that moment was that she was the resident counselor of the center, but I would soon learn that she had the real power around those halls because she gave the okay to out-process everyone. She was like a goddess and every time you took a trip to her office, it was judgment day. The only way to enter the pearly gates to freedom was if she said, "Well done."

"Good afternoon, girls," Patricia spoke. Her voice was softer than what I had expected, but I could tell by the way she glided into the office, that she could still control a room. She sat down in her seat and I was pleasantly surprised that a nice looking woman such as herself was using her time to tame riled-up teenage girls instead of being seen somewhere, but I figured there was a story to that.

"How goes it, Patty?" Tatiana smiled. Patricia merely glanced over at Tatiana with an unamused look on her face as she said nothing back. I looked to my left and noticed the cocky smile Tatiana donned quickly faded and I couldn't wait to see what she was in for.

"I have a bone to pick with you. You know that, right?" she finally responded. Tatiana just stared back at her while sinking down in her chair. She was in major trouble, and she was trying to charm her way out of it, but by the looks of it, such antics could not move Patricia. Seeing them correspond made me realize that I would have to rely on more than just my way with words to get out of whatever trouble might find me there.

Patricia glared at Tatiana for a few more moments and then turned her attention to me and said, "So, you must be Eve."

I still wanted to try my hand at alluring this woman onto my side, but since I could tell she had a bullshit radar, I simply nodded.

"Well Ms. Eve, welcome to Bennings Detention Center for Young Women. I'm Patricia Donnelly, but you can call me Patty. I'm the counselor here."

She sat in her chair, leaning to one side, sizing me up. She had done this way too many times to count and I'm sure to her, I was just another nobody delinquent ordered to do some time. There was something in her eyes and even the way she spoke that said there was something more to her, like there was a bigger reason she was there. She was certainly pretty enough to be a model. Her amber skin was impeccably smooth and blemish-free, and her light brown eyes were breathtaking. She had a short afro of defined natural curls that made me a bit envious of her. Maybe she was one of those crusaders on a mission to make "troubled girls" better, or maybe she was in it for the glory of it all. With one thorough look, I did my best to size her up too, but in the back of my mind, I knew what I was seeing wasn't all I would get.

"Nice to meet you," I replied. I wanted to keep it short and sweet so I wouldn't be confronted with the same mean mug Tatiana got.

"Unlike Tatiana here, you're new and I'm required to meet with you independently, so with that being said..." she looked at Tatiana and nodded towards the door. "Scoot. I'll be seeing you later."

Tatiana rolled out of the chair and rolled her eyes before saying to me, "Good luck, princess," and slamming the door.

I kept my eyes trained on Patty, who seemed entertained enough by the comment to crack a smile.

"I see you met Tati," she said to me, still smirking.

"Yeah, we've uh, become good buddies," I remarked.

"Well don't get too close to that one. She's one more jumped fence away from being sent to max hall, and I'm sure you want your time here to be drama-free, correct?"

I nodded.

"Good. Now, let's take a look at your file again," she said, snagging it from the top of the stack.

"Eve Isabelle Johnson, 17, from Riverside, Ohio. Hmm, rich kid I see." She proceeded to further investigate my file, flipping through document after document, all the while, her eyes were telling a story of their own. I could tell there was a mix of "*How does this rich kid get into this much trouble?*" and "*Damn, this girl is messed up.*"

"You have quite the track record. I'm honestly shocked."

"Shocked? Why?" I retorted. Her eyes zeroed in on mine and she began her rundown of just how much of a headache I was to society.

"Well for starters, the reason you're in here is a big one."

"I had nothing to do with it. Next?"

Her eyes found me once more and this time my gaze stood up to hers. When she saw I would not back down, she smirked and continued revealing my rap sheet.

"Everyone says they're innocent. And I guess you getting caught up for drugs, prostitution, and assault is a fluke too, huh?"

"You forgot petty theft. And no one got hurt in any of those cases."

Patty looked down at a file for a moment. "It says here you stabbed a girl."

"With dull scissors and let's be clear, I didn't really stab her; I had them in my hand, and as she walked by, she walked into them," I said, smirking a little. Were my intentions to send the girl to the hospital? No, but my intentions weren't pure either. The only thing that stopped that situation from being news was that dear old dad paid the girl's hospital bills and insisted that the police not file a report, which they seemed to do anyway. What no one knew at the time was that Stacy was basically trying to extort me for my allowance and threatened to beat me up every time I told her to scram. As far as I was concerned, that situation was buried, so it irked me to no end that people kept bringing it up.

"Look, what do you want me to say? Yeah, I did all of those things. But I'm not here for all those things, I'm here for something I had no part of."

I ranted on more for a good five minutes, while Patty just sat, listening attentively. Her face did not change, and judging by the stale, annoyed look on her face, she was not feeling what I was saying at all.

"... so basically, they OJ Simpson'd me," I finished, crossing my arms and sitting back in my seat. Her eyes perked up, and she became amused.

"What's so funny?" I asked.

"Oh nothing," she chuckled. "I just don't think I've ever heard of using someone's name as a verb, but it's effective."

"So, you get my drift, then."

"I do–in fact, I get everyone's drift. It's my job." She took one more glance at my file before closing it up and setting it back on the large stack of papers. She sighed while never looking away from me and it made me uneasy. I felt a bit violated and like I was being judged or something.

"I will tell you what I tell everyone when they come here-you're here for your own good. You don't see it now, and maybe you won't for a while, but I guarantee that you will appreciate this experience when it's all over."

I scoffed. "Yeah, I doubt that."

"Why?"

"Because nothing good comes from being in prison. I've seen *Orange Is the New Black*, I know how this all goes down."

She laughed again. "First of all, they're at a female prison. And you're not in prison-you're at a juvenile detention center."

"Same thing."

"No, it's not-not by a longshot, but you'll learn that soon enough." I rolled my eyes as she continued.

"Second, that's a show. This is real life, and I'm telling you, this experience will only make you better."

I found it odd that she tried to glamorize this place as if I did not just see two girls trying to bash each other's skulls on the hard linoleum floor minutes ago.

"I love the fact that you've convinced yourself that this place will change the lives of every single girl who walks in here and that it isn't a complete waste of taxpayer dollars. Optimism is a great quality to have," I responded dryly. She stared at me with a look mixed with annoyance and sympathy and it gave me great pleasure knowing I was slowly getting under her skin. Just when I thought I would catch her breaking a sweat, she smiled a sweet smile that drained all the pleasure I got from messing with her.

"You're an incredibly smart girl. I think your intellect will be put to great use here," she said getting up from her chair. "I'll need to complete my paperwork, but your time seems incredibly valuable, so I'll let you go. Bates will walk you to the intake room. Try not to give him any trouble. It's his job to bring you back down to size, so if you test him, he will answer. I'll be seeing you tomorrow morning to start your program."

She jotted down quite a few notes on a blank sheet before I even realized that our meeting was finished. I slowly rose from my seat and wouldn't take my eyes off Patty as she continued to scribble nonsense onto her notepad.

"Let's go," Bates growled, which startled me. He held the door open for me to exit and when my body left the threshold of Patty's office, the door slammed behind me and I began my walk with Bates.

"You know, I-"

"Move along," Bates grumbled. He hated his job, and it translated through his talk, his walk, and everything else about him. He was pushy and grumpy and just plain unpleasant. If the other COs were anything like him, there was no doubt that I was going to be a soldier in a war that I could not win.

I decided not to poke the bear because I knew his bite was going to be way worse than his bark, and instead I stayed trained on my surroundings. The outside of the place was one thing, but the inside was another.

The center was strange; it didn't strike me as a prison for teens at all, but more so like a boarding school. There was an awful lot of positivity jumping off the myriad of posters and bulletins that lined the hallway walls, and it made me sick. The minute I stepped foot in the building, I was offended at the sight of the great windows that let the light in from the outside. It was patronizing to be able to see the sun but not be able to feel it, and I began to loathe this place a little more with every step we took. To have a bunch of girls locked up in a place like this with constant reminders of the world that's moving on without them was sinister, and maybe that was the point.

Tatiana told me it was newly renovated, but I couldn't imagine what more the center could have needed before it fell off the line of being a detention center and became a halfway house. Aside from the fresh paint job and waxed floors, the center added on a whole new wing that could house about 30 more girls, a bigger library, and a couple more classrooms.

The center became privately owned right before its renovations. The woman who owned the company and now the center believed that troubled youth deserved redemption, even if given to them in an alternative setting. Marie Trumbull believed the link between the improved conditions and access to an alternative learning program positively affected imprisoned youth. So, her first step in proving her point was to buy Bennings, make it over, adopt a new, rigorous learning and behavioral system, and pump out little rehabilitated and productive members of society.

At least that's what the pamphlet Bates handed me before slamming the room door in my face said. Before leading me to my new room, Bates directed me to the changing room where the COs took all my clothes and gave me a royal purple sweatshirt and gray sweatpants to put on.

"Can I get another color?" I asked the lady. She shook her head and explained that all intakes wore the purple and it would only be for 30 days. I groaned loud enough so that everyone in passing could hear, but no one reacted. No one cared about my discontent, and they were used to worse forms of displeasure.

I stood in front of the room door for a good minute, hoping that the doors would open right back up, or I'd snap out of some high daydream I must've been having after consuming one of Johnny's infamous edibles, but there was no come-to moment. I was there. For real.

I glanced around, taking in my new room for the next month in all its penitentiary wonder. It wasn't half bad, but it looked like the painters missed this room and I would have preferred carpet instead of linoleum. The space was compact, and it was shocking to see how the planners of the place stashed three bunk beds in what otherwise wouldn't have even been enough space for one of us in my world. The room was smaller than my own room at home and having to share it with five other girls was about to be a struggle I would not get used to. Each bunk sat against a wall and had a nightstand right next to it. There was one lone dresser for all our clothes, each of us able to take a drawer. Normally I would have objected and threw a fit, but they only gave me a change of clothes for four days, so I had more than enough space. I placed my sweats, t-shirts, and long johns in one of the empty drawers before taking deep breaths to keep myself from going off the deep end.

There were two unclaimed beds already fitted with sheets, one right above the other on the left side of the room, so I tossed the blanket CO Bates gave me on the bottom bunk. I avoided reminding myself that I was locked up just long enough to make up my bed and make myself comfortable. I didn't even have time to complain about how hard and lumpy the cheap mattress was before Tatiana strolled right up to the room door, accompanied by a larger, female CO whose tag read Jones.

"How the hell you beat me here?" Tatiana glared at me. I glared back at her and scoffed. Lord knows what she had gotten herself into between Patty's office and the room, but whatever it was, I didn't care, nor did I feel like figuring it out. I rolled my eyes and turned my back to her so I was facing the wall. I knew it would tick her off, and I could hear her heavy footsteps stomp towards me with rage. Without looking, I knew Tatiana was fuming, but I had no clue why. All I knew was she was going to take every chance she could to pick on me and this was just one of many.

"Get up. I need the bottom bunk," Tatiana demanded. I slowly turned over just so that our eyes could meet and smirked at her. I wasn't getting up. Not if I could help it.

"Nah, I'm good," I told her. She paused and then took a deep breath.

"Look princess, the bottom bunk is usually mine, so get up." I ignored her request and informed her that I wasn't getting up and that she should try the top bunk for once. I guess she figured that threatening to kick my ass was going to make me quiver and jump to the top bunk, but she must've also forgotten that I didn't like her and wouldn't do anything for her, no matter how nicely she asked.

Sure, I could have gotten on the top bunk. It wouldn't have bothered me any, but it was the principle of the matter. You don't come into a place demanding your "needs" be met and expect people to cater to you, especially when we're all equally considered trash in said place. Only a millisecond passed after I uttered "over my dead body," before I felt a strong tug at my sweatshirt. I'm not sure how I expected Tatiana to respond, but her dragging me out of the bed and throwing me across the room was not what I pictured. As I held my head after it hit the ground, I watched Tatiana plop down on *my* bunk that I claimed fair and square. She kicked off her shoes and made herself comfortable as she stuck her tongue out and taunted me.

After being dramatic earlier that day and making the mistake of letting someone like Tatiana see me get emotional, I decided I would not be a punk. I marched myself right over to her, both of us making eye contact, and cracked her square in the face. I didn't mind the searing pain in my right hand because I was so busy giving myself a pat on the back and then defending myself against Tatiana, who was at least my weight and a half. Some other girls, who I presumed were in our room based on their purple tops, watched and cheered outside of the room door as we wrestled and rolled around on the floor. I was glad that I at least got one good hit in because Tatiana went beast mode on me and unleashed the best she had, which was more than I could handle.

four.

A Couple Hours at Bennings. The room was quiet. Patty sat on the edge of the front of her desk, eyes on fire and steam coming from both her ears and nose. Tatiana sat crossed armed with a bruise on her cheek and a few scrapes while I sat in the seat right next to her with an ice pack on my eye.

CO Bates and CO Fillman, a taller, lanky and pale female guard who monitored the low risk girls, broke us up, but not before we both got in some good licks. They both stood behind us, giving Patty a report of what they witnessed before Patty brought her attention back to us. I knew when Patty closed her eyes and took a deep breath that she was about to light us up. I just couldn't believe that I got into so much trouble, and I hadn't even been there two hours.

"Both of you girls are practically grown, so I'm just going to ask, what the hell is wrong with y'all?" Both Tatiana and I tried to explain, but she cut us off and started with Tatiana.

"You get five more days in intake because you know better. How many times do we have to go through this with you, Tati? You know, if I didn't know any better, I would think you enjoyed being the center of drama around here."

"I mean, I *may* have a problem," Tatiana stated with a smirk. Patty's annoyance level went from about a six to a straight 10 so quick, I couldn't even revel in the punishment Tatiana was about to get served.

"Get her out of here," Patty instructed CO Bates.

"I'm sorry, I was just messin' around!" Tatiana explained. When she saw that Patty wasn't playing games, she began deflecting and turning things back on me.

"Well she started it! She punched me first!" to which I then yelled, "Yeah, because you dragged me and flung me across the room!" We exchanged a few more words before CO Bates grabbed a firm hold of

Tatiana and carried her out. Once the door closed, I looked at Patty who was staring straight through me.

"I know," I sighed.

"Do you? Do you *really* know?" Patty retorted back. The question was rhetorical, but the answer was no. I didn't. I couldn't help myself. Being incarcerated and having to come to grips with that just made me crazy. I couldn't bring myself to be the bigger person or take the high road because I'm not the bigger person and my inner GPS doesn't recognize high roads.

"You haven't been here for half a day and you're already starting off on the wrong foot," Patty insisted. I remained quiet because I knew what was good for me.

"You can't breathe life into people like Tatiana," she began. "I haven't even finished developing your program yet and you're already making it harder for yourself," she followed up. The rest was static. As she rambled, I kept my eyes trained on the grain of the wood on her desk. I trailed each line across as she spit chastising and disappointed words at me. When she finished, she cleared her throat, and I looked up at her.

"You're right," I told her. She raised an eyebrow. "I'll do better. But to be fair, I didn't start this, and-"

Patty put her hand up and shook her head. "Uh-uh, nope."

"What?" I cowered.

"You're not doing the blame thing. You *both* acted out of line. You're going to be with and around Tati until either of you go home. Get used to it and adjust."

Tatiana was high risk–no surprise there. I don't know what she did to end up at Bennings in the first place, but whatever progress she made before was for nothing because she ended up in the same position I was, yet again. Patty could only say so much about Tatiana or any other girl's background before it violated confidentiality, so she treaded lightly, but I caught her drift. Tatiana was a dangerous cookie and was mentally disturbed. She was not someone I needed to spend too much of my energy on. She would only be trouble.

I let Patty know I understood, and she sent me away, but not before requiring me to come see her first thing the next morning. I nodded and made my way back to the intake bunk with CO Fillman. As I walked up to the room, I noticed that Tatiana was sitting on the top bunk, with an enormous smile on her face as she chatted with the other intake girls. CO Fillman opened the door and almost closed it on me before I could walk all the way through it, leaving us alone once more. Tatiana and I locked eyes, but I guess she had time to calm down because her vibe wasn't as hostile as before. The rest of the girls got quiet and stared at both of us like there was another showdown on the schedule.

"So, look, I'm sorry for rippin' you out that bed. I shouldn't have done it."

I couldn't believe *she* was apologizing to me *first*. I stood wide-eyed with my mouth gaped open, which caused her and the rest of the intakes to chuckle. Surprised at Tatiana's sudden change of heart, I found that high road everyone talked about and apologized too. After all, I didn't *have* to punch her.

"And I'm sorry too. I overreacted and you know what? You can have the bottom bunk. I really don't mind taking the top." Patty would have been proud of both of us; we were handling ourselves like big girls and I for one was proud of myself. Oddly enough though, Tatiana declined my offer, not that I minded.

"Nah, it's yours. Fair and square," she said with a sweet smile on her face. I smiled back at her and hopped in my bed ready for a nap.

"Besides, Pissy Penelope used to sleep there, and I know for a fact they didn't clean that mattress good." My eyes shot back open.

"Wait, don't you mean Pukey Penelope?" mocked one of the other girls.

Tatiana giggled. "Oh yeah! She sure did used to pee, doo-doo, *and* throw up in her bed!" The girls all laughed and while they enjoyed their taunting session, I was getting tangled up in the starchy blankets trying to fight my way out of the bed. I pulled back the fitted sheet and there it was; a *huge* stain that covered a good portion of the bed surrounded by much smaller, dingier stains. I did my best not to throw up, but gagging was out of my control. With no other recourse, I remade the bunk and laid on top of the blanket, completely disgusted and annoyed.

five.

*S*econd *Impressions*. My nap was anything but relaxing and nowhere near long enough. I still managed to sleep while Tatiana and the rest of the girls, Violet, Ricki, Dylan, and Jordyn, cackled and roared about nonsense. It wasn't until the room was too quiet for too long that I woke up, feeling confused and like I was missing something. I let my eyes readjust and squinted at the clock that sat right above the doorway. It said 5:40 p.m. Shoot. Dinner.

Evening mealtime started at 5:30 and ended at 6:00, with all 50 girls eating in one shift. By the time I got to the mess hall, got my dinner, and sat down, I would only have 10 minutes to eat. I looked down at my stomach and figured I could go a night without a meal. I wasn't nearly as hungry as I thought I would be, probably because my stomach was in knots about the change in scenery on top of the anticipation building up about my proposed program. Before I could lay my head back down for a good two minutes, another officer, CO Rivers, called to me to get up and get to dinner.

Without looking at him, I murmured, "I'm not hungry." I could tell that he didn't budge and wasn't going to until I complied, but I waited for him to become demanding.

"You sure? You won't be able to eat until tomorrow morning." Though I still didn't care to stuff myself with cheap and/or fake food, I figured I should get a little something to hold me over. I let out a sigh, slipped on my shoes, and headed to the mess hall but froze in place when I got a good look at the man who got me out of bed. The firm grip I imagined his arms could hold me in on top of his clear, milk chocolate skin and easygoing brown eyes made me only dread my status as a delinquent even more. He was so fit, and for a second, I wished that I was free and that I would have met him in a place less drab and in circumstances way less devastating. I wished that I could get his number and text and call him all day, every day. I wished we could lay in his bed, him holding me tight while I rub my fingers along the abs I just knew were under his perfectly fitted officer uniform. He was beautiful and a distraction.

This would not be good for me.

I was a pro at not showing my interest despite burning and yearning for him, so I pretended to look for something. I grabbed one of the other girl's hair ties from a side table and put my hair up in a top bun. As I walked past Rivers, I flashed him a cute, flirty smile but after a few steps, I realized that I could milk my newbie status for all it was worth. I turned back to him with a smirk.

"Can you take me to the cafeteria?" I asked him sweetly.

He raised an eyebrow. "You don't know where it is?" he asked.

I shook my head. "Nope, it's my first day." He thought for a split second and then led me to the cafeteria. I did know where the mess hall was, in fact, I passed right by it on my way to the room when I first got in, but I needed to keep my eyes on CO Rivers for as long as I could. When we arrived, he stepped aside, and my smile quickly dropped. All 50 girls were packed in the cafeteria to the point where those sitting on the ends of the tables had to use their leg to prop them up to keep them from falling. They filled almost all the tables, and everyone was talking to each other and chumming it up like it was some girls' summer camp.

"You okay?" Rivers asked me. I nodded, trying to save face even though I was scared out of my mind. For a time, I had forgotten I would be among real criminals until I saw one girl whose face was all scarred up and looked like she had been in a dozen knife fights. Another one was so big and sweaty, she looked like the mere thought of exercise would send her into a frenzy, not to mention her strong hands looked like they could break through walls. I didn't know anyone, not that I wanted to, so scoping out a good seat would be a task. I brazenly strutted down the main aisle of the cafeteria, hoping to give off the impression that I wasn't one to be messed with. As I passed each table, the girls stared, and I just knew they were plotting against me.

I glared at everyone staring at me as I jumped in the back of the line. I felt uneasy about how comfortable everyone seemed with staring me down. Then I remembered that these girls didn't care about norms, or else none of them would be there. My lack of comfortability shifted to complete disgust once I laid eyes on what would be my dinner. The food was so unrecognizable. They had name plates in front of the platters and I *still* wasn't sure what they were serving us.

I took a deep breath, grabbed a tray, and eyeballed the rest of the girls in front of me as they took the slop given to them without a fuss. I was getting sick just seeing what they claimed to be spaghetti with some meat sauce but nearly threw up in my mouth when the smell hit my nose. I immediately could taste the sour-smelling meat and most likely old canned sauce and shivered before being snapped at by the head "chef" whose tag read Donna.

"You want some or not?" she barked. Her deep, husky voice startled me and I didn't want to agitate her further, so I nodded my head and reached my tray out for her to toss a scoop of the spaghetti and a bread roll on it.

She then growled, "Go on, new girl," before pointing down the line, where the girl right in front of me was getting a juice cup. Before grabbing one for myself, I glanced back at the crowded hall and zeroed in on an unclaimed space in a corner of the room, right underneath a window.

I made my way through the lion's den once more as most eyes were on me, and I was so relieved to sit down in one piece. One look at my food caused me to say a prayer over it-something I rarely did-before scarfing it down to avoid savoring any tastes. It didn't taste nearly as bad as it looked, but I would've been lying if I said that I didn't crave a burger with some fries and wouldn't have done just about anything to get it. I finished with only a few minutes left before the end of the shift and since I didn't have anyone to keep me company, I headed back to my bunk.

It was my intention to keep as far away from Tatiana as possible because she seemed to love using her energy to make me even more miserable, so it shouldn't have come as a surprise when I ended up face down on the dirty linoleum floor as Tatiana and her gang taunted me from the table right next to me. There was no way to hide the fact that my arch nemesis tripped me in front of everyone, but I could at least try to hide the humiliation I felt. Tatiana had already felt my wrath before, and though that fight ended in a draw, I wanted her to know that I could square up with her and win if I wanted. I was face to face with her and before I could backhand the dog mess out of her, I glanced at CO Bates, who was eyeballing us hard. He had his hand ready to grab whatever was on his waist and though I would have loved to give Tatiana a good punch to the throat, I knew that ending up in Patty's office for the third time on my first day would not fare well for me. Besides that, I *still* didn't have a program set up, and it was already clear that Patty would not be easy on me.

"What you gon' do?!" Tatiana roared in my face. I looked her in her eyes and walked away. Once I was out of the cafeteria and I was clear from anyone's view, I dashed towards the nearest bathroom and screamed as loud as I could. I let it all out to the point where I was sure the girls in the cafeteria could hear it if they listened.

What a day it had been. The judge's decree ripped me away from my home, my friends, and my life and threw me to a pack of wolves, leaving me to fend for myself for seven months. It was only day one and I couldn't find the will to go on any longer. The only thing that gave me solace was getting a hot shower.

I always felt like a brand-new person after a shower; washing up felt like I was washing the day away and could start over the next. Before getting myself prepped for the shower, I tested the water to see how hot it would get, or should I say, I tried to. I turned the knobs, but no water came out. I thought to check another bathroom but saw CO Fillman and asked her why the showers weren't working. She responded with some nonsense about a schedule and only being able to shower at certain times of the day. I remarked that it sounded like a prison and though she got the joke and even laughed, she didn't hesitate to remind me that I was being held as a prisoner.

"You can either shower in an hour or tomorrow morning," Fillman explained. I rolled my eyes and waved her off, telling her I'd just do it tomorrow. I couldn't be bothered with anyone else's crap, so I kept to myself for the rest of the night. Despite having to stay in the same room with Tatiana, I somehow ignored her and the other girls, and they eventually left me alone.

The next morning, I arose bright and early. Well, not bright, just early. The little window above our bunks showed that the sun still hadn't peaked just yet, leading me to believe that it was almost 6 a.m., which meant the showers would be unlocked and I could wash myself in peace. I shamed myself because I went a whole day without showering, but I then gave myself a pass because it was a hard day. Despite the day before being a struggle, I wanted to have my head on straight for my meeting with Patty; perhaps there was some time to redeem myself and get an easy program. Even if I was way past that point, it wouldn't hurt to start my second day off right.

I was the first one waiting outside the bathroom with just a towel wrapped around, my shower shoes, and a prepackaged caddy with liquid soap, a toothbrush, toothpaste, some lotion, shampoo, and conditioner. I usually took some serious time to wash my hair, but since I was strapped for time, didn't have my usual hair products on hand, and wanted to be sure to make a positive second impression, I massaged my scalp and let the conditioner sit while I quickly washed up. Smelling fresh and feeling good, I scampered to the cafeteria where again, I was the first one there.

"You're here early," noted CO Bates.

I shrugged and responded, "Well, the early bird gets the word, right?" He glanced at me with suspicious eyes and corrected me.

"It's *worm*, but yeah, that's right." I could still feel his stare as I pranced across the cafeteria, happy that I was the first in line and was most likely not going to have to deal with a lot of people. I was about halfway finished with my bagel, sausage, and fake egg when some other girls began trickling in. A few of them eyeballed me, but most of them pretended like I didn't exist, which was exactly how I wanted it to be.

With a few minutes to spare before my scheduled time to meet with Patty, I paced to her office and noticed that she was just settling in. When I knocked on the door, I caught her by surprise, but she seemed impressed that I was there early. We made small talk as she got herself situated, and I had hoped that she wouldn't bring up yesterday's debacle. She sipped on her coffee as she examined her computer screen, the glare from the blue light casting its light in her eyes.

"So," she began. "After careful consideration of your file, our conversations, and yesterday's mess, I have concluded that you are high risk and once your 30 days are up, you will begin your program with the rest of the high risk girls."

For a second, I couldn't believe it, but when the initial shock wore off, it made sense. Was it that big of a surprise? Not really, but I had hoped that Patty saw through all the crap and realized that I was harmless. Instead of blowing up like I wanted to, I took deep breaths and put on a fake smile. She read right through me, as I hoped she would.

"You have an objection?" she asked, semi-uninterested in my answer. As calm as I could, I attempted to explain how I saw things. She wasn't buying the talk about "first impressions can't be everything" or "give me a chance to show you who I really am." She had heard it all before and I had no redeeming qualities to prove that I was as good as I was trying to make myself out to be.

"Not an objection, but can I ask *why* I'm high risk? One fight with a girl who seems to try everyone's patience can't possibly be enough to warrant putting me in the same category as real criminals." She smiled and shook her head. Again, she was seeing right through me.

"Believe it or not, that fight yesterday had very little to do with my decision, though it didn't help any."

"So, what was it?" I asked, very annoyed now.

"I'm not sure if you're fully aware of what *all* is in your file, but your rap sheet is extensive and it's not all petty stuff."

I immediately objected once more. "But I've never been charged with anything!"

"True. But the cops who brought you in took some serious notes on you." I shoved my face into my hands and screamed into them, muffling the squeal. She let me go for as long as I needed to, and I think she appreciated that I didn't make a bigger scene. When I finished, she just looked at me.

"You good?" she asked. I nodded.

She sat back in her seat, intertwining her fingers, and I knew she was about to hit me with some crap I didn't want to hear, so I prepared myself to tune her out.

"To be fair, I don't think you, yourself is high risk. However, I have guidelines I have to follow when creating programs and you being involved in a robbery attempt, having extensive reported drug use, and stabbing a girl with scissors doesn't help make your case."

"But I've already explained to you-"

"And I've explained to *you* that I have no other choice." She shuffled through a cabinet behind her desk and brought out a notebook, a binder, a couple pencils, and a composition book for keeping a journal. I took one look at the package and shook my head.

"Don't expect me to do any work until I'm placed with the low risk girls," I told her.

"Fine," she said. "I can't make you do anything, but don't expect me to have sympathy for you when your release date gets pushed back because you decided you wanted to be difficult."

She had a way of getting people in line without having to yell or scream. She was stern and direct, but most of all, she was sincere in her words. I couldn't believe I was giving into this woman–even my parents couldn't get this cooperation out of me. I suppose I realized there was more at stake now. Or maybe I was growing up a little? Whatever it was, I convinced myself that going against a big dog like Patty was going to hurt me later, so I grabbed my supplies and huffed. She smiled, happy that she got her way, and rambled on about my program.

six.

The First Math Class. I left Patty's office feeling defeated and villainized. She claimed she understood me, but she was still putting me with girls I didn't belong with. I would have never said it out loud, but I was scared. I didn't know how this would go for me and based on my first day, it would not be good at all. As CO Bates escorted me to my first class, I played Patty's words over like a skipping CD. She assured me that being high risk wasn't as bad as I thought it was, but having that label seemed stigmatizing. I thought being high risk meant I would constantly be policed and escorted because they believed I was a danger to myself or others, but it was more than that.

The programming was Trumbull's idea, but Patty and the Principal of Academia, Ms. Jenkins, expanded on it and turned it into a full rehabilitation program. They created the two groups, low risk and high risk, to categorize the girls and give us the proper attention we needed. It was implied that us high risk girls were the most troublesome, but we were the ones who needed the most love and help, be it tough or mushy. Our programs were based on what Patty and Ms. Jenkins believed would benefit us most individually, so my program wasn't the exact same as the next high risk girl. I couldn't wait to see how it all worked... or failed.

"Go on in," CO Bates barked. I stood in front of my first class of the day, legs feeling heavy and feet glued to the ground. I wanted to strut into the class like I owned the place, but something fierce was holding me back.

"Don't make me have to get rough," he howled again, this time shoving open the door and nudging me in. Suddenly, my feet could move, but now I was stuck in place by the dozens of stares shooting daggers at me.

"Good morning, Eve!" the instructor, Mr. Kole, greeted me. He was a younger looking version of CO Bates, but his bright smile proved that his personality was nothing like his.

"Good morning," I said back quietly. I kept my eyes trained on the floor, careful not to make eye contact with any of the girls. Mr. Kole directed me to the only open seat in the back of the class, next to a bookshelf only half filled with heavily used books and a girl wearing a bright blue sweatshirt signifying that she was low risk. She looked way too young and innocent to be in a place like this, but that only made me think she could secretly be one of the most diabolical.

"Hi!" the girl hailed. Her face was small and round, and her eyes were big and brown, reminding me of a cartoon character. Her friendly aura and smile would have occupied my focus, but it was her glasses that won my attention. They were larger frames that took over half her face and looked like glasses a grandma would wear, but she made them work for her. She was adorable, young, and seemed harmless, so I greeted her back with the same spirit she had.

"Welcome to Bennings!" she exclaimed. I thanked her and tried to catch up with the little that I had missed in the class and soon realized that there had to be a mistake. Mr. Kole was instructing the class on the order of operations, and I learned that in, like, the 3rd grade. Everyone in the class, apart from the girl sitting next to me, looked like they were in high school, so I was shocked and thoroughly confused at how and why we were learning something everyone should have mastered in elementary school.

"I think I'm in the wrong class," I mumbled, as I tried to slide out of my chair. The girl next to me put her hand on mine and shook her head.

"No, you're not. This is a standard lesson. Trust me, I've tried to get Ms. Jenkins to change the curriculum, but she insists that it's the state that chooses what we learn. You're lucky, though. Last week we were going over long division, and I nearly died of boredom." We giggled together as we quietly watched Kole attempt to explain PEMDAS.

"I'm Roz by the way!" she told me, sticking her hand out to shake mine. I smiled at her and shook it with as much enthusiasm as she had.

"What are you in for?" she asked me casually. My smile quickly faded as I flashed back to that night I so stupidly went with Johnny and his goons, the night that would haunt me forever. She saw that I was a bit disturbed and tried to take her question back, but I assured her I was okay, and I told her. I *may* have embellished some details, like I *might* have been keeping a look out for the guys and that I *might* have been the one who came up with the idea to rob the credit union, which I also claimed was a well-known bank.

The lies just rolled out so naturally and I didn't think I was setting myself up to get called out on my lies later on, so I went with it. When I finished explaining, Roz looked shocked and even shuttered, pretending to be afraid of me. I cackled out loud, which then caused Mr. Kole and the rest of the class to look back at me, annoyed. I pulled my sweatshirt collar over my mouth, pretending to hide away, but Mr. Kole wagged his finger at me and Roz anyway. I promised him I was sorry and would be quiet, and when he turned back to the whiteboard, Roz and I giggled to ourselves some more. We agreed to talk later, and she shared some past work they had done in the class, all of which she received an A+ on.

After the first two classes of the day, I was over everything. I was so exhausted, and it was weird because in my normal life, I would have been doing the exact same thing as I was now, minus the whole incarcerated part. I waited patiently in the lunch line, which slowly moved as each girl took her time deciding whether to get the processed burger or processed hotdog. The girl who led the line was throwing a fit about the steamed carrots not being cooked enough and it caused a couple guards to get involved. I looked around to see if I could find that *fine* guard Rivers, but he was nowhere to be seen. Thinking about him made me think about my girls, Mackie and Rachel, and how much fun we had scoping the lunchroom every day, talking about the same guys and the gossip that followed them. It was like clockwork; Mackie would bring the tea, Rachel would offer her commentary, and I would sip it all. We were such a dynamic trio, and I missed them so much. I had hoped that they were thinking of me and missed me too.

"Whatchu' want, girl?" Donna snarled. I snapped out of my daydream and looked down, noting that the line wrapped around the room and then I pointed to the burnt burger and corn on the cob. I gave her a smile, hoping she would see that I was harmless and that she would lighten up, but she rolled her eyes and motioned for me to move down the line. I sighed, grabbed a juice box from the drink cooler, and I felt immediate dread.

Once again, I was facing the hard task of finding a place to eat in a crowded cafeteria where I knew no one. I studied the room once more as I slowly put one foot in front of the other. I was beginning to think that I would have to pull a Cady Heron move from *Mean Girls* and eat in a bathroom stall, but a familiar, happy little face caught my eye. Roz energetically waved to me and I could see a light shine on her. It was then that I accepted her as my savior.

"Hey, sit here!" she said, patting the placement in front of her.

The rest of the cafeteria was full, but for some reason, the section of the table we were at was empty. I then wondered if Roz was the reason for that. I mean, she seemed nice-too nice, innocuous even, but she was also in the same place I was. Maybe she did something so bad that people wanted nothing to do with her, but she was low risk, so that couldn't be it. Maybe she was just annoying. I couldn't be sure, and though the thoughts reeled in my head as we sat and ate, I didn't mind not being squished like all the other girls seemed to be.

"So, how's your first day going?" Roz asked me. I shook my head, annoyed.

"Exhausting. I'm so tired of everything already." She nodded in solidarity of my strife.

"Yeah, it's like that, but you'll get used to it. How long are you in for?"

"Seven months."

"Yikes," Roz said, patting me on my hand.

"Yeah. This place sucks, but it's not what I thought," I told her. She nodded in agreement and began going in-depth about why Bennings was the way it was. Apparently, it was once one of the worst places to get sent to if you were a troubled kid. Parents would get their girls back completely broken. There were reported abuses in *all* aspects of the word, ranging from money being embezzled by top management, to starvation, to sex abuse by a few of the guards. Some intakes tried to bring attention to it, but they were either shut down or paid off. It was even rumored that one girl killed herself after trying to report a guard that was raping her and her friend. Then Marie Trumbull came along. I guess she did her digging, realized all the problems Bennings had and fired *everyone*. Bennings was closed for about a year while she renovated the center, vetted, and hired new staff. This year was year four of the "revitalized" Bennings Center and since reopening, not a single negative peep had been uttered about the place.

I sat in complete awe as Roz casually explained everything to me and it only made me happier that I got there when I did. Had I come when I "stabbed" Stacy with the scissors, I may have ended up a lost cause like some of the others before me, or worse.

"All right, lunch is over. Head to your next class, now!" CO Bates yelled out right after the bell rang. Roz and I both looked at each other with wide eyes and with no words, dumped our trays and headed to our next classes. It turned out that we had social sciences class together right after lunch, so we linked and agreed to stay at each other's sides when we could. Day one shaped up to be much better than intended and I could breathe a little easier, even if I still had a long way to go.

seven.

*O*ne Week at Bennings. One week in, and I was finding my groove. I kept to my shower schedule and every morning CO Fillman commented on how early I was up for the showers. I said the same phrase I did to CO Bates my first morning, but said it right, before she'd open up the bathroom for me. After my showers, I'd quickly get dressed, not that it took much time anyway, and went to breakfast, where again, I was the first one in and the first one out. I soon began beating Roz to class, and I soon learned that she was not only a complete nerd but was also on track to graduate school early. I stuck by her, because even though she was a couple years younger than me, she was smart and the kind of person I needed to be seen around.

We became fast friends and I would even say inseparable. Though we only had two out of the four classes and meal times together, we cut up whenever we were around each other. Mr. Kole quickly got annoyed with me and I'm sure was beyond over me constantly apologizing for being disruptive, but he admired Roz and I think he learned to appreciate me because of her.

Dinner came, and just like the previous days, our table was left open for us. Every time I sat down, I'd examine Roz, noting how innocent she appeared with her enormous glasses and her two French braids. Based on her appearance alone, I couldn't see her doing anything worthy of ending up here and personality-wise, she was a jewel. She was sweet and fun, so what did she do that was so bad? I never wanted to ask though, because I wasn't ready to accept that my friend might be a maniac.

Not too long after everyone settled at their dinner tables, CO Bates, CO Rivers, and CO Jones came in, and they were escorting a small group of girls, at least five, whose wrists and ankles were shackled. The cafeteria grew still as the guards unleashed the girls from their chains. As they did, Roz, as energetic as she was, began waving at two of the girls in red sweatshirts, to which then they both smiled and nodded in her direction. A shiver creeped down my back and it was becoming clear why Roz was left alone. She either befriended just any old person, or her friends were not to be messed with, and judging by the scar on the Latina girl's neck, it was the latter.

Once all the girls were free, CO Bates told them to "Get on to gettin'," and they scrambled to be the first in line to get food.

"Are they your friends?" I asked Roz, notably nervous.

"Gigi and Brit are, but don't worry! They're cool!" Her words were reassuring, but the looks of the girls caused me to second guess my trust in Roz. I ate and watched as the two who acknowledged Roz whispered to each other, constantly looking back at the other girls they came in with. Based just on how mean their mugs were, I guessed that they were sworn enemies to the others and that something could pop off at any time. Both girls were the first out of the group to get their food and they swaggered their way over to what had been mine and Roz's table for the past week. Both were tall and noticeably thick; they looked like they could win any fight they came up against, including those against boys. They both had pretty faces, which only made me even more weary of them, and when they sat down, I tried to keep calm through my panic.

"What up Rozzi boo! What we miss?!" the Black girl heralded. She had a husky, deep voice, but she seemed very positive and bright. I thought I even saw a twinkle in her eyes when she smiled at Roz. Both girls hugged on Roz, causing her smile to be even brighter than normal. I could tell that she was happy to be amongst her friends.

"I see you survived without us," the Latina mentioned, as she tickled Roz's side. Roz let out a little yelp before covering her mouth to muffle her laughter. It was cute to see them together, but I felt like a complete outsider, like I was watching them from the other side of a two-way mirror or something. It was like I wasn't even there.

"Oh guys! This is Eve! She's new here," Roz introduced.

"That's Brit," she said, speaking about the Black girl who was sitting next to me.

"And this is Gigi," motioning to the Latina who didn't waste her energy to give me eye contact. Brit looked over at me and smiled.

She nudged my shoulder, saying, "What up Eve! Welcome to heaven in hell," before beginning to devour her hamburger. The other girl just looked at me with her light brown eyes. I quickly looked away, not just because I was scared, but because she gave me "deeply troubled" vibes, and though I could probably relate to some of her plight, I just knew I wouldn't be able to relate to *all* of it.

"What are you, scared?" Brit asked of me, casually noting that I was trembling.

I shook my head to get her off my back and Roz chimed in with, "No way she's scared! She's high risk like you two crazies." Brit and Gigi both looked me up and down and busted out laughing to themselves. I was offended for a second, but then realized that since my second day at Bennings, I had been acting so timid. It was my way of alerting the other girls that I meant them no harm and didn't want trouble, but perhaps I was setting myself up for failure. I watched as they mumbled to themselves and looked over at me laughing and knew that I could no longer be the shy girl who didn't want to ruffle any feathers. If I was going to survive among the roughest and toughest, I was going to have to *show* that I could hang with these girls.

"There's no way you're high risk. What you do?" Brit probed. I started to plead my case, but Roz jumped in and took it away.

"She robbed a bank and then led a high-speed chase and even hit a cop!" Brit's thick eyebrows perked up, she looked over at me with an approving smirk and said, "Not bad." Gigi, on the other hand, was hardly impressed, in fact, she kept her gaze straight ahead as Brit gave me my props for what was really a lie.

"She also punched Tatiana her first day here, so, if that's not enough for you, I don't know what is," Roz finished. Her comment threw me off because I didn't even mention what happened between me and Tatiana to her. Roz looked at me and smiled.

"Word travels fast around here."

Brit howled and shook me as she commended me on "putting a nice one" on Tatiana. Apparently, Tati wasn't liked by *anyone*.

"That bitch always has a punch coming her way around here. I'm just shocked it came from a new girl," Brit stated. I glanced over at Gigi who was doing her best to hide a smile and for some reason, I felt better. The tension I had pinned up the whole dinner disappeared, and I felt myself opening up as if I was back at school, at lunch with my friends.

"So, how was max hall?" Roz asked the girls. They both looked at her with the same "girl, please" look.

"Same old, same old," Brit responded, sucking her teeth.

"You guys shouldn't have even been in there. It was clearly self-defense!" Roz argued. Brit agreed and went on about how she told Patty that and pleaded for her to let her and Gigi off the hook, but Patty didn't take the bait. They were subject to spend the max time-five days–in the max security hall for the "yellow infraction" also known as fighting.

"Besides, Coco only lost a little blood. It wasn't a big deal," Brit continued, shrugging off the otherwise very serious offense. As Roz and Brit continued to catch up, I stared at Gigi, who remained quiet and reserved. I never made it a point to figure anybody out, but she was so intriguing. There was something about her that attracted me to her. She was tough and carried herself like a true badass, but there was also a virtue I saw in her. Like, she didn't just *do* things because she could; she had her reasons. Whatever it was, it made me want to get to know her, and yet, avoid her all at the same time.

"You know Coco had to go get stitches, right?" Roz mentioned to Brit. Brit was so animated with her response that it was funny to watch her reaction. Her eyes grew wide and her mouth gaped open as she tapped Gigi, who was spaced out, and gave her props.

"My girl Gigi's hands are lethal weapons, I swear to ya'!" she exclaimed as she got up out her seat and began punching the air. Roz was entertained, but Gigi remained stone-faced. It was almost like none of it phased her, which made her even more scary to me.

"Sit down, Brittany!" CO Rivers called out to her. She stopped fighting the air and turned her attention to him and I could see based on her body language that she felt the same way about him as I did.

"Oh, I'm sorry Rivers. Love you!" she called to him, blowing him a kiss. He winced at the act and rolled his eyes. CO Bates' eyes were like laser beams and once Brit caught them in her sights, she sat down and behaved. She continued to make heart eyes at CO Rivers, who kept his eyes away from our table, before turning her attention back to us and commenting on how fine CO Rivers was.

"If I wasn't locked up..." Brit said, licking her lips. "Anyway, how did you end up hangin' out wit' Specs?" she asked me. I looked around, confused.

"Who is Specs?" I asked her, embarrassed that I didn't know. Roz then raised her hand, unapologetic about the suitable nickname, and I chuckled.

"Oh, um, Mr. Kole put me next to her in math."

"And we've been best friends ever since!" she smiled as she munched on her hotdog. I smiled at her as I offered her a napkin to wipe the ketchup off her cheek and then asked how she and Gigi met Specs.

"We all came in around the same time a few months ago. Specs was one of the most annoying people in intake, but she's super smart, and you *always* need someone super smart in your crew," Brit explained.

"Besides, Specs don't mean no harm to no one. She wouldn't

hurt a fly."

This was it. I spent so much time trying to figure out what it was about Roz that got her in a place like this and now was the time to ask. There was no better moment than to bring it up now.

"Okay, so if you're so sweet, what are you doing here?" I asked Specs. Brit, with another animated response, asked her, "What? You didn't tell her?!"

Specs shrugged and said, "She never asked!" Brit began to geek out and cleared her throat to tell me what, I presumed to be an epic story.

"So, you know how I said this girl is super smart, right?" Brit asked me. I nodded.

"Well, she's not just super smart. The girl is a genius! An *evil* genius!" Brit laughed. I buckled up for this wild ride, and I was not disappointed.

Specs was extraordinary. She never had issues in school, in fact, when she was in just the third grade, her teacher insisted that she skip *two* grades because she was *that* advanced. Her grandmother, who she lived with, was astonished, because no one else in her family had ever shown so much promise in school and she worked hard to keep Roz on the right path. Roz didn't end up skipping grades, but she was considered for every magnet program in her city and when she entered middle school, she was offered a chance to take high school-leveled classes, which she did. Because of this, Roz spent most of her first year in high school not in class. Although she had taken most of her classes well in advance, only seniors could leave early if they had more than enough credits to do so, so the school agreed that they'd keep her busy during the couple hours she wasn't taking a class with her peers. What I quickly came to learn about Roz was that a bored, unproductive Roz will find something to do to pass the time.

Her school, like most schools, had an online grading system that she quickly hacked into, because again, boredom, and she started plucking around. One day, one of her friends complained to her that her biology teacher kept giving her failing grades on her quizzes and tests and was confused because she knew the material. Her friend began comparing her tests to one of the other kids who got A's on his and realized that her answers matched, and that the teacher was failing her for no reason. Specs vowed to handle it and she knew just the way to do it.

Specs took matters into her own hands, and not only changed her friend's grade to what it should have been, she went into the system and changed every failing grade to a passing grade. She improved the scores of hundreds of students, and not only that, she created some hardware that would lock the teachers out from changing the initial grades. The best part about that story is that Specs never got caught. The school had no idea it was her or that any unauthorized person had access to the system. Specs cleaned her slate and made it appear that she was never there. When the investigation ended with the school district's IT department, they concluded that it was a system error that they couldn't fix. Specs got off scot-free, her friend passed the class, and all was well, but that's not where it ends.

Specs knew her abilities, and she was going to take them as far as she could. Her grandmother, who was not just taking care of her, but also her younger twin brother and sister, was having a hard time staying afloat. She was ruthless, though; she did what she had to do, but Specs saw her grandma get burnt out day in and day out working multiple jobs when it was her time to relax and enjoy retirement. Now a superb hacker, Specs managed to breakdown the security software at a bank and once she got in, she routed funds to her grandma's account, enough to keep them going for a while, but not enough to draw any crazy attention to the random deposit.

"Who did you steal it from, again?" Brit asked Specs. Specs smirked and said it was from a "wealthy man who wouldn't miss it." Her grandma was shocked and took it as a blessing with no questions asked. Once again, no one was the wiser and Specs got off with stealing or should I say "redirecting" money. Hacking became more of a game for Specs and she just *had* to one-up herself.

One day in her government class that she popped in on now and then, they learned about local, state, and federal taxes and how those taxes trickle through the government and fund the country's operations. Specs saw a massive opportunity in front of her, and no amount of projected jail time was going to persuade her from at least trying to do what she ended up doing–stealing from the government. Well, not stealing from the government, per se. She knew *that* was going to be a tsunami, but stealing from those who worked in the government would be a more of a 20 foot wave.

"I'm so confused right now," I said, rubbing my temples. There was so much going on in my head that I was getting a headache thinking about what it took to do all of that and *succeed.*

"What is there to be confused about? Specs stole money from a bunch of stuffy congresspeople and kept it for herself!" Brit cleared it up. Specs, pleased with herself, sat quietly as Brit continued to tell me how Specs not only stole the money by hacking into the government's payroll system and rerouted upcoming paychecks to some random account, but she hid the money from the government.

To this day, they *still* don't know where it is.

"And they'll never find it," Specs interjected. "Even if they did, they wouldn't be able to do anything with or about it."

"Why not?" I asked.

Roz then explained, "Because the money is no longer in a U.S. bank, nor is it in U.S. dollars." My mouth, already aching from being held open the entire time, almost hit the floor.

"You mean to tell me that the money you stole is in some, like, offshore account or something?" Roz laughed and shook her head.

"Absolutely not! I'm pretty sure the government can seize offshore accounts, that is, if they know about it, but I did one better." Brit and Gigi, who already knew the punchline, sat smiling at Specs, while I sat flabbergasted at my friend, the embezzler.

"So?!" I snapped. Roz continued.

"Okay, yes, I put the money in an 'offshore' account, but if-and that's a low possibility if-the government finds the account, they'll only find, like, $300 collecting interest. That's because I bought gold with the rest of it using random currency."

"Gold? Why gold?" I asked.

"Because, gold will always have value and it's a hot commodity, so it sells easily. It was the best thing to buy."

"Where did you get it and how?" I probed more, hoping to take a few mental notes for later.

"I can't tell you that, but I have my sources," she said playing coy. "And before you ask, the gold is hidden. I will never tell anyone where it is."

My head continued to spin into a frenzy. Everything she explained was beyond my scope of knowledge, and I knew a thing or two about money. After I let the idea of Roz literally owning a gold mine settle, my biggest question now was, if they never found the money or the gold, what was she doing at Bennings?

"They never found any of it, but let's just say, it's almost impossible to hack the government without them knowing where to find you." My eyes grew wide once more as she explained that on a day, not too long after she moved the funds and bought the gold, that the FBI came to her grandmother's door asking for her. Roz laughed hysterically as she described how shocked they were that Roz was only then 14 years old.

"They didn't know whether to put me in the deepest darkest cell and throw away the key or ask me for tips."

"Get to the best part, Specs! Tell her what they said!" Brit egged her on. Roz shook her head no.

"No way! I shouldn't have even told you!" she exclaimed. Brit nagged Roz until she couldn't take it anymore. Roz took a deep breath and got on with the final act.

"Okay. So, they were mad, especially since I wouldn't tell where the money was. They told me I was looking at serious time for what I did and threatened legal action."

"So that's why you're here then?" I asked her. Roz nodded.

"I mean, I get what I did was wrong, but I figured those nuts on Capitol Hill didn't deserve it as much as people like my grandma did. After all, it is *our* tax dollars that pay their salaries." So, Specs was like a Robin Hood for the 'hood, only she didn't steal from the rich and give to the poor, she just stole from the rich and hid the money for later.

"About two weeks later, I received a special letter. I had never gotten mail before, and the letter was unmarked, but we knew it was from the government. My grandma was scared because she thought it was a letter laying out what they would do to me, but we were both shocked to see what it was really about."

"And?" I poked.

"The CIA offered her a job after she finished college. There! I said it!" Brit announced, ruining Specs' moment. My head whipped over to Specs' so fast, it made my headache worse.

"Are you joking right now?!" I asked her. Roz shook her head.

"The letter itself didn't say much, but it had a number to call. I spoke to someone and let's just say they recognized how my skills could be of use to them."

"Are you sure it was the CIA? How do you know it wasn't some random person?" I asked.

"Oh, it was them," she said with a smirk. That was such big news, but Specs didn't seem too thrilled at having a job with the most powerful intelligence agency in the world after college.

"That's crazy awesome! My friend, a CIA agent!" I exclaimed, Brit also rejoicing with me.

"Keep it down!" Spec shushed us. "You guys aren't supposed to know. If they ever found out that I told anyone, the deal would be void." Specs eyeballed us with such intensity that I immediately zipped my lips.

"So how much longer do you have here? It's the perfect time to look for colleges and-"

I stopped. I saw Brit and Gigi's face quickly turn down and then I looked at Roz, who suddenly looked worse than sad; she looked defeated. I immediately knew that I said something wrong.

"I- I don't really know," Specs admitted. Gigi patted her back, giving her the comfort that I took from her when I probed so deep.

"I'm supposed to be getting out in a few months, but my grandma's been in and out of the hospital after having a stroke. They won't release you if you don't have a stable home, so either they'll place me in a home away from my brother and sister or they just won't release me." I continued to regret my decision to speak at all, but Specs was my friend and I wanted her to know that she was going to be okay.

"I'm so sorry I made you upset. I didn't mean to." Specs peered over her glasses with glossy eyes, but she smiled and nodded.

"Your grandma will be okay, and she will pick you up along with your siblings and you'll be able to be all together. You'll graduate from high school, and then college, and then become a CIA agent," I explained. I was so serious and almost passionate about my words, but they didn't resonate with the rest of the girls the way I wanted them to. They immediately cracked up laughing at me, including Specs, and mocked me for the dramatic monologue. Though I was sincere in what I said, I was happy that Specs wasn't upset at me or her situation.

"Well, while we're on the subject of how we all got here, I have to admit, mine was pretty crazy too," Brit offered with a wide smile.

"Oh God, here we go," Gigi uttered with a smirk. I watched them roll eyes and laugh at each other for a moment before I cut in because I was curious about it.

"So, what did you do?" I asked once there was a moment of silence.

"Joyriding," Specs answered for her. Brit looked annoyed, not only because she wanted to tell it, but because Specs summed up the entire ordeal with just one lousy word.

"First of all, I didn't just hotwire any old car, so get that straight," Brit snapped.

"I stole my boyfriend's car, crashed it, and then lit that sucker on fire causing a 20-car pile-up on a freeway to get back at him for cheating on me. That highway was backed up for hours," Brit laughed to herself.

Once again, I was stunned. These girls never ceased to amaze me and though crashing a car wasn't nearly as epic as syphoning money from the government, I knew Brit's story had more legs than she let on.

"Uh, your boyfriend was one of your teachers and he 'cheated' on you with his fiancé," Specs corrected her, dramatizing her air quotes around the word "cheated."

"Just tell all my business, why don't you!" Brit said between her teeth.

"So, hold on. You were having an affair with one of your teachers? That's disgusting," I commented, though I had *no* room to talk. I never even dreamed of getting with a teacher, but perhaps that was because most of my male teachers were "one step into the grave" as me and my friends used to say. Besides, getting with a teacher was just so messy and as cool as Brit was, it was appalling how much of an amateur she was.

"What can I say, I have a thing for older men I can't have," Brit shrugged. "Speaking of..." she said looking at CO Rivers. I glanced over too because he was perfect eye candy. I didn't blame Brit at all for her love for older guys–hell, I was at Bennings because of my own obsession with being wanted by someone I shouldn't have, but Rivers was secretly mine. The only thing that stopped me from saying so was Brit's size and the fact that she had *just* come out of max hall after helping send a girl to the hospital. Me declaring my lust for him would not get me anywhere good with this group, so I kept my mouth closed for my own sake.

"I can't wait to get a piece of Rivers. When I get out, my first stop will be *his* house!" Brit called out with no shame. CO Rivers and the rest of the cafeteria heard all of it, just as Brit wanted, and Rivers blushed but then got annoyed.

"You just don't learn, do you Brittany?" he asked her, shaking his head and rolling his eyes.

"Maybe you can help me out?" she flirted, while the rest of the girls in the cafeteria, including me, cheered on her bold proposition. Unfortunately, CO Bates nipped the fun in the bud and demanded Brit stop or else she would get written up again. Brit brushed him off, but quickly stopped because she had gotten written up before and she was on her last one before getting a red infraction. A red infraction meant her release date would get moved, and because of the fight, her date was already pushed back five days.

Once we all settled down, I focused back on the conversation, which was getting *really* good.

I looked over at Gigi, who was finishing her fruit cup and asked her, "So, why are you here?" Had I known that asking Gigi anything personal was off limits, I wouldn't have even thought to ask. I would have shelved the thought, or asked around, but no, I was too bold and too dumb to catch the vibe she was sending me. Specs and Brit got quiet and awaited Gigi's reaction, which they knew was going to be intense. Without making eye contact or even acknowledging my presence, she sucked back the remaining juice in her fruit cup and slowly turned to me with the most intimidating scowl I had ever seen on a girl.

"I slammed a girl's head into a wall because she wouldn't mind her business."

I suddenly forgot to form actual sentences and couldn't stop stuttering.

"I'm so sorry, I didn't mean to be all up in your business. I- I just thought since we were talking about-" I apologized, still fighting my newfound stammer. She wasted no time in hearing what I had to say; she swiftly got up from the table, dumped her tray, and asked CO Rivers to walk her back to her room. I sat speechless and on the verge of tears. I was clearly not prepared for that reaction and once again, I regretted opening my big mouth.

"She doesn't like to talk about it," Brit divulged. I felt so bad; I didn't have a clue about what it could have been, but I knew it had to be something deep. I examined Specs and Brit's faces, which were both somber, and I attempted to plead my case. Thankfully, they understood and even tried to help me calm down.

"Don't worry about it," Specs said. "It's just a sore subject for her."

"She hates me, doesn't she?" I asked, hanging my head low. Brit patted my back, comforting me.

"Nah, not completely," Brit said before stabbing her juice box with the straw.

eight.

***O**dd Girl Out.* I spent the last few minutes of dinner silent. My mouth was only getting me into trouble, as usual. I listened to Brit and Specs continue to catch up, Specs talking about what was happening in her classes and Brit talking about some letters she received from her "boyfriend" the teacher, who not only wasn't in jail for being in a relationship with Brit, but also was audacious enough to still keep in contact with her.

"We have to be on our best behavior for the weekend!" Specs mentioned, clapping her small hands together.

"Oh yeah! I can't wait! We finally get a break," Brit responded. I ended my speaking strike for a moment to figure out what they were talking about.

"What's happening this weekend?" I asked. Specs eyes lit up with excitement.

"This weekend, we are having the Day of Empowerment! We get to go outside and do a bunch of fun stuff like games and contests and stuff!" The thought of getting to have a little fun in this hell hole made me excited too.

"Yeah, the owner thinks it's a good idea to let us have some fun now and then," Brit scoffed. "God bless you Marie Trumbull."

The Day of Empowerment was like a reward for positive behavior and an incentive for the girls to take the planned workshops that day. The idea was, you take part in the exercises in the morning, you get to enjoy yourself in the afternoon.

"Patty told me that if we do well in the courses, it could help us get into the Gems and you know what that means..." Specs told Brit, to which Brit then responded, "Early release!" They gave each other a high five and began strategizing about how they would avoid drama at all costs. I cut in once more to get more clarity because an early release was just what I needed to hear.

"How do you get into the Gems?" I asked.

"It depends," Brit explained. "You have to be on your best behavior, do really good in school, and be helpful around the center." I sighed because I had already gotten into a fight my first day there, so I already failed the behavior part. I spaced out for a minute to figure out how I could help around the building and prove that I should get out earlier. Getting good grades in school and behaving would not be a problem from then on, but I wanted to focus on showing myself useful.

The bell rang, letting us know that dinner was over. My mood immediately turned sour after realizing I would have to go back to my room with Tatiana, the pest. Specs gave me a big hug and Brit gave me a fist bump.

"If you can sneak out of your room, come over to the red room. That's where us high risk girls stay. We all usually hang out there," Brit told me. I nodded and smiled, feeling great that I was being included and that I might just have a group of friends to get me through this otherwise dreadful situation.

"Okay!" I replied before shuffling back to my room.

After the first night, I was lucky enough not to hear much from Tatiana. Other than the occasional stupid comment about me being a "lightweight" or her calling me "princess", there weren't any real issues between us, which was how I liked it. I still couldn't stand her presence and she made it clear she couldn't stand mine. When I got to the room, the door was open and the rest of the girls, including a couple new intakes who had taken the place of a few of the girls who had moved to the red or blue rooms, were playing cards. Noticing that they were so immersed in their game, I casually slid my way in and found a little comfort on my bunk.

"Look at her, the princess doesn't even come in and say hi to nobody," Tatiana began. I knew to ignore her because that tactic was old, and I couldn't let her bait me into a reaction I would regret. The other girls snickered and scoffed and despite me having my back to them, I could feel them all staring at me and even plotting. I could sense movement in the room and knew that Tatiana and her new goons were readying themselves for a battle, so I turned to face them with a straight, unbothered face. They all stood sprawled throughout the compact room, prepared to take me on from all angles.

"She ain't gon' last the full 30 days here, I bet," declared Tatiana, addressing the room as if she was the queen and the others were her subjects. She then laughed at how angry I looked, which prompted the rest of the girls to mock me. I was beyond heated, but I tried my hardest not to let those broads know they were getting under my skin.

As I turned my back on them again, Tatiana poked me in my side and then my back, adding more remarks about how I was a crybaby and wasn't going to do anything to them, blah blah blah.

Without even looking at her, I told her, "Stop talking shit before you see how I really am."

The other girls shifted back like I knew they would, but Tatiana didn't budge. I could still feel her presence on top of me and before I could say anything else, Tatiana grabbed the back of my sweatshirt and my sweatpants and yanked me out of my bed with all her might. I don't even know why I didn't expect that, but I was in such shock at how much power and strength she had behind her grip and pull that I just succumbed to the jerk and let her do it. Before I knew it, she had me pinned up against the wall and the other four girls backed her up in a semi-circle. I could only see one way out of this–getting my ass kicked.

"I'm sick of yo' mouth, hoe! I know you used to bein' the center of attention and all that, but this here is *my* house, and I run this shit! You gon' stop disrespectin' me!"

I gasped for air as Tatiana's grip on my neck tightened and her hot breath invaded my personal space. I kept quiet and fought back tears as I immediately thought back to the last moment before leaving the courtroom. My parents. My brother and sister. Their reaction to my verdict was so dry and dead. They didn't care that I was being locked up, nor did they care what might happen to me while in here. After warring with myself for a few moments, I surrendered to my emotions and let the tears fall. I tried to wiggle my way out of Tati's grip and when she could feel the fire on the inside of me getting out of control, she let me go. I bent over, gasping for air and coughing, and then pushed through the other girls blocking my way to the room door and poked my head out, screaming for help from a guard.

"I need to go to the bathroom!" I yelled. I couldn't even be excited that it was CO Rivers who answered my call. He took one look at my face and gestured for me to take the lead.

"What's wrong?" he asked me. I ignored him and dashed out. He called out for me to stop running, but he didn't chase after me.

I stood in front of a sink, avoiding the mirror at all costs because I was nowhere near decent, and let everything go. I sobbed. I screamed. I cursed. I let the world melt around me and took the time I needed to feel what I needed to feel. My body felt light, but my heart was heavy and was beating so quick, I almost called for help. I took deep breaths to relax myself, an old trick one of those therapists told me to do when I felt myself "going over the edge," and it worked. I guess the money my parents paid to "fix" me wasn't a *complete* waste.

"It's time for you to come out now," CO Rivers announced, knocking on the door.

"Give me a minute!" I growled back at him. I waited for the water to get warm and finally glanced at myself in the mirror. I was a mess. My hair was all over my head, my eyes were bloodshot red, my cheeks were puffy, and I looked pale.

I thought back to what that cop, Rickers, said about me. How he remembered a different little girl, and he was right. All of a sudden, I could see blue and red lights behind me in the mirror and when I turned around, I was back inside the car with Johnny, Big Rob, and Merv, screaming at them to let me out as the police trailed us. Trying to get away from the thought, I closed my eyes and turned back to where the mirror would be and then saw nothing but black. When I looked up, I could see the stars, millions of them, shining brightly above as we hid in the gravel pits below. Johnny was whispering to me and holding me tight, and though I felt comfort in his wrapped arms around me, I couldn't settle my mind because he was the one who got me in this mess. I shook my head, telling myself to get back to real life, but then I saw myself in front of Judge Basin, slamming her gavel as she deemed me a menace to society and told me I deserved what I was getting.

I slumped to the dirty tile floor, crying as I began picturing Mackie and Rachel heading to homecoming without me. We were supposed to go together and meet up with others later for an after party. I could see them having so much fun without me. They were going to forget about me, that was for sure. Seven months is a long time to be away. With school having just started, I would miss *all* of my senior year, all because of something I couldn't take an ounce of credit for. CO Rivers knocked again, this time sticking his head inside the bathroom.

"Seriously, you need to come out now."

"Okay! One more minute!" I snapped at him again. I took my time getting up, my body now feeling heavy as bricks. I took a few more deep breaths and rinsed my face off, scrubbing my skin until it felt brand new. I opened the door, just as CO Rivers was about to knock again, and didn't even make eye contact; I just scooted out of the bathroom and made my way back to the room to face the same girls that caused my mini mental breakdown.

"Hold on, stop!" Rivers called out to me. As he walked towards me, I noticed how concerned he was, and it made me even more emotional.

"Are you all right? Did you get it all out of your system?"

I looked into his beautiful brown eyes and shook my head. Feeling myself get weak, I collapsed into his arms and sobbed again. I didn't care that it was against the rules for us to touch. I needed his support, and after a few moments of him wondering if he could, he wrapped his buff arms around me and patted my back. He didn't hold me tight like I wanted him to, but I appreciated him for letting me be vulnerable in his arms.

"It's hard, I know," he said to me as I struggled to breathe and choked back tears.

"Let's go sit," he told me, walking me over to a nearby table. He carefully guided me like I was an old lady with no sense of direction or balance, and he sat down across from me. I nuzzled my head into my folded arms on the table and continued my weeping session. He sat quietly as I calmed myself down with every sniffle and whine.

"I hate it here," I told him. He scoffed at my obvious response, but he made it a point to mention that I was not the only one.

"Nobody likes a place like this, but we all are here for a reason." I turned my face up at him because he was sounding like an after school special and I couldn't stomach the dramatics. He saw how annoyed I was at his response and he sort of laughed it off, realizing that he sounded a bit corny.

"Okay, maybe that's a bit cliché to say," he admitted.

"Yeah, you think?" I snarled.

"But seriously, though. You're not here because you're innocent." I glared at him once more, preparing to give him a mouthful, but I stopped myself because he was right. Though I really had nothing to do with Johnny's poorly planned out robbery attempt, I was guilty for a whole lot of other things. My mere decision to associate with him made me guilty. It was becoming clear to me that you are who you keep around. That was one lesson I really wished I would have taken from my parents.

"I'm *clearly* not used to living like this," I said poking fun at myself.

He laughed too and said, "Yeah, I can tell."

I didn't expect to bounce back so quickly from such a devastating moment, but CO Rivers was as personable as he was attractive.

With a smile on my face, I wiped the remaining tears from my cheeks and boldly asked him, "Would it be okay if we talked sometimes? I like talking to you and you seem to calm me down."

His head cocked back at my request, but I was serious. I felt like he would be the only person to keep me from becoming unhinged and besides being a calming force for me, I would be around him more and get to know him. Who knew what we could be once I got out? After a few seconds of thinking, he smiled and nodded his head.

"Sure, why not?" he said. I smiled back at him sweetly. As we walked side by side back to the intake room, Rivers instructed me on how to deal with Tatiana.

"Ignoring her is her biggest weakness. She chills out once she realizes she can't get to you." I nodded and before he closed the door to the room, I thanked him for the talk. When he smiled back, I nearly melted away. I watched him and his muscular body walk away through the glass and when he was out of sight, I turned towards the rest of the girls who were making crying sounds and sad eyes. Without fail, Tatiana began hurling more insults and making fun of me, but I did as Rivers said and ignored her. As far as I was concerned, she no longer existed. I plopped down on my bunk, my back to the other girls and with a few deep breaths, I was fast asleep, imagining myself cuddled up with CO Rivers in a bed much more comfortable than this one.

nine.

Visitation. I sat in Patty's office in slightly better spirits than I was the day before. I didn't want to bring up the debacle from last night, and though something told me that Patty already knew, she didn't mention it either. Instead, she sat back and listened as I spouted off all my issues. It was customary for the fresh meat to have a one-on-one "accountability session" with Patty to further discuss the events that led up to why we came to Bennings. I didn't get the importance of it, but I guess the formality made it easier for her to understand us better–at least that's what Patty claimed, but I didn't completely buy that.

I went into my whole spiel, talking about my oh-so-perfect parents and my ever-so-wonderful brother and sister, who, if it weren't for me, would have the perfect life and be the perfect family. I rambled for a while and I probably only saw Patty's eyes twice because she spent most of her time jotting down notes. Of course, I brought up Johnny and his friends–they were the reason I was mixed up in the robbery to begin with. She took particular interest in mine and Johnny's relationship. She focused on the age thing and tried to persuade me that I was being taken advantage of.

I laughed in her face. I wasn't trying to be disrespectful, but the mere notion that I had no idea what I was doing and that I was somehow brainwashed was pure comedy. It almost seemed like I was in a perpetual intervention. I had heard it all before and I was so bored of it.

"How did you meet Johnny, if you don't mind me asking?"

"I do mind," I said. Patty glared at me, her nostrils flaring.

"Is there a particular reason why you mind, or you just don't want to tell me?"

"Both."

"Eve, work with me here."

I got the feeling that she was trying to be of help, and though I knew she couldn't rewire me, I played the game. I told her about how Johnny practically stalked me while I was shopping for a party one weekend. I was with Mackie and Rachel, and they were creeped out, especially since they knew who he was and had heard some rumblings about him, but I was intrigued. He was cute and fit. He had this sleepy gaze that made it obvious he was high all the time, but he managed to show love through them even still. When he flashed his smile, it was like sunshine. That was his secret weapon. Dark and handsome, that's how I liked them, and Johnny checked those boxes and more. I walked right up to Johnny, asked him if he liked what he saw, and when he smirked, I had to grab a hold of the clothes rack next to me to keep from trembling. We exchanged numbers and we didn't waste any time.

"Did you know he was much older?" Patty asked as she continued to write on her notepad. I shook my head no. I knew he was "older", but I didn't think to ask by how much. He had such a youthful face and presence about him, I didn't think it mattered. It was only after I saw people post on his Instagram, "Happy 25th," that I even knew the guy was in his 20s. Even after I found out, I didn't ask. Actually, I felt even better knowing that I was able to pull an older guy. Even though my parents had money, he always took care of me and made sure I was good, so I couldn't stand the fact that people judged him for being with me.

"So, when can I get visitation?" I asked quickly changing the subject. Patty was a bit surprised at how quickly I bounced from one topic to another, but she plunked at her computer, checking to see the exact date I would be eligible for visitors.

"It looks like you are eligible now, but no one has requested a visit yet. My shoulders tensed up and my brows furrowed. I knew my parents wanted me there and all, but I had hoped that they would come visit as soon as they could.

"My parents know they can come, right? I mean, they're aware of the scheduling and stuff? Have they at least called? I'm sure-" I ranted. Patty stopped me and attempted to calm my nerves, though what she said only made them worse.

"Trust me sweetie, they know when they can come visit you and they signed an acknowledgement form stating they understood their rights as visitors. And no, no calls." I wanted to say so much, but nothing came out. It was just like them to cast me out and forget about me. I didn't know why I thought they would be different this time.

They always did this to me; they'd leave me alone and let me do whatever I wanted to do, but as soon as I got into trouble, they suddenly cared enough to bail me out and wag their fingers at me publicly. Then, once the heat was off them, they'd pretend like I didn't exist anymore, and the cycle continued, only, this time, I was out of the game for a while. I just knew they were happy I was locked up and were probably planning the "Eve Is Gone, Whoop-de-do!" party as I spoke with Patty.

As I imagined my parents continuing their lives, throwing dinner parties and galas, popping champagne bottles, and cackling to themselves about how they finally got rid of me, I began shaking uncontrollably. Patty kept telling me to breathe deep and to calm down, but I couldn't. I was going to blow up, and the question was when and who was going to trigger the meltdown.

I sauntered to math class, feeling more depressed and less hopeful than I did a few minutes before. Specs did her best to keep a smile on my face, making me little doodles and cracking jokes on Mr. Kole, who wore very tight pants that made his butt bubbly and luscious. We couldn't for the life of us understand why he would wear pants that accentuated his features knowing there were horny teenage girls who were deprived of contact with boys, but we decided that Mr. Kole was just a clueless puppy who just knew a thing or two about math. Though Specs did her best and got an occasional giggle and knee slap from me, I still felt like I was in a gutter, surrounded by the crap that was being shoveled my way.

I didn't expect lunch to be much different, but Brit and Specs tag teamed and had me pounding the lunch table in hysterics. They were shaping up to be great friends to me and I was so grateful for them, but what really shook me was when Gigi got into the mix. After that very awkward exchange between the two of us, I avoided talking to her when I could, careful not to risk getting her angry or making her even more uptight. I didn't expect her to warm up to me any time soon, but when she joined in on the make-Eve-feel-better brigade, I was a tad alarmed. What was her angle? She *did* practically threaten to beat me up when I asked her about why she was at Bennings just the day before, so why the change of heart? It didn't really matter though because I needed the cheering up, and she was only helping.

For the rest of the week, I kept myself out of trouble and more importantly, I kept my self in a good mood. The Day of Empowerment was the next day, and it was all anybody could talk about. I had only been at Bennings for two weeks and I was having the hardest time of my life. My saving grace was that I had some new friends to keep me from going too far into the depths of depression. Specs and I sat in our usual corner in the back of the math classroom, talking and carrying on, when Patty popped her head in, zeroing her eyes right on me.

"Eve, can you come with me for a moment, please?" she asked. I nodded, and as I got up, all eyes were on me. I waved bye to Specs, as I didn't expect to see her again until lunch and followed Patty out the door and through the hallways.

"What's happening?" I asked as we made our way towards the meeting room. Once I recognized that that's where we were headed, I got giddy. I wasn't told that I had visitors coming, so I figured it was my parents coming to surprise me. I had it all planned out. I had given a lot of thought to this whole situation and wanted to take responsibility for my part. I was going to apologize profusely, let them know that I was sorry, and that they made their point. I figured I'd even throw in going to rehab, making sure I graduated high school on time, and going to college to spice up the mix. They were sure to be proud of me and demand my release so I could go home with them.

"You'll see," Patty smiled. Her smile let me know that my assumptions were right, and that I would finally see my parents. She opened the door to the meeting room and my smiling face quickly turned, but only for a second. Once my brain registered who I was looking at, I screamed and howled, completely ecstatic.

"Rachel! Mackie! What are you guys doing here!?" I yelled at them, bringing them both into an embrace. I took a step back to get a good look at them; I was so used to seeing them every day, but I was glad to see not a thing changed. Without fail, Mackie was in her track pants and t-shirt looking ready to run a marathon in a minute, and Rachel looked just as cute and dainty as always in her flowing sunflower dress. My emotions bubbled up, but I couldn't bring myself to show how overwhelmed I felt, though a few tears escaped my eyes. The girls both wiped my face, and we laughed at how pathetic I was for crying.

"How did you guys get here? Better yet, how did you get *in* here? You have to be 18 to come by yourself," I interrogated. They both looked at each other and smiled deviously.

"My brother agreed to take us," Mackie explained. "He signed us in and then pretended to have an important meeting, so he's outside on a fake conference call." We laughed together in our little huddle and then sat down so we could catch up.

"Tell your brother I said thank you, and I owe him one," I told Mackie. She brushed me off and assured me he didn't mind.

"So, what about school?" I asked them. They ditched an entire day of school to come see me for a few minutes, and though skipping school was something we all were used to doing, I felt horrible they were doing so under these circumstances.

"Girl, it's Friday! There is nothing going on in school. Besides, you're our girl and we *had* to come see you!" Rachel interjected. All the feelings of being alone and forgotten by my parents didn't hold a candle to the fact that I was so loved by my friends, new and old. I didn't want to waste too much more time on the how's and why's of their visit because there was so much to catch up on. I was only out of society for two weeks, but I felt like I was gone for an eternity.

"Okay, tell me everything! What are people saying about the case?" I probed them. They looked a bit uneasy. It was obvious they didn't want to tell me, but I pushed them to spill. A large part of me wanted to know the truth, even if it was not in my favor.

"Girl!" Rachel began. "Johnny and those guys are going to federal prison! They're being held at county now, but they're supposed to get sentenced soon."

"Yeah, it's not looking too good for them. Especially Johnny," Mackie cut in. My eyes averted from theirs as I thought about how hard Johnny was taking things. He had to have been going through it, and then it dawned on me that I hadn't thought much about Johnny since getting to Bennings, aside from being asked about him. Once the wheels turned, my empathy for him turned off and I realized that he deserved whatever he got too.

"Did you know he had pictures of you?" Mackie asked me. My eyes shot back to hers.

"Yeah, we took pics all the time, why?" They both shook their heads and Rachel sat with her head down as Mackie continued to explain.

"No, sis. He had nude pictures of you. It was all over the news. They not only got busted for the robbery, but when the cops got a warrant and searched Johnny's place, they found tons of drugs, a stash of pictures and even a video of you guys doing... you know." I buried my head in my hands, thinking back to when he could have taken the photos and video and couldn't remember anything that would lead me to the answer. I was stumped and didn't want to believe that he would take them without me knowing, but he had to have.

I'll be the first to admit, I was far from virginal. Technically, Johnny wasn't my first, but my experience between my first and Johnny was so different, I might as well not claim the other one. I liked Johnny so much, and I knew he liked me too. Maybe I just wanted to impress him or maybe I was just some tramp, but it didn't take us long to start fooling around. When I thought about it, I remembered that we hooked up the first day we hung out. Then, when I *really* thought about it, we only messed around a couple times before he let Merv and Big Rob join in, and most of those times, there were drugs involved. I genuinely hated being with those two; they constantly smelled of Hennessy and were very rough, but I convinced myself that if doing that meant Johnny was happy, then it was worth it. Sitting across from Mackie and Rachel with no freedom wearing a recycled sweat suit made me realize that none of it was worth any of what I thought Johnny could give me. In fact, he took a lot from me. It was then that I decided that Johnny was absolute trash, and so was I for being with him.

I tried my best to keep my cries to myself, but I let out a sniffle and a whimper or two, prompting Rachel and Mackie to comfort me the way they always did. They held my hands and hugged me as I let out my anger and frustration through my bawling. Again, I wiped the snot and tears from my face, and swiftly moved on to the next subject. I asked them what people at school were saying about everything and they became mum. They were so apprehensive and refused to tell, citing that I'd get even more upset, and I decided that they were right.

"Fine. How are you guys doing? How's school and the college search and all that?" I asked them. They both held on to me as they took me through our daily school ritual they were performing without me. It was the usual-football games, house parties, and working. Rachel had just started dating Colton, one of the star basketball players who could get a full-ride scholarship anywhere he wanted. She had been crushing on him since freshman year, so it was sweet to hear that he finally asked her out. Mackie was still "playing the field" and was having her own load of fun. She never mentioned who she was dealing with, but she insisted that she was happy *and* satisfied. Mackie still hadn't made up her mind about which schools she wanted to go to, but Rachel was set on attending USC to study directing. She had been in the theater scene, and though never on the stage, she was a brilliant planner and had a good eye for visuals, so it made sense that she'd take her dreams to the next level.

The more they talked about their plans, the more left out and dejected I felt. Their lives were a hell of a lot more appealing than mine, and I had once lived it with them. I had taken my high life for granted and being locked up in this center was what I deserved for deliberately disregarding it. Soon, Patty walked up to us, clearing her throat, and warning us that we only had about five minutes left of the visit. We were chatting for almost 30 minutes, but it only seemed like two. Before I went back to my new life and they went back to their normal ones, I asked about my parents.

"How are my mom and dad?"

Rachel said, "Honestly, they seem the same, but to be fair, they've always had great poker faces." I brushed off Rachel's comment with an eye roll and then asked if they told either of them when they'd be coming. I knew neither one of them would have come without telling my parents, so I knew they had an answer. They both looked at each other and had a silent conversation with their eyes, going back and forth between gazes, fighting about who was going to tell me.

"Can one of you just spit it out?" I demanded. Mackie zipped her lips and looked at Rachel, who then took a deep breath.

"We went to see your parents last night to see if they had anything for you or anything they wanted to tell you..."

"And?" I probed. Worried, Rachel finally broke her silence.

"Your dad told us to tell you he was sorry, but they're not coming to visit you. They think it would be best if they didn't come." I let Rachel's words play and replay in my head several times, and each time, her voice sounded more and more like my dad's. Once I could hear his voice clearly, I could feel him taunting me through his words. I could even see my mom, right beside him, saying nothing. I couldn't articulate how hot my blood was boiling or how cold I could feel my heart turning. I had done such a great job of containing myself that entire meeting, but I finally released just a pinch of that bad energy when I balled up my fists and slammed them down on the table.

"Those assholes!" I shouted, prompting CO Bates, who had popped in the room at some point, to say, "Watch your language!" Patty was nowhere to be seen, but I had to talk to her.

"Bates, take me to see Patty," I demanded. I walked out, but then stopped and rushed back to Rachel and Mackie, who were still in shock at my outburst.

"I love you," I told them hugging and kissing the both of them on their cheeks, before stomping off through the meeting room doors and through the maze of hallways. I felt horrible that I left my friends there like that, but I had something I had to do in that moment. I stormed into Patty's office, and she wasn't having any of it. I demanded that she call my parents, and she folded her arms, insisting that she would not be doing anything as long as my tone was as harsh as it was. I plopped down in one of the chairs opposite her, took deep breaths, and then asked her again as I gritted my teeth. She still wasn't happy in the manner that I approached her, but she studied her Rolodex of contacts and dialed a number, putting it on speaker phone.

"Hello?" a sweet, cool voice answered.

"Mom! How could you do this to me!? Better yet, how could you let dad do this!? Am I not important enough to you?!" I screamed into the phone. Patty immediately interjected and told me to calm down, but I refused. They *all* were going to hear my mouth, and I did not care. I could hear a shift on the phone, and I knew my mom was handing the phone over to my dad who was who I wanted to address anyway.

"Eve, have you lost your damn mind?! Don't you ever call here and speak to your mother like that ever in your life, do you hear me?!" He screamed back. I got louder, and we proceeded with our shouting match. I cursed him out, and he cursed me out. I told him off and he told me off. It was the same song and dance we were used to doing, but this one hurt more.

"You didn't even have the decency to even call me and tell me you weren't coming. You had Mackie and Rachel tell me!? You're both cowards!"

"What good would coming to see you do, huh? We would do the same thing we are doing now. You never wanted to listen to us, so why would we think you would change now? You are there because of *you*, now sit in there and do your time!" As I prepared to rip my dad a new one, I could see Patty shifting in her seat, completely uneasy at our interaction.

"No dad, I'm here because of *you!* You never paid attention to me and that's why I did everything! You never cared about me!"

"We never cared? Listen to yourself! We bailed you out, paid for your problems to go away, and continued to give you freedoms when we should have stripped them away. *We* never cared?! You are ungrateful and a stain on our family's good name. Why couldn't you just follow your brother and sister's lead instead of wandering all over town like some who-"

My eyes widened as Patty took the phone off speaker and grabbed the handheld.

"Okay, this conversation is not productive or healthy at all and I'm cutting it short." I smashed the speaker phone button and screamed, "Screw you, dad!" with all the strength that was in me.

"I wish I was never born in this family!"

I could hear him yell back, "You would've ended up right where you are now, regardless!" I went to retort when a brawny hand gripped my shoulder, pushing me back. CO Bates held me in my seat as Patty took the phone back off speaker phone again. I struggled to get air and couldn't stop blubbering. I felt so low and scummy and couldn't believe that my own father fixed his mouth to call me a whore. Patty continued to listen to my dad hurl insults about me, probably saying I didn't deserve their love or that I was a lost cause. Once Patty finally got a word in, she told father dearest that she would need to speak to him privately another time when tensions had cooled down.

She eyeballed me as she hung up the phone, searching for the right words to say. She knew there wasn't anything that could be said to mend my hurt feelings. I wasn't going to accept any excuse on my dad's behalf, so I got loose from CO Bates' grasp, ran out of the room, and screamed as loud as I could for as long as I could. There were still classes going on, and the teachers and some students poked their heads out to see what all the fuss was about. I'm sure all they saw was another spoiled little brat making a scene over a sour phone call, but I felt my entire world shatter, taking my heart with it. I genuinely thought there was hope and that I could prove I deserved another chance, but it was clear that my parents hated me, so I needed to hate them.

I parked myself on a wall and slunk to the ground, again releasing the last and loudest of my cries before suddenly being bombarded by arms surrounding me. I didn't look up as I was too embarrassed at the scene I was causing but hearing Specs and Brit's voices whisper to me was soothing enough.

"Here, get her up," Gigi told them. They helped me back up and as they led me down the hall towards the red room, I glanced around to see CO Bates and CO Rivers trailing us to make sure I didn't snap again.

"I hate them," I said to myself. "I hate them."

ten.

Step In The Right Direction. Gigi directed the girls to guide me to her bunk. If my head wasn't so discombobulated from my hysteria, I would have thanked her for offering her own bed for me to rest on while I pulled myself back down from my fit. The girls sat around me as I explained what happened with my friends' visit and the call. They hugged on me, wiped the sweat from my face, and even fanned me as I sobbed into Gigi's pillow. I closed my eyes and the last thing I remembered hearing before knocking out was Gigi whispering to me, "It's okay. Let it out," as she stroked my back.

I missed my second class, but Patty wrote an excuse note for me. She would have made any other girl go back to class or risk getting written up for insubordination but listening in on that call gave her a perspective no one else had about my life. Yeah, I was a spoiled, obnoxious, and selfish girl from a rich family, but I needed more help than she thought, and she got a glimpse of why.

I had been out for about an hour or so and was awakened by a crowd of girls piling into the room.

"Eve," Specs whispered to me as she lightly shook me awake. "Are you coming to lunch?"

Groggy and still tired, I stretched out my arms, releasing much of the tension I built from being completely still during my nap, and nodded. As I slowly gathered myself to get out of the bed, Brit came up with the rest of the girls from the red room and presented a huge card made from taped together construction paper.

Brit handed it to me and said, "Here, we all signed it! We hope you feel better."

I examined the card, noting that everyone from the red room and Specs signed it, however, my gaze zeroed in on a name I never thought would be on anything for me: Tatiana. I looked up at her and she nodded her head in my direction and even smiled. I smiled back and thanked everyone and had hoped that no one would notice me getting emotional, but Gigi told me to suck up the tears because I had done enough crying for one day.

"It's time to eat!" she said, intertwining her arm with mine. I looked over at her and noticed the smile on her face and felt like I finally made it in good with her.

"And just letting you know," Brit began, "you got family right here!" A room full of smiles, a giant card, and the appeal of having people who cared enough about me to consider me family was all I needed to forget the pain I felt earlier. CO Tankard, another female guard who kept a close watch on the high risk girls, commended everyone for rallying around me.

"You girls showed true sisterhood right there. For that, I'm giving you all good marks towards your weekly goal." The room cheered because weekly goals were another hurdle we had to jump over in our journey towards getting out on time or early. If you met your weekly goal, you increased your chances of joining the Gems and getting an early release, or at least being on the good list. If you failed to meet your weekly goals consistently, Patty, Ms. Jenkins and whoever else had power could hold you back until you got your act together.

Tatiana strolled over to me, and though I prepared myself to fend her off, she thanked me for having my breakdown so she could get herself back on track to get out of intake on time. She extended her hand for a fist bump, and I happily fist bumped her back. Arm in arm with both Gigi and Specs, we started our march to lunch, but then I stopped when I saw CO Rivers. Since he had agreed to let me vent to him, I knew this would be a good time for me to rant about my abandonment issues.

"You guys go ahead. I need to do something really quick," I told them. They nodded and agreed to save me a seat. I watched as all the girls in the red room headed to lunch and when the last one was out of sight, I glanced over at CO Rivers, who already knew what I wanted. He pointed his head down the hall towards the rec room, which wasn't too far from the cafeteria. I walked beside him in silence, figuring out what to say first.

"I heard enough," CO Rivers told me, as I sat across from him with my head propped up on my folded arms. I shook my head, embarrassed at the entire ordeal, but more than anything, ashamed because my parents had forsaken me so easily.

"I don't get it," I told him. "I mean, I know I wasn't the best daughter, but you don't throw people away."

"That's how you feel?" he asked me, and I nodded.

"I feel like they couldn't wait to get rid of me. Believe it or not, I had some good moments. There were times that I stayed out of trouble and did what I was supposed to do and was still made to feel like the bald-headed stepchild of the family." CO Rivers cocked his head to the side, doing his best to hide a smirk.

"How so?"

I explained my family dynamics; my parents were the "model" of what a middle-aged Black couple should be. They were both successful and made their wealth the proper way; mom, a successful business owner, and my dad, a real estate mogul. They were hard workers and pillars of the community. People looked up to them and I understood why. Then there was my brother. He was the first born, so he was the guinea pig, but whatever failures my parents experienced with Kobi didn't affect how he operated in the real world. He was everything a parent could want in a kid; smart and studious, good-looking, athletic, and made good choices when it came to girls. There was absolutely nothing stopping him, and when he announced that he was going to law school, my dad was ecstatic.

My sister, Chelsie, was also an overachiever, but she was more technical and logical than me or my brother. Chelsie knew from the moment she could pick up any tool that she wanted to create things, so she went the engineering route. Again, my parents were beyond proud of Chels, not only because she wanted to study such a financially rewarding career, but because she would be one of very few Black female engineers, which could open even more doors for her if she ventured down the right paths.

"And then there's you," CO Rivers stated. He was careful in how he said it; he wasn't poking fun at how different I turned out or anything, but the statement alone brought a lot of baggage with it and reminded me of just *how* different I was from my entire family.

"Yep. Then there's me. Troublesome, stupid, rebellious me." He cut me off before I could hurl anymore insults at myself and told me to stop putting myself down.

"You're more than that," he said.

"Oh yeah, I forgot whore. According to my dad and probably the rest of the world, I'm just some little hoe who did everything in her power to ruin her parents' reputations." He looked at me with sad eyes and tried to refute my statement. The fact was, there wasn't anything to dispute. On the outside looking in, I was a nuisance. I was so blatant and deliberate about how little I cared about how bad my family could look, and maybe the robbery was the final straw.

"You're not a whore," CO Rivers strongly insisted. I peered into his eyes and could see how contained he was, though his tone was contrary.

"But I am. I was with an older man. I let him and his friends do whatever they wanted to me and apparently, they went far beyond what I wanted because there are pictures and a video of me somewhere that I had no idea about. For all I know, they're circling around the internet, giving pedos pleasure. So yeah, I'm a whore." He perched his head on his arms and leveled with me. We looked into each other's eyes and for a second, a moment, I wanted to kiss him. I almost went for it too, but he had to ruin it with sensible talk.

"That doesn't make you a whore. In fact, it makes you a victim. What he did to you was illegal in so many ways and just morally wrong."

A victim? There was no way. I couldn't be a victim. I was willing—well, at least when I was aware of it. Plus, I was now 17, 16 at the time we started hanging out. I was in on the game and wanted to play. I couldn't be a victim and I refused to accept that. When I tried to get Rivers to walk back his words, he doubled down and demanded that I see it his way. I fell silent and did everything in my power to take my mind away from imagining myself as a victim.

"Look, you've made some serious errors in judgment, but that doesn't make you a terrible person. You're misguided, but that's why you're here, to get on the right path." I appreciated him for attempting to cheer me up, though he only made me think about some things more seriously. My stomach grumbled so loud we both could hear it, so after sharing a chuckle, he escorted me to lunch.

"I admire you. You know just what to say," I said to him with a smirk. He chuckled a little, shaking his head.

"Believe it or not, I know a thing or two about being abandoned, but I didn't let it break me. I let it motivate me and now I'm trying to help people like you and the rest of these girls get over the hurdles I faced."

"You really are, like, the only one who can cheer me up," I noted as we stood in front of the cafeteria doors.

"Nah, I think your new friends do a good job of that. I see how you are with them." I thought about that, and I smiled as I glanced into the room and saw Specs, Brit, and Gigi all staring at me with smiles on their faces as they waved for me to hurry and come in.

"Yeah, I guess they are making me better day by day," I said.

"You can do the same for yourself, you just need to know you have permission to grow and be better," CO Rivers said to me with a sincere smile.

eleven.

*T*he *Day of Empowerment.* *"... you just need to know you
have permission to grow and be better."*
    It was Saturday, which meant it was the Day of
Empowerment, a day that everyone had been waiting for. My head
was still spinning from the drama the night before, so I couldn't bring
myself to care enough about it. To get my head on straight, I
sauntered to Patty's office, where I found her filling the last of the
folders for the day. She wore a bright green blazer with a white
undershirt and some jeans and looked so done up but dressed down
all at the same time. She even had a certain pep about her, and I
assumed that she was also excited for the day, which only made me
more annoyed that I didn't share the feeling.
    "How you feeling, Eve?" she greeted me with a concerned smile.
    I shook my head and said, "Not good. Not good at all."
    She stopped stuffing the folders and invited me to sit down as she
sat on the corner of her desk and peered down at me. She extended
her hand out to grab mine and for a second, I hesitated, but I knew
Patty meant no harm and this was her way of perhaps transferring
her positive energies and good vibes to me.
    I explained how heartbroken I was about what happened with
my parents, and in particular, my dad. I told her I wasn't going to
make it the full seven months to which she reminded me I had no
choice.
    "You're stronger than you think you are, Eve," Patty said, lightly
running her thumb over the back of my hand. "Besides, you only
have a couple weeks left before you're in general pop. Being with
your friends and getting into the groove of your program will make
the time go by quicker and smoother."
    I stared at her and said nothing, but I'm sure my expression
screamed doubt and helplessness.

"If it makes you feel any better, your friends requested another visit with you next weekend. It's obvious that they love you."

Hearing that my girls were willing to make the trip out to see me again made me feel lighter, loved, and wanted. I smiled a little and Patty's face lit up, only making me smile wider.

"See? You have people who love you and want you at your best. They seem like great girls, your friends." I nodded.

"Yeah. They're more than great. They're the best."

"Your parents will come around, I know it," Patty insisted. My smile faded as the thought of them sitting in the court room unreactive as I got carried away in cuffs played over in my head once again.

"You're wrong about them. They won't come around because they don't want to. They've already convinced themselves that I'm beyond saving. You heard that yourself yesterday." I sprung up from the chair and decided that Patty wasn't being very helpful.

"Eve?" she stopped me. I turned around to her, not saying a word.

"Are you participating today?" I cocked my head to the side.

"Yeah? I thought we had to?"

Patty chuckled to herself and said, "No, you don't, but we knew all the girls would love the activities afterwards, so we made the workshops mandatory in order for everyone to enjoy the festivities."

I had an out; I didn't *have* to take part and could spend the entire day in my bunk, sulking about my life and my inherited misfortune. I watched Patty as she continued to stuff the last of the folders and figured that it wouldn't hurt to attend. Besides, the change of pace would be good for me.

"Yeah, well, I was planning on going anyway. I'm going to meet up with my friends now. Thanks for the talk."

"Well, I'm all done here. I'll walk with you," she said, gathering her materials. I had hoped I could take my time and think on some things alone, but since Patty had already insisted that we go together, I could get some brownie points and help her out. Without being asked, I grabbed a pile of the folders as she grabbed her rolling crate filled with more folders, a tablecloth, pens, pencils, and other supplies. With a smile, she thanked me for helping her out, and off we went.

I kept my mouth shut, hoping she would take the hint that I wasn't interested in talking anymore, but she continued her crusade in my parents' honor.

"Your parents will be so proud of how different you'll be... They won't know what to say or do... I know it's hard to see it now, but blah

blah blah blah blah."

She talked my ear off, thinking she was cheering me up, and to her defense it was her job, but she was only making me hate my family even more. Based on my past, I could disprove every affirmative thing she said would happen, and I hated that Patty didn't get it. She was acting like she knew my family. She knew nothing about me or them, so how was she so confident that she'd be right? I wanted to snap at her. I wanted to tell her to save her spiel for someone else, but when I looked at how assured she was, I bit my tongue. Perhaps it was better to just let her think her ideas would be reality. Maybe if I started believing in them, they could very well come true.

"You're *so* smart and you have so much potential," Patty said. "You can go far in life, with or without your parents' help or approval."

I appreciated her compliment, though I felt like it was a standard go-to catch phrase people in her position told people like me. Her optimism was becoming rather annoying, but a part of me was absorbing every word and burying it in my soul. I knew her words would ring true eventually, but at that moment, they just didn't seem applicable.

"You could even be fast-tracked into the Gems if you do what you're supposed to do. The Gems group sets the girls up for success outside these walls and you'll excel without a doubt," mentioned Patty. Though I had already gotten the rundown on the Gems and what that program would do for me, it hit different hearing Patty tell me that I would be a perfect candidate for it. Maybe I wasn't giving Patty enough credit; this was more than just a job for her, and maybe she really did believe in all of us.

We made it in front of the auditorium, the doors already opened, and most of the girls were already sitting down with some still trickling in. Out of the corner of my eye, I could see some arms flailing, so I looked and smiled when I saw Specs, Brit, and Gigi waving me over.

"Thanks for the pep talk, Patty!" I said as I handed the folders that were in my hand to CO Fillman who was on guard at the door. I scurried over to my friends and they greeted me with hugs and fist bumps. Specs pulled out a fruit cup from underneath her shirt, which officially made my day.

"Since you weren't at breakfast, I figured you'd be hungry. This was all I could take out without being seen," she said as she sneakily passed it to me as if it was contraband. My heart fluttered a little. Her gesture was equivalent to a "hey, have you eaten?" text and it made me love her even more. I gave her another hug and drank the syrupy juice before funneling the peach and pear chunks into my mouth.

"Why were you with Patty? You good?" Brit asked me.

I nodded and replied, "Yeah, I'm cool. I was just helping her bring her stuff down." Brit gave me a thumbs up and even Gigi, who I felt was now warmed up to me, smiled at me. I still felt like a pile of poo dropped out of a car in a brown paper bag on a freeway and left to rot, but I realized that I wasn't the only abandoned piece of crap. I was surrounded by throwaways, and maybe, just maybe, I could learn to accept my place amongst them.

"All right, all right! Who's ready for an amazing day of empowerment?!" Patty called into the microphone. All the girls, including myself, screamed, cheered, and clapped in response. As the crowd settled, I casually watched as the girls around me gushed with their friends and squirmed in their seats. I had only been around for a few weeks, but it came to my attention that this was the first time in a long time that the girls around here would have any fun outside of what they created themselves. Apparently, the center piloted the Day of Empowerment a little over a year ago with some success, but it required some fine tuning and tweaking, so it was a real treat to have the program back and in effect.

"Before we start, we need to set some ground rules."

There wasn't a single girl in that room who didn't roll her eyes or groan, but Patty ignored it all and continued her speech and the rules were as one would expect. Clearly, we had to be policed and kept track of, so that was the bulk of the intro, though Patty felt it necessary to reiterate that no fighting or disrespect would be tolerated. Finally, she went into the agenda for the day, which for some reason, piqued many of the girls' interests.

"There are four workshops available, three of which you have to attend today. Two of the classes are breakout sessions, which means they will be held at the same time. Everyone here has their own folder and in it will be your designated schedule. You *must* attend all classes and your assigned session only. If you're found in a class you're not supposed to be in, you won't be able to take part in the field day, so follow your schedules!" Patty explained as Ms. Jenkins and a few of the COs started handing out the folders.

"The first class starts right after I finish, and everyone needs to attend. It's called 'Girls Empowered: Taking Back Yourself from the World' and Ms. Jenkins will facilitate that one. The second block is for the breakout sessions, the first option being 'Understanding Your Worth' and the second called 'Leveling Up in the Real World'. We have assigned each girl to a workshop according to your program, your progress, and what the staff here believes would most benefit you. Please understand that you may not be with your friends, but it will only be for an hour, so you'll be okay."

Somehow, I knew I would be one of the unlucky ones ripped from her group to be in a different class that I didn't really want to be in.

It was CO Rivers who had our folders, and as he handed them to me to pass down, he smiled and winked at me, which caused my heart to thump out of my chest. Sure enough, when I opened my folder and compared my schedule to the rest of the girls, I was the only one not in the same breakout session.

"Understanding Your Worth? This is bullshit," I said closing my folder shut.

With a smile, Brit remarked, "Clearly not," prompting Brit and Gigi to giggle with each other.

"Don't listen to them, Eve. You'll be fine," Specs whispered to me, caressing my hand. Though annoyed, I nodded and agreed to attend, but not be present.

"Finally, everyone will come back here for the last workshop of the day, Charm Etiquette School. That will be two hours, but it will be fun!" Patty promised.

She introduced Ms. Jenkins to the podium for the first workshop of the day, to which then I zoned out completely. I heard bits and pieces of the first session, but if I had to sum up the class, it was about making your own way in the world and not letting people influence you–you know, the usual crap after school specials force feed you.

I snapped out of my bored trance when Specs waved her hand in my face to get my attention.

"Knock, knock! Anybody home?" she asked, knocking against my skull. I shot her an annoyed look, but she giggled and let me know that the first session was done.

"We'll see you in an hour, pal. Have fun 'understanding your worth,'" Brit told me as she and Gigi continued to taunt me.

I waved goodbye to them with a sour look on my face and headed towards the opposite way they were going. We had a couple minutes between sessions, so I roamed around before ending up right at the room. I was surprised to see Patty setting up; I figured since she helped plan the whole day, she would sit out teaching, but this was her thing. She was in her element.

"Hello again," she greeted me with a genuine smile. I stood in the doorway with my arms crossed and my eyes zeroed in on her as she continued to organize the seating arrangement.

"Are you okay?" she asked. I shook my head.

"No. I'm not." She stopped what she was doing, looked me up

and down, and scoffed before continuing to place her materials on each seat.

"Are you going to tell me what's bothering you or do I have to read your mind?"

"Oh, I'd love to hear what you think I'm thinking... this should be good," I told her, plopping myself down in one of the many empty seats. With one finger tapping on her pressed lips, she examined me as if trying to find the answer to the equation that is my mindset.

"Let's see... you're upset because you're not in the same class as your friends?"

"Gee, how did you know?" I asked sarcastically. She shook her head and finished placing the last few mirrors on the remaining desks.

"You're not the only one who I figured would be upset, but believe it or not, this is for your own good."

"How so?"

"The fact that you even have to ask that is a big reason you're in here."

Confused and getting more irritated, I got up from my chair and walked towards her.

"Honestly though, why do you have me in here with the low self-esteemed girls? I mean, mirrors? Seriously? What are we going to be doing, giving ourselves pep talks?"

Just as Patty went to answer, a slew of girls piled into the room, laughing and messing about. As they all took their seats, I made my way to the back of the class to the desk closest to the door. When Patty saw that everyone who was supposed to be in the class was present, she cleared her throat.

"Eve?" she addressed me. I looked up at her and didn't say a word, but I nodded so she knew she had my attention. "Would you mind moving up? There are a few seats closer to the rest of the group."

I stayed put, but only for a second because I then remembered that my behavior would also determine if I got to join field day, and Lord knew that if I had to sit through this crap, I would definitely enjoy myself afterwards. I got up and as I walked towards the front, I located the empty seat right in front of her and popped a squat.

Clasping my hands together and with a sarcastic smile, I asked, "Is this better for you Ms. Patty?"

She returned the sarcasm back with a fake smile and remarked, "It's perfect, thank you," before welcoming the rest of the girls to the course.

"Welcome to 'Understanding Your Worth'. You're all in this class for one reason: because the staff believes in you and we want you to believe in yourself."

Oh, brother! I thought to myself, doing everything in my power not to allow my eyes to roll to the back of my head. As Patty continued to talk, I racked my brain wondering how her or any of the staff felt like I wasn't confident enough in myself. I mean, I exuded confidence; I walked with my head held high and didn't care what anybody thought of me. I did what I wanted and for damn sure was confident in my decisions, even if they were stupid, so for the life of me, I couldn't figure out why I was there.

Patty began the course with breathing exercises. She coached us on how to decompress whenever we felt pinned up anger boiling up inside. One of my therapists taught me this too, but he had me lay down on a mat as he placed his hands over my chest. He claimed he was making sure I was breathing deep enough for the exercise to be effective, but I knew when he'd place his hand over my boob and leave it there that he was bullshitting me. I jokingly told Mackie and Rachel this once after a session and the horror on their faces was both shocking and funny. I didn't know why they seemed so disturbed at it–it seemed as innocent as it could be but after knowing what Johnny did to me, I realized that I was taken advantage of many times without even knowing it, and that feeling sucked.

I always felt control over myself. I never ever considered that I was being abused because I was willing... or... maybe I thought I was? I never said no, and it wasn't like I didn't like the attention or the touch. It felt good feeling like I was attractive enough or that I had the "right stuff" that any person would want. It made me feel empowered and in even more control because I had the grand prize. I had what they wanted, and they had to impress me to get it. At least, that's what I think I thought. I didn't know why this breathing exercise made me think about all that, but when I opened my eyes, I realized that I was thinking a little too hard and for a little too long because the rest of the girls and Patty were just staring at me, some concerned and some annoyed that I was taking so long.

"Are you good, Eve?" Patty asked me. I took a deep breath and nodded, looking around the room with apologetic eyes, hoping the other girls would accept my nonverbal apology.

"Good. On to the next exercise."

We cycled through a ridiculous amount of self-image drills, one where we expressed how we hoped others viewed us versus how we viewed ourselves, and another where we went around the room and gave every girl a compliment. When it got to me, my heart raced because I couldn't be sure what the girls would say. Most of them didn't know me and wouldn't have a reason to say anything nice to or about me.

"She's sort of quiet, which is cool, especially around here," one girl said, prompting laughter from the rest of the girls.

"I think she's cool," another said.

"I don't know why I think this, but I have a feeling she has great style," another chimed in.

I actually laughed out loud because, though she was right, it was even funnier that she made the baseless assumption since all any of us ever saw each other wear were sweatpants and sweatshirts. Compliment after compliment, some genuinely sweet, and some obviously made up to get through the exercise, I took them all in.

"She acts like a princess, but she can hold her own in a fight," the last girl said. I did a double take when I saw that it was Tatiana. I must've been in my own little world because I didn't even notice that she was in the class too. I smirked at her and she shook her head, trying to hold back a smile.

It was down to the last 10 minutes of the workshop and everyone was getting restless. That fruit cup that Specs gave me, though good, didn't hold me over at all and my stomach was screaming for some food. I had wondered if the lunch menu would be different today since it was a special event, but I couldn't even care because all I wanted to do was to eat something.

"All right girls, we're almost done. Everyone should have a mirror on their desk. That's yours to keep, but for now, I want you to hold it up in front of you. Look at yourself. I want you to tell us about a time when you felt the proudest of yourself."

While everyone began spouting off moments like when they aced a spelling test, learned how to drive, or got their first job, I couldn't think of a single thing. It wasn't like I wasn't proud of myself at all–I accomplished a lot, after all, I was still living, but my mind was blank, and I had nothing to draw from.

Patty called on me and I just stared at her and then back at my reflection. I stuttered and stammered until I asked to pass. Patty cocked her head to the side and told me to think harder and that she knew I had something to be proud of. I closed my eyes tight and even clenched my fists, hoping that something would pop up in my head so Patty would get off my back, but again, there was nothing.

"I- I don't know. I don't think I have something I'm proud of," I admitted to the rest of the group. I hid my face in my folded arms and hoped that Patty would move on to the next person, and after a quick pause, she did. I fought my angry tears hard and thankfully had my sweatshirt sleeves to soak up the stream that flowed its way out of my eye. Before I picked my head up, I wiped away any trace of sadness on my face and tucked away the sense of failure I felt.

"Perfect!" Patty said, clapping her hands together. "You guys made it through this class, and I have to say, I'm proud of each one of you. I think you guys are understanding just how special you are. You may not feel this, and it may even be a bit sappy to say, but the world needs you, your talent, and your light. Each of you brings something a little different that makes this world better. I need you to remember that as you finish up your time here. So, for this final drill, I want you to look back into your mirrors and in a few words describe how you feel about yourself in this moment."

Everyone raised their mirrors and admired themselves. Even I played along with this game, though I wasn't feeling up to playing. For the last time, the girls went around the room and shared what they thought of themselves. *Capable, awesome, gifted, funny, smart, worthwhile,* and *trendsetter* were just a few of the words the girls used to describe themselves. Finally, it got to me, and with all eyes pointed in my direction, I stared hard at myself and saw nothing good. I stared up at Patty, who was trying so hard to read me, and I suddenly found the perfect way to describe myself in that moment.

"A work in progress," I uttered right before the bell rang. Patty nodded her head in approval and said, "Good," before the rest of the girls stood up in unison and shuffled out of the room.

"Thank you for participating," Patty said to me as I headed out of the room. "I'm proud of you."

I nodded and headed back towards the auditorium, hoping that seeing Specs, Brit, and Gigi would get me out of my funk.

twelve.

*A*ll *Together Now.* Specs and Brit would not stop geeking over their session. As the speaker for the Charm Etiquette School gave a rundown of how the class would work, Specs and Brit began make-believing scenarios that they might find themselves in when they got out and what they would do.

"Your class sounded like fun," I told them, still jealous that they all got to be together.

"Yeah, it was fun! You would have loved it, Eve! How was your class?" Specs asked.

I shrugged and said that it wasn't half bad, but I would have gotten more out of their class. Brit cracked another lousy joke about how she hoped I had "recognized my worth" before cackling to herself, while Specs, Gigi, and I stared at her, unentertained. This time, I was sitting next to Gigi, so I turned to her to see how she liked the class. She had a stale look on her face, which told me she didn't care for it. Before I said anything, Specs interjected and mentioned that the guy teaching the class said that Gigi would do well in the real world because of how well she responded to the scenarios. Gigi rolled her eyes and remained quiet. As the instructor asked for volunteers for the table etiquette part of the class, I leaned over to Gigi and asked if she was okay.

"Yeah, I'm cool. That workshop was just a waste of time for people who don't even know if they'll get to be out in the real world again."

I fixed my mouth to ask what she meant by that, but after getting threatened the last time I asked her about her situation, I knew to stay quiet. Instead of saying anything else, I just patted her hand that laid balled up in a fist on the arm rest. One by one, the volunteers sat at the table set up on the platform in front of us and the instructor, Mr. Simpson, who owned an etiquette refinery school not too far from

Bennings, began explaining proper table manners. The entire thing made me laugh because I could remember being forced to attend those classes as a kid and absolutely hating it. I had a hard time paying attention in the class, but I still remembered that utensils were placed according to when you would use them, starting from the outside going in. I knew never to place my elbows on the table, no matter how comfortable or into the meal I was, and I always asked to be excused. When it came time to graduate from the school, my teacher, Ms. Wise, was shocked that I knew everything and had no choice but to pass me despite me being disruptive and being kicked out of class on a regular basis.

Mr. Simpson cycled through a few more rounds of volunteers for the table manners portion before switching gears and shifting to actual roleplay. This part took the longest, but it was the most entertaining. He gave us scenarios where we would have to make sound decisions and based on the decisions most of the girls chose to play out, these girls were not rehabilitated. For giggles, Specs and Brit volunteered, and they acted out a scene where Brit was offering Specs some drugs. The prompt was boring and so overdone, but Specs made a complete joke out of it by being as dramatic as she could, while Brit played the best drug dealer I had ever seen. The auditorium was in an uproar and even Patty, Ms. Jenkins, and Mr. Simpson were fighting back fits of laughter, but Mr. Simpson reigned them in and told them to be serious or let someone else do it. Specs agreed and told Brit she didn't want any drugs and that she would report her to the authorities in a monotonous voice, causing some of the girls to snicker in the audience.

We ended the course with a quiz that reiterated everything that we discussed, and it was cake. Mr. Simpson gave us the last 20 minutes to take the 15-question quiz, and I was the first one done with 15 minutes to spare. I handed the quiz to Patty, knowing I aced it, and with a raised eyebrow, she thanked me and handed it to Mr. Simpson who began grading it.

One by one, the girls handed in their papers, and finally the last girl handed in her quiz with still a few minutes left to spare. Mr. Simpson finished the grades and stepped up to the podium where he announced that everyone passed the course, prompting cheers and group hugs. Passing meant we all could take part in field day, but Mr. Simpson didn't seem to be aware that most of us didn't actually care for his lecture or that we passed, but that we all could go outside. He clapped his hands along with us and Patty took the mic to give us the instructions for the second half of the day.

"In order for this to go smoothly, we need everyone to line up in a single-file line in front of CO Fillman and CO Jones who will escort you out to the yard for the games and food."

With no more direction, we all sprang out of our seats and did our best to get in a line, though it didn't take long for there to be a problem with line cuts and girls screaming about their feet getting stepped on.

"Girls! You will all get out there, so please relax!" Patty called to us in the microphone. CO Fillman, annoyed with how dramatic some of the girls were being, started placing girls in the line so it could move. After minutes of getting us all organized, the COs, Ms. Jenkins and Patty walked us out to the yard where we all stood in amazement at the set up. There were white and red balloons tied everywhere, a few carnival games with real prizes, and a ticket booth manned by one of the staff stood next to a couple food stalls that had pizza, hot dogs, burgers, popcorn, cotton candy, and even boxes of movie theater candy. In the middle of all the activities was a large, open space with speakers and a projector screen.

While I stood enamored at how well the staff not only set up the yard, but how stealthily they set it up without us knowing, the rest of the girls hightailed it to every inch that the carnival covered. Brit and Gigi didn't seem as impressed as the other girls because they stood by me while everyone else hopped from stall to stall.

"Where did Specs go?" Brit asked us. Gigi and I both looked around and then I spotted her running back towards us, practically out of breath.

"Dunk tank. CO Rivers. Come on!"

Our eyes quickly shot to Brit, who seemed to bubble with excitement.

"Dunk tank!? Let's go!" she said, pulling Specs towards what Gigi and I realized was in fact a dunk tank with Rivers sitting right above it being taunted by most of the girls in the center. Gigi and I took one look at each other and laughed before jogging over to join in on the fun, and though I didn't want to admit it to Gigi or anyone, I couldn't wait to see CO Rivers soaking wet.

"You feeling better from yesterday?" Gigi asked, taking my attention away from Rivers and the crowd of restless, thirsty girls. I smiled at her and nodded, thinking about the card everyone made me.

"It really boosted my spirit."

"Hey, that's what friends are for," she said before turning her attention back to CO Rivers and cheering on the next girl up to dunk him. Before then, I had wanted Gigi to think of me as more than just some girl her friends kicked it with, but to hear her acknowledge that we were friends made me feel so good. It was weird to admit, but I valued Gigi's opinion of me more than anyone else's. I didn't know why–probably because she was the most closed off and it would be a challenge to crack her open, but that confirmation seemed to seal some deal between me and Gigi and I felt like we were on another level.

"Hey," I grabbed her shoulder. "You can talk to me about anything if you ever need to. That *is* what friends are for," I told her.

I had hoped that she understood that I was just as serious about our budding friendship as she seemed to be and wanted to make the deal sweeter by offering a listening ear. Perhaps with us now officially being friends, she would open up to me and tell me more about herself. I would have been lying if I said it wasn't eating me up inside not knowing what she did to get sent to Bennings. Gigi had already turned away from me and continued cheering on the shenanigans, so instead of making this a moment, I followed suit.

Specs was now up and had already made two failed attempts. Brit was in her ear whispering to her and pointing to the bullseye, giving her a serious pep talk. Specs, as focused as I had ever seen her, threw her third ball. It barely tapped the release lever and caused her to strike out. We all supported Specs by giving her pats on the back, but now it was someone else's turn to dunk Rivers.

"Who's next?!" Rivers yelled out to us, laughing at how badly we were failing at dunking him. No one else wanted to embarrass themselves and take a turn. I thought about it, but I didn't want to set myself up for failure, should I strike out too, so my hand only got halfway up before I stopped myself from volunteering.

Gigi must of saw me from the corner of her eye because she grabbed my hand, raised it up, and screamed, "Eve wants a try!" as she walked me to the front of the crowd. The rest of the girls clapped and cheered me on as Brit became my coach for the moment.

"Focus!" she said to me.

I nodded and trained my eyes on the target. It glared at me and the more I stared at it, the bigger it seemed to get. To give him a chance to say goodbye, I glanced at him and smiled, to which he then called out to me, "Go easy on me!" finishing his plea with a wink. My palms got sweaty, and I even took a step back to catch myself. The smirk he had on his face was just as devious as it was inviting, and I knew I had to sink him, not just for myself, but for everyone. I threw the first ball, but it slipped and landed about a foot in front of the target. The rest of the girls laughed as I tried to hide my embarrassment, but Brit, being a good friend, told them to shut up so I could concentrate and patted me on the back, telling me I got this. I took my time and threw the ball as hard as I could, and this time, though it didn't trigger the lever, it tapped the target, causing everyone to lean forward and then throw their fists towards the air when it didn't stick. I stomped my foot and watched as Rivers, who looked terrified, wipe the sweat from his forehead.

"Oh, screw this!" Brit yelled. I swear, the world shifted into slow motion as Brit ran over to the target and pressed the lever herself just as I was gearing up to take him out. I saw his eyes grow wide as he waved his hands at Brit to stop, but there was no stopping her. He plummeted into the tank and when his body hit the water, every single girl jumped forward to get a good look. As he emerged, I noted how his skin glistened as the sun beamed down on his wet skin, how seamless he pulled himself out of the tank with a giant smile on his face, and how tight his wet shirt was against his body. I no longer had to imagine what he looked like underneath this uniform because I could see his defined six-pack making its impression against his top. CO Jones helped him out and wrapped a towel around him as the girls gathered around to laugh and taunt him. He looked over at me and shrugged, still smiling before being whisked away so he could change.

"I'm next!" CO Bates clasped his hands together. We all turned and watched him as he walked up to the dunk tank with confidence and took his place as the next victim. I knew what I was thinking, and when I looked around at every single girl around me, I knew we were all on the same page. We waited patiently as Bates got himself situated, making himself as comfortable as he could get.

"All right, who's up first?" he asked us with his hands held out wide, as if he was embracing this experience open-heartedly.

"Get him!" Specs yelled as she led the charge of about 10 other girls who bum-rushed the tank. Bates didn't stand a chance. Within seconds, he was submerged in the tank and the entire crowd yelped and hollered. As far as any of us were concerned, this was a small dose of payback for all the hostility he aimed at us every day, but he was bummed that he didn't get to savor his moment at all. CO Fillman helped him out of the tank so he could dry off and change and insisted that we all go find something else to do for a while.

I had forgotten that I had been without a proper meal all day, so the first thing I did was grab a corn dog with ketchup and some fries along with a soda and watched Gigi, Specs, and Brit cycle through the games before getting their own food.

The sun was slowly setting, and the sky became a pinkish purple with hints of blue splashed throughout it. White puffy clouds floated in the sky and reflected the cool colors that the setting sun allowed the sky to dance with. The girls and I sat in our own space on a palette of blankets the COs handed out so we could watch the movie. The girls got to vote on the film, which I somehow missed out on, so we were watching the live action version of *Aladdin*. The mood had settled from earlier in the day and now everyone laid on their own blankets, watching the movie. Brit, who announced she was bored only minutes into the movie, took down my hair that was slapped in a bun and began braiding it, while Specs laid in Gigi's lap. I was sure Specs was knocked out and when we heard a little snore from her during a quiet moment in the movie, we knew that she had used up all the energy she had for the day.

"Do you guys think they'd do this thing again?" I asked Gigi and Brit. They both shook their heads.

"Probably not. And if they do, it'll be after we're all long gone," Brit predicted. I hadn't even thought about it, but I didn't even know when Brit was leaving, or how long she had been in for that matter, and since I knew Brit didn't mind, I asked her.

"I've been in for about three months now. I still have a while though. March 1st, that's my date, as long as I don't do anything stupid to get it pushed again, that is," she chuckled to herself, Gigi joining in, careful not to disturb Specs during her nap.

"Patty pulled me aside like, a week ago and she reminded me, yet again, that I could have gotten into the Gems, but that fight didn't help my chances of that."

I looked over at Gigi who seemed uninterested in the conversation. I kept my eyes trained on her body language as best as I could while Brit held my head down to finish the first braid. It appeared Brit was reading my mind because she asked Gigi when she was supposed to be getting out. I pretended not to be interested in the question, but my ears perked up.

Gigi grunted. "I don't know, girl. Last I heard, they'd get back with me closer to my birthday, but my situation is different, so I just don't know."

Gigi carefully moved Specs head off her lap, got up, and wiped her sweats.

"Y'all want some popcorn or something?" she asked us. We both shook our heads and Gigi shrugged us off, leaving us alone.

"What's Gigi's situation?" I asked Brit. I could sense her shaking her head behind me.

"It isn't my place to say," Brit told me. I sighed and watched Specs as she slept so peacefully.

"What I can tell you is the reason is very serious. In her last meeting she had, her case worker told her that the judge was still considering moving her to an adult prison once she turned 18."

"My God," I said out loud. It was killing me not knowing what happened, but whatever it was, her not knowing when she was leaving pointed towards rough times ahead for her. Before I could even ask a follow-up question, Gigi popped up with a big bag of popcorn that Brit immediately dug her hands in.

"Aye Brit, I thought you said you didn't want any?!" Gigi growled. Brit smashed the handful of popcorn into her mouth and mumbled, "I changed my mind," and then kept doing my hair.

"You're gross, yo," Gigi laughed, shaking her head.

She sat down, carefully moved Specs head back to her lap, and then began stroking Specs' cheek, smiling as she did it. I probably looked like a complete creep watching Gigi like that, but it was hard not to pay attention to her. She was such an enigma. Here she was, so calm, so cool, but something was looming over her head. Whatever she did, she would have to pay the price for it eventually and that price seemed to be bigger than what she was willing to pay.

thirteen.

ecember 21st. The Most Wonderful [-ly Dreadful] Time of the Year. Christmas time at Bennings felt so strange to me. The rest of the girls were excited, but I felt like the fact that we weren't free to celebrate the holidays was being thrown in our faces. I was feeling down because this was my first time I wouldn't be home taking those stupid, fake matching pajama photos, watching old holiday movies, and sneaking a peek at my gifts early, only to pretend like I was surprised Christmas morning. Some of these girls were used to being indisposed of, so it didn't seem to faze them, but their giddiness about the holiday just didn't sit well with me. The only real saving grace was that I was finally a "red", meaning I made it through the intake process and was amongst the other girls in the high risk population, which also meant that I could now be with Gigi and Brit.

After the Day of Empowerment, I stayed on my p's and q's because the closer I was to getting the red sweatshirt, the closer I was to becoming a part of the Gems, and the closer I was to getting an early release. Seeing Rachel and Mackie every other weekend also helped me tremendously. They had no idea, but them making the effort to show up was more than what I needed. I felt like I still had a leg out in the real world whenever they came and gave me the tea and other updates on what was happening. Every time we left each other, I wondered what they thought of me. Did they look at me as less than because of everything that happened? I wondered if they had to field questions at school about me or how often they had to defend me and my stupid actions against my peers and their negative comments. I wondered if they would get tired of driving hours out to see me for only a 30-minute visit. I wondered if they would abandon me once I got out because I wouldn't be in the same place as they were in life.

They did a great job of not letting on that any of my thoughts would come true and constantly assured me that they had my back and that we were girls until the end. They never told me what people said about me or what was happening in the news, other than to tell me that Johnny was going to prison for a long time. That gave me a little peace for some reason.

Their last visit was a few weeks ago. They said they weren't sure if they'd be able to make it out if the weather was bad, but they promised they'd call me if they couldn't. I told them I understood and not to worry. Mackie and Rachel both floated me two crisp $20 bills while holding my hands, and though I more than appreciated the sentiment, I told them to keep it. They could use that money way more than I could, seeing as how the canteen didn't even deal in cash and there was nothing worth even buying from one of the girls. They hesitated, took the money back, and left me with a great big hug and hints of their Victoria Secret scents on my sweatshirt. Later that day, I got word from Patty that money had been added to my canteen wallet–$40–and that she had a special message from Rachel and Mackie: "Merry (early) Christmas, Evie! We love you!" and I loved them for that.

I stared at the paper snowflake garlands that lined the walls in the red room and noted how especially chipper everyone seemed to be. Not that I was keeping close track of time, but I was more focused on the fact that I still had five months left in this place than I was that Christmas was only a few days away. At the beginning of the month, the staff gave us supplies to decorate the rooms, hallways, and classrooms so that the festive mood of Christmas would not die just because we were at a detention center. I was beginning to think we weren't at a center at all because I had never heard of so much leeway being given to people who were being reproved.

Thankfully, we had already finished our classes because I was just not in a mood to deal with anything else. Gigi and Brit sat at the foot of my bed chatting about what they would have wanted for Christmas and soon enough, Specs pranced into the room, perky as usual. She must have gotten some good news or heard from her grandma or something because she couldn't wipe the grin off her face.

"What's up, Specs? What you all smiley for?" Gigi asked her. Specs shook her head and shrugged.

"Nothing in particular! It's just a good day!" Brit and Gigi groaned at her positivity and I rolled my eyes and pulled my sweatshirt over my head so that no one could see or feel just how annoyed I was. Before I could even take a deep breath, I felt two hands shake me out of my comfortable curled up position.

I slowly pulled the sweatshirt back down off my head so that they could see only my eyes. Specs stood over me, still smiling from ear to ear.

"Ms. Patty wants to see you. She said she has something for you." Without a word and just a head nod to Specs, I inched out of bed and took my time getting to Patty's office. I had been on my best behavior so it couldn't have been anything bad, at least I didn't think it could be. Once Patty and I were face to face, I asked her what was up.

With a big smile, she said, "It looks like you got more money put on your books for the canteen."

I perked up. "Really, how much?" I asked her, intrigued.

She reviewed her computer screen and responded, "It looks like $100."

I was shocked. I had heard little whispers here and there about people getting $30 max added to their wallets, which was plenty for the items in the canteen, but I wondered why I got so much and who sent it. There was no way Rachel and Mackie sent that amount, considering they had already sent me money, they were both working minimum wage jobs, and those checks got eaten up by their shopping habits. I was shocked they even thought to give me money at all.

"Your dad added it last night, and this came in the mail too," she said handing me an envelope. Dear old dad gave me money. For a second, and I mean a second, I thought it was genuine. I casually ripped open the envelope and had to take a second to process what it was I was seeing... and *not* seeing.

"Happy Holidays from the Johnsons!" the card read. My eyes slowly drifted from left to right as I recognized each face on the card. Dad looked tall and strapping. Mom looked poised and classy. Kobi looked confident and accomplished. Chelsie looked bright and beautiful. There was one thing missing–me. The card said it was from the Johnsons, but how could that be if I wasn't on it? I examined the photo one last time and knew it was recent because my sister was wearing the watch my dad got her for her birthday, which was right before she left to head back to college in September. I remembered that watch because I showed him the watch, hoping he'd catch the hint and get it for me, and he up and bought it for her. I was heated and felt like I didn't exist and those same feelings I felt when Chelsie gleamed over the diamond-studded watch as she unboxed it, were the same feelings I felt now. I angrily glared at the holiday card that didn't have me or even my name on it and knew they sent it to me to destroy me.

"Eve, are you all right?" Patty asked. I stared at the card, breathing harder and heavier with each breath I took. "Eve, please say something." I glanced up at her with tears of fire brimming from my eyes and ripped the card up as small as I could.

"Give him his money back. I don't want it. As a matter of fact, call him and tell him to go straight to hell."

I stormed out of the office, slamming Patty's door shut, and I was sure that something on her wall fell because of the force. I ripped through the hallway and as soon as I turned the corner, I ran right into CO Bates, who was casually patrolling the hallways along with CO Rivers. I bounced backward, but Bates grabbed a hold of my arm before I could fall on my butt.

"Hey, watch where you're going!" he told me. Ignoring CO Rivers and what he would think of me, I looked right into Bates' eyes and said, "Suck my-"

Before I could finish, he snatched me up like Johnny once did when he was high and drunk.

"And watch your mouth! What is wrong with you?" he growled at me as he hovered over me like a bear about to attack. I could see Rivers trying to pull Bates away from me, but I was ready to square up, despite being half his size.

"Get off of me!" I screamed to the top of my lungs. I swung on him and missed, but I quickly got my other arm free and landed a good slap to Bates' face. He turned red and as Rivers continued to hold him back, I continued to fight and wail and I think I even saw Bates lunge at me, which made me go even crazier. I wish I could say I blacked out; I wish I could say I had no idea what I was doing, but I knew exactly what was happening.

When I saw Patty and two female COs run towards me, I stopped and stood still, eyes stinging from the burning tears, hands hurting from the blows I landed on Bates, and piercing screams escaping from my mouth as if no one else was there except me and God. Tankard and Jones grabbed a hold of Bates as he caused more commotion with whatever crap he was spewing and escorted him to another part of the building, while Rivers kept a firm hold on me. Patty tried to contain the attention I was bringing to myself by shooing the girls who had peeked their heads out of the nearby rooms. I could hear Rivers telling me to keep calm, but I couldn't and didn't want to. I held him tighter than he was holding me, and I bawled into his chest.

"She's shaking!" he called to Patty, who rushed over to me.

"Breathe sweetie, breathe!" Patty told me. I wanted, with every inch in me, to do just that, but I couldn't. I was shaking uncontrollably and heaving, all while doing my best to breathe. I could feel my chest constricting, which only caused me to breathe heavier, trying to maintain the air I needed to regain the sense I left in Patty's office.

"Eve? Eve! Talk to me!" Patty yelled at me. Her voice muffled and soon all I could hear were mumbles and screeches. "She's having a panic attack. Get her to my office!" Patty instructed CO Rivers. When he tried to get me to walk, I wouldn't budge. He gave me the option to walk on my own once more, but when I wouldn't move, he scooped me up and carried me bridal style back to Patty's office, where he carefully placed me in a chair and slowly backed away, closing the door on me so I was alone with my racing thoughts and broken spirit.

I struggled to calm myself down, but I got to where I could sit still and listen. Patty knelt down in front of me with a box of tissues and a glass of water and handed them both to me when she saw I calmed down. I could feel the confusion radiate from Rivers as he stood in the doorway, making sure nothing else would pop off, but I saw how disappointed Patty was.

"You were doing so well," she said, shaking her head at me. As I slowly gulped the water, I watched Patty make notes in my file and I turned off. I heard nothing she said for the rest of the meeting, but I noted how upset she was at my regression. I'm pretty sure what she was telling me was important and would affect my program or even my release date, but at that moment, I didn't care. I just needed to get out of there.

When Patty dismissed me, CO Rivers walked over to me with his hand extended out to help me up and I knew she was done chastising me. I got up without even looking at Rivers and led the way back to the red room, where I knew I would be greeted with noise, questions, and more annoyances.

"What is going on with you? What was all that about?" Rivers asked me as he escorted me. I didn't answer. I liked Rivers, and I didn't want whatever might come out of my mouth to make him look at me even more differently, so I kept my mouth shut for my own good.

"You don't feel like talking?" he probed. Again, I didn't answer. After asking me if I was okay a few more times, he stopped attempting to make sense of everything and opened the door to the red room. I made a beeline straight for my bunk, avoiding all eye contact and questions being hurled my way, and smothered my face in between my sheet and my pillow. I had hoped that everyone would take the hint and leave me alone, at least for a while, but no. Of course, there had to be one person to try me, and of course, it *had* to be Specs.

"Eve! Eve, look what I made!"

I ignored her, but she kept pushing me and pushing me and trying to get my attention. I was trying to show her I wasn't in the mood without having to tell her, but instead of just answering her so she'd leave me alone, I did the worst thing I could do. I ripped the pillow from on top of my head, eyes still blazing, and snapped at her.

"You are the most annoying thing I've ever met! You're like a bug! You're not wanted here, so go away!"

The room fell silent. I wouldn't have even known that all the red shirts were there, or that Rivers was still standing at the door and witnessed the entire thing, or the shock and disgust on everyone's faces. All I felt was anger and frustration, and all I saw was Specs, tears welling up behind her big glasses and her ponytails flying in the air as she sprinted away from me, crying. It was almost in that instant that I snapped back from the devilish version of me to the reasonable side of me. I glanced around the room, not realizing the damage I had just caused, but then I looked at Brit who was mortified and Gigi who was fuming and knew I messed up bad.

"What the hell is wrong with you?!" Brit screamed in my face before chasing after Specs. The room was still quiet, but now the rest of the girls scattered about, pretending to be about their own business but still watching and listening as Gigi confronted me.

"Are you on your period or something?" she roared. I sat back down on my bunk and stared straight ahead, ignoring her. "Hello! I'm talking to you!" She snapped her fingers in my face. Still avoiding any more conflict, I laid back down on my bunk and curled up in a ball. I should have known Gigi wouldn't leave me alone. Specs was like a little sister to Gigi, so me telling Specs to scram would not sit right with her. She began nudging and pushing me, trying to get a rise out of me, and she did.

"Why you actin' all stank all of a sudden, huh?" she barked, to which I attempted to bite back.

"I'm acting how you act every day, now leave me alone!" Gigi stood in front of me still as a board. Her face didn't report on her inner thoughts or feelings towards me at the moment, but a light chuckle left her lips after a long, somewhat awkward pause, which made me even more agitated.

"Oh, you got balls now, Ms. I-pretend-to-be-badder-and-tougher-than-I-am? Square up then." I glared at her and she glared at me and the challenge was on. I stood up, my gaze never leaving hers, and she hopped backwards with her chin in the air and bit her bottom lip hard. She was mad, but so was I. She took one look at me as I prepared for whatever was going to happen and she laughed again, this time revving up the rest of the girls in the red room to egg on the fight. When she turned her back to me and began giggling with a couple of the other girls, I slammed my fist against Gigi's head from behind and suddenly the other girls' faces went from entertained to horrified. Gigi toppled over to the side but caught herself and held the side of her head. She looked at me with piercing eyes as she held her head, as if to keep it from falling off. When she knew she was okay, she wiped the dirt off the bottom of her shoes, like how I used to see the basketball players do during games to keep them from sliding on the floor, and she geared up to tackle me.

We bumped into just about everything, side tables, the bed frames, even the cement half walls that separated each set of bunks. Bruised but still not beaten, we rolled around the floor, still wailing and aiming to get the last hit in. We scrapped a little before being broken up by Rivers, who grabbed Gigi, and Jones, who grabbed me. Gigi continued to scream insults at me, but I paid no attention to her. When I looked at Rivers and how disturbed he was at me and my actions, I couldn't care about what anyone else was saying, doing, or thinking. I was drained and gave up the fight all together. I let Jones cuff my hands behind me and completed my walk of shame with Gigi being escorted right behind me. I kept my head down and tried to hide, but I still felt so exposed.

Before leaving the room, I looked up to see Brit cradling Specs, who was still highly upset. They stared at me, eyes big and wide. Brit looked like she wanted to punch me square in my face and Specs looked like she was too afraid to even look at me. As tired as I was of everything, I still shed a few tears and I had hoped that Specs would see that as my way of saying sorry.

fourteen.

Max Hall. I was now standing in the one place I vowed not to end up while at Bennings. I didn't need to watch a show or any documentary to know that maximum security hall was the worst place to go while locked up. The little that Brit told me and Specs was enough to make me want to be on my best behavior, and yet, I was standing in the middle of an almost empty cell that was barely big enough for me to move around. CO Rivers stared at me for a few seconds before closing the door, which caused me to jump.

I kept my head low, staring at my feet and then at the cracked cement floor that looked like the Hulk had a small temper tantrum. The longest crack went from the doorway right to the cheap cot with deep stains that laid flat on a solid cement block. Just a few feet to the side of the cot was a shiny, clean toilet, which was the oddest thing to me. The four walls that separated me from everything else were undoubtedly thick and I knew that if I dared scream, no one that mattered would hear me.

Max hall was in a completely different section of the building, separate from the rest of the girls and most of the amenities. Unlike the rest of the center, this part of the building had no windows, so the only way I knew the time of day was to track the meals I decided I wasn't going to eat.

I sat upright on the hard mattress and knocked my head against the wall. Maybe I'd get some sense into me, or maybe the feelings and memories I had that caused me to flare up in fits of rage would somehow dissipate with every bang, but for some reason, those thoughts only intensified. I did my best to squelch my tears by keeping my eyes closed tight, but when I felt, it was extreme. My anguish and hate for my life and myself appeared, this time, in tears and screams.

I hated myself. I hated where I was, how I got there, and who I had become. I wasn't always like this, but if you were to ask me to remember a time when I wasn't, I wouldn't be able to recollect anything. My transformation happened over time; I didn't just snap and become this unbearable twit. This version of me had been a long time coming and maybe dad was right. Regardless of my path, I would have ended up right there, in a small, damp and dark room all alone, wondering why I was even alive.

"Shut up!" I heard someone faintly yell. Loud bangs on what I assumed was another room door vibrated through the hall and that mixed with my screaming and my now throbbing headache and racing thoughts caused me to overload, and in an instant, I passed out.

Somehow, someway, I went the rest of my time in max without speaking a word. A revolving door of COs and subpar meals came and went, but I stayed glued to my bed. When CO Rivers came to bring me food, he'd watch me eat because one of the other COs called themselves "telling on me," claiming I wasn't eating and that I was tossing my food in the toilet, which I didn't deny.

In the middle of the first night, I asked myself, *How did I get here?* I replayed so many moments that, in hindsight, I could have avoided. Getting mixed up with Johnny and his mess was my biggest regret. I had already been up to my antics before him–the prostitution bust, though again, I hadn't technically done anything wrong at that point, the assault on the cop, though again, he roughed me up for no reason, so in my eyes, he deserved what he got, and stabbing Stacy with the scissors. I beat myself up over that one because, despite her trying to bully me into giving her money, Stacy didn't deserve that.

Could I be sick or crazy? I thought to myself. In the many hours I spent sitting in front of a therapist, I was never once given an official diagnosis aside from the narcissist thing, an observation I never disputed.

What's wrong with me? My inner voice yelled out, causing an echo throughout the walls of my mind. Though I couldn't bring myself to express my confusion about my existence and purpose, I let my inner self shout as loud as she could. I didn't know it was possible, but when I closed my eyes, I saw inner me. She was so young, and I could tell from the large tears that fell from her face that she was even more confused than I was. I saw her running in darkness, looking around, calling for someone to help her, but with no avail. She needed to escape or to find help, and when she couldn't, she sunk to the ground and buried her face into her knees, her whimpers almost unbearable to witness. I wanted to help her, to comfort her, but I couldn't because I *was* her. When I last saw her face, she looked up with large streams trickling down, her bottom lip quivering, and she uttered, "I give up," before disappearing in thin air.

Whenever I thought about that girl, I cried. She was me, but she didn't seem like me at all, and maybe that's why I had so much sympathy for her. She was so little. How scared she must have been to have no one there to help her. It was almost pathetic how helpless she was... *I* was.

"Shit," I said to myself as I wiped another tear. I think I was at the start of a breakthrough and funny enough, I didn't need some hack therapist to tell me that that's what it was. The hardest thing for me to reconcile with was how I would survive after getting out of this room. I was sure that my main cheerleaders-my girls, Rivers, and Patty-all had different views of me now. Specs feared me, Brit couldn't stand me, Gigi hated me, Rivers wouldn't be able to look at me, Patty was disappointed in me, and it was all my fault. No matter how much graveling and kissing butt I did, I would forever be marked by how I handled everyone and I couldn't stand the thought of not having any of them on my side nor could I stand myself.

To pass the otherwise slow time, I hummed to myself, reenacted my favorite movies, and even tried to do yoga. I did everything I could to keep my mind busy so I wouldn't think about the vision of little me crying out for help. It only took a day for snapshots of little me to sneak in now and then, torment me, and remind me of how sad and hopeless of a human I was. In those moments, I could do nothing but shut my eyes tight and whisper to myself, "I'm sorry I did this to you."

"All right Johnson, let's go," CO Jones called from the other side of the door. I could hear her keys jingling around and her turning the key in the door. She glared at me with an eyebrow raised and cocked her head to tell me it was time to leave the cell. I didn't want to move because a small part of me believed it was a trick; I just knew Jones would slam the door in my face as soon as I reached it and cackle at how pathetic I was for even believing I deserved to be free from that room.

"Come on Eve, we don't have all day."

I quickened my pace out of the room and as she slammed the door shut, I had to do a double take because I could have sworn that I saw my inner self still standing in the room. I almost lunged for her, to grab her up to hug and hold her, but when I blinked, she was gone.

I kept my head down for the walk, hoping I wouldn't cross paths with anybody that I might've pissed off a few days ago. As soon as CO Jones stopped, I looked into the room we were in front of, and I took a step back so I couldn't be seen.

"It's okay. Go ahead in," Jones comforted me as she gently pulled me into the room.

I did my best to avoid CO Rivers, CO Bates, Patty, and Gigi's gazes, but I knew what this was about, and I was being forced to face all of them whether I liked it or not. I inhaled and exhaled a couple times before bringing myself to stare all of them right in the eyes. My stare went right to Gigi, whose intensity was just as strong as mine. With her furrowed brows, I couldn't tell if she was ready to fight me again or if she was in deep thought, but whatever she decided to do, I figured I'd let her do it.

"How are you doing, Eve?" Patty asked me in a somewhat cold, detached tone as she glanced through what looked like my file. I said nothing and just nodded. When she didn't hear me say anything, she looked up at me and waited for a verbal answer. When she realized she wouldn't get one, she huffed and moved on to what we called a mediation meeting. Whenever girls were sent to max hall for fighting, they'd do their time and then attend a mandatory mediation, where they'd be forced to "put their differences aside" and talk things out. I was all for it, but I had nothing against Gigi and as I watched her gaze get softer, I didn't believe she had a real problem with me either.

"Eve, do you have something you'd like to say?" Patty asked, clicking her pen and carefully placing it next to my file. Sure, there were lots of things I wanted to say, some productive, some reductive, but I looked over at CO Bates, who was standing stiff with his head down, and I knew exactly what she was alluding to.

"CO Bates, I'm truly sorry for what I did to you. I shouldn't have hit you, and I was totally out of control." I bowed my head in an effort to show just how sorry I was-because I was-but I felt like I could sense some apprehension or disbelief amongst the others.

After a few moments of silence, Bates responded with, "Apology accepted, kid," before walking out of the room. I felt lighter when he left, feeling like I made good progress with him, but there was another, larger elephant I needed to address and that was my behavior and how it got out of hand in the fight with Gigi.

"Can either of you explain how all of this happened?" Patty inquired, breaking the silence. "It appeared that you two were getting very close to each other, not to mention you were both well on your way to becoming Gems." Mine and Gigi's glances shifted from each other to Patty. I couldn't speak for Gigi, but I felt the most ashamed sitting in front of Patty with the knowledge that I had been doing well enough to advance to the one group that would have given me the quickest access out of there. I hated myself before, but I despised myself now.

Neither of us said a word. I think we were beyond pointing fingers and just wanted this all to go away and for us to start fresh–well, at least that's what I wanted.

"I'm only going to ask one more time. What happened?"

After another awkward silence, Gigi threw her hands up and then blurted out, "It was Eve. She started it." I didn't even flinch when she said my name. I couldn't dispute what she said because it was my fault. I didn't even care that she threw me under the bus, I just wanted to get the meeting over with.

"I know who did what. I want to know why," Patty responded. I spoke up to defend myself because even though I hit her first, she kept instigating.

"Look, I got mad because she was picking and poking at me. She saw that I was aggravated, so it pissed me off when she wouldn't leave me alone."

"I only did that because you hurt Specs' feelings! That girl did nothing to you for you to say what you said!"

I scuffed and begged to differ. "Specs was the main one getting on my nerves! I purposely ignored everyone for a reason. What made y'all think I wanted to be bothered?!" I asked, this time raising my voice a bit. Patty raised her hand towards me, letting me know I was getting worked up, so I settled down and sat back in my seat with my arms crossed. Gigi's glaring eyes were piercing. She was still pissed, but so was I.

"She was only trying to get your attention so she could give you a Christmas card she made you. She made cards for everyone in our room and while you were meeting with Patty, she was handing them out. If you would have opened your eyes and stopped being so selfish, you would have known that, and we wouldn't be in this shit."

Patty shot her a death stare and cleared her throat. Gigi recanted and apologized to Patty for her language. I sat completely silent with my mouth gaped open. When I thought back to that moment, I remembered seeing the construction paper card. It didn't even dawn on me that it might've been for me. I didn't know what it was, but I couldn't care in that moment because I was in my own head. None of those girls were around when I blew up on Bates, so they couldn't have known what I was going through or what I was feeling. I felt worse than horrible; I felt like complete scum and I wished that I could give Specs the world, but even that wouldn't be enough, so in the least, I wanted her to know I was deeply sorry.

"Do you know why Eve was upset?" Patty asked Gigi. Gigi shook her head.

"No. We didn't even get a chance to ask because she snapped on us."

Patty directed her attention towards me. "Would you like to explain why you were upset?"

I shook my head. "It doesn't matter. Gigi doesn't care and it won't take back the fact that I hurt Specs' feelings."

Patty and Gigi cocked their heads at the same time and had the same confused facial expression.

"I don't know that to be true, Eve."

Gigi cut in. "Of course, I care. That's what friends are for."

I stared at them for a moment as I argued with myself on whether I should divulge what felt like some deep, dark secret or if I should avoid answering the question. I bowed my head and persuaded myself to just spit it out.

"I-I was upset because my parents haven't come to see me yet. It's been months and even my friends from school check up on me, but my parents refuse to have anything to do with me." I twiddled my thumbs as I choked back the tears, remembering how low I felt getting that Christmas card.

"And then there was the card..." I told Gigi. I looked up and saw that she was focused on me, so I continued.

"They refuse to come visit me, but they cared enough to send me a Christmas card I wasn't even on and add money to my canteen wallet as if that was supposed to make up for it or something." I could hear Gigi inhale and release a deep sigh which let me know that either she sympathized with me or that she thought I was being a big baby.

"And why did that make you upset?" Patty asked, helping me get to the real point.

"Because, I feel like they're all taunting me. They're so happy out there without me and it's like they wanted me to know that."

With what I assumed was a genuine and well-meaning smile, Gigi responded with, "Well, hey, at least you got money for the canteen, right?"

I glared at her wondering how she could think that some money for some junk food and extra tampons was a better alternative to feeling wanted by my family, but then I remembered that she didn't actually know anything about me or my family. She only knew what she saw and what I told her, which wasn't much.

The girls could tell I was "privileged" by the way I spoke or how I walked through the halls like I owned them. What they didn't know was that the facade I showed them was all taught. It wasn't at all how I felt. I probably felt more scared and out of my mind more often than I felt in control-aside from when I was with Johnny. Instead of answering how I wanted to, I shook my head.

"You don't get it, and that's okay, but trust me when I say this—this is a game to them, and I am one of their pawns. They don't really care about me and the money doesn't mean shit. They're just doing what they always do."

"And what's that?" Patty asked.

"They're keeping up appearances—this charade of a life that my dad has been so desperate to create. He's delusional, and I read right through him."

Patty and Gigi just stared at me, sort of unsure of what to say.

"I'm sorry you feel that way, Eve. Despite all that's happened, I do believe that *both* of your parents love you dearly."

"If that was the case, they would have been here and wouldn't have sent my friends to tell me they weren't coming to visit me. If they cared, they would have skipped the holiday card this year because I wouldn't be there to take it, or in the very least, they could have left me off the mailing list." I got choked up again but stopped myself because I didn't want to shed anymore tears because of them.

"You know, I was going to apologize to them for everything. I wanted to tell them that I would make it right, and I would have meant it. But I see what I'm worth to them and they don't get shit from me now."

A few seconds passed and something compelled Gigi to get up, walk around the table, and embrace me.

"I'm sorry your parents are scummy," she said with a tone that made me laugh through the pain I felt in my chest. I stood up and we hugged again, this time swaying together, letting our vibes take us away for a moment. CO Rivers and Patty stared at us in silence as we continued to violate the no-touching rule and basked in all the love we had for each other.

"I'm sorry for picking on you," Gigi whispered to me.

I whispered back to her, with a smile, "I'm sorry for sucker punching you."

We giggled into each other's necks and when we let each other go, Gigi looked up at my hair and pointed saying, "Your hair is a mess," with a laugh. I felt my hair, which was frizzy and literally all over my head, and laughed along with her because it hadn't even dawned on me that I had gone a full three days without doing anything to it. Patty smiled and commended us on how quickly we reconciled.

"I think you girls are good to head back to your bunk. Your release dates are safe for now, but don't make me regret my decision," she said giving us a stern look. Gigi grabbed my hand, which made me smile. She grinned widely and promised that this was the last she would hear from us.

"Well, I can't promise that, but we will try," she said with a chuckle. Rivers also snickered at Gigi's remark and Patty could only shake her head, though she also found Gigi's honesty amusing.

"You girls got out just in time too," Patty mentioned. "The Christmas Eve dinner is tonight and you both shouldn't miss it."

Gigi and I skipped down the hallway as Rivers and Jones followed and no one would have been able to tell from looking at us that we had just spent three days in separate small, dank rooms all alone and left with our thoughts. Since Gigi had already been to max a couple times, she was completely unbothered, but as I stood just a few feet away from the red room, I knew I could never go back in there.

"Hey, you did good today," CO Rivers applauded. He extended his hand out for a fist bump, but I ignored it and went in for a firm bear hug, to which he eventually accepted.

"Thank you. Can we talk later?" I asked him, staring up into his beautiful, almond-shaped eyes.

He nodded with a smile and remarked, "Of course."

I needed that hug, especially since I was about to step back into what could potentially be a lion's den. I left these girls in a fit of rage, so I was sure their opinion of me wasn't very high, not that I cared. The only ones I needed to know were okay with me were Specs and Brit. As I stepped over the threshold, the room got quiet. I could feel all eyes watching me as I strutted right to Specs, who was being held back by Brit. Gigi gently pulled Brit's arm away from Specs, which made Brit step back. Finally, face to face with Specs, I stared in her eyes and flashed back to how distressed she looked when I left her. She was so innocent, and I couldn't stand myself for how I treated her. I wanted so badly to just bring her in for a hug, but I wasn't sure how she'd receive me.

"Specs, I want to say to you in front of the entire room, that I'm so sorry for what I said and how I said it. I didn't mean it at all. I was just angry about something that had nothing to do with you and I took it out on you. Please forgive me?" I asked. I would have begged on my hands and knees for that girl. She was my first friend at Bennings and if it weren't for her, I wouldn't have Brit or Gigi either. I stared at Specs and noticed her eyes sparkle just before a smile flashed across her face. I let out a sigh of relief because I knew, without her saying anything, that she was okay and that she had forgiven me. She scooped me into a surprisingly tight hug and then jumped up and down as she clapped her hands.

"Of course, I forgive you! I'm just glad everyone is friends again!"

Before I could respond, she ran over to my bunk and grabbed the Christmas card she made for me and I gleamed at how thoughtful it was. Specs seemed to love her sparkles and glitter, as she had put too much and it was rubbing off on my hands and clothes, but I didn't care. I just loved that she loved me enough to make a card for me.

"Oh, let me get in!" Brit chimed in as she formed a group hug with the three of us. I knew if Specs was cool with me, Brit would be cool with me too, and we re-solidified our friendship with a fist bump and a head nod.

"So, are you guys good?" Brit asked, pointing at me and Gigi. I looked at Gigi, who looked back at me and smiled.

"Yeah, we're great."

fifteen.

February 1st. Three Months Before My Release. Gigi was gone all day and though Specs, Brit, and I tried our best to keep ourselves busy, our group was just not the same when one wasn't around. After the whole max hall debacle, there was a shift between us, a good shift. I had a heart-to-heart with the girls and explained some things. I admitted that I wasn't involved in the robbery and that I had no idea what was going on. Somehow, they all knew that already and wouldn't have believed it, even if I did have something to do with it. I took offense to that, but their cracks were all in fun.

The dynamic between me and Gigi changed too. It was like we understood each other better. After mediation, we just sort of clicked. I couldn't explain why, but she let down her walls and made it possible for me to get close to her and I saw the real her. With our relationship quickly budding, it only made me closer with Specs and Brit too. If Gigi trusted me, then they knew they could trust me, though Specs never had a problem with that.

Shortly after we got out of max, both Brit and Specs were inducted into the Gems, which was a huge deal because not only were their release dates quickly approaching, but they could potentially get out early. Specs found out that her grandmother was healthy again after overcoming complications with her stroke, so when she got out, she would go home with her family.

Brit's release was in just one month, and Specs was leaving shortly after. We tried our best not to think about how drastically different things would be once they were both gone, but we assured each other that we would still be "the girl gang," as everyone else called us, and that we should make the best of the rest of the time we had together.

Watching Specs and Brit get inducted into the Gems *and* improve themselves was a sight to see, and I couldn't wait to be a part of the group. Specs was already so sweet, kind, and super smart, but the Gems helped her improve her confidence and it showed in the way she interacted with the staff, the other girls, and how she viewed herself. She walked with her head held high and with her bright smile visible for everyone to see. She lit up every room and lifted everyone's mood.

Brit lightened up too. She always came across as edgy and boisterous. She claimed Patty told her that those qualities were great to have, but she needed to use them in positive ways. Brit learned to use her voice for good and became Bennings' unofficial cheerleader. Like Specs, she often livened up everyone's day, but contrary to Specs' approach, Brit was in your face, patting you on the back, telling you, "You got this!" and a host of other very entertaining and theatrical declarations. They were both so happy when they got into the Gems and they wore their green sweatshirts with pride.

I wasn't *completely* jealous of them; I was happier for them than anything else but being in the Gems meant you were on a positive path and that you were on your way out. Not only was I ready to be out of Bennings, but I would miss them both when they left.

After a few hours of being MIA, Gigi finally emerged back into the red room where Brit was teaching me and Specs how to play Spades. When we saw her, we dropped everything and rushed over to her, but her face caused us to stop in our tracks. She looked flushed and looked like she just had a meltdown.

"Everything okay?" I asked her, placing my hand on her shoulder. Brit locked her arm with Gigi's, Specs embraced her from the front, and I from her side. She hadn't even told us what happened yet, but whatever it was, it seemed devastating to Gigi.

"No, everything isn't okay. Not at all," she said, stammering. We walked her over to our table, where we surrounded her like the supportive friends we were. We let her take her time and get her thoughts together. I *still* didn't know what she had done or what her situation was at all, so I had no context, but Specs and Brit knew, which explained why they were more concerned than I could be.

"My life sucks, man," she said, burying her face into her hands. After catching her breath, she told us what she knew.

"Not only are my little brother and sisters in foster care, but the judge is leaning toward proceeding with a preliminary trial."

My mouth hung open and Brit and Specs immediately crowded Gigi and gave her a hug. It was bad news all around, but unlike anyone else at the center, Gigi never let on how bothered she was by anything. She sat there, stone-faced as she was being safeguarded from the world by Specs and Gigi and not a groan, a scream, or even a much-needed sob left her mouth. She just sat there, and it only made me think how maddening everything must've been for her. To not feel free enough to release must've taken some toll on her emotionally. She must've felt trapped. As I watched her keep a straight face, I just knew a war was happening within her and that she could blow at any moment.

We gave Gigi a little space after receiving the news, and we let her nap while we went to lunch. She claimed she wasn't hungry, but Specs promised to smuggle something back from the cafeteria, just in case. As we ate, I couldn't help but stare at Specs and Brit's sweatshirts.

They must've noticed because Brit said, "They're cool, right?" as she pulled on her own. I nodded and forced a smile. They really weren't any different from the red or blue sweatshirts, but the meaning behind the sweatshirt is what I craved. However, I still had months left at Bennings and though I had been on my absolute best behavior since spending a few nights in max hall, I wasn't feeling like there was much hope for me in becoming a Gem soon.

"You want to know a secret?" Brit asked me in a hushed tone. I stared at her with an eyebrow raised and wasn't sure if I really wanted to know what Brit was dangling in front of my face, but I shrugged and nodded.

"Word is you and Gigi are next to become green."

My eyes got wide and my heart raced. I wanted to jump up and dance a little jig, but then Specs nudged Brit, which gave me pause.

"Brit!" she said with her mouth full. "Don't tell her that! You don't know that for sure."

I knew it was too good to be true. That little tinge of elation disappeared with any hope I had of becoming a Gem sooner rather than later.

"I do know for sure! I heard it with my own ears," Brit replied back, rubbing her arm. My ears perked a little.

"How though?" I asked. "How are you sure?"

A smirk spread across Brit's face and Specs rolled her eyes as she continued to devour her sandwich.

"I may have overheard someone say something about you two being up next," she revealed trying to play coy.

"Can you just spit it out?" I asked her, banging my fist on the table. She pulled back for a second and put her hand up to her neck as if to clutch some pearls.

"Well, excuse me," she said in a high-pitched voice. "I overheard Patty talking to Ms. Jenkins about her recommendations. You, Gigi and a few other girls came up."

"That was it?" I asked. Brit nodded and shrugged.

"Well, I didn't stay for too long or else they would have known I was ear hustlin', but yeah, that's it."

I gave Brit a blank stare and continued to eat my food, pretending like Brit never told me anything.

"I told you not to say anything," Specs shrugged. For the rest of the day, I remained sort of irritated that I wasn't making any progress. I was good, did my classwork, wrote in my journal, reported to Patty whenever she summoned me–all but got down on my knees and begged, and still I got nothing. Though Brit gave me a little hope, her observation held no real merit since she didn't listen to the rest of the conversation and that my name being brought up didn't mean something would happen. My patience was running thin, and I felt myself reverting to my old ways. Seeing Specs and Gigi in green, prancing around the center knowing they were above us all was starting to make me feel some type of way, so I told them I would be in the library and spent a few hours of uninterrupted silence there while reading a book, something I hadn't done in a *very* long time.

I felt refreshed and like my internal battery was recharged after leaving the library. Time away from everyone and everything was something I didn't realize I needed, but once I got that first dose of peace, I decided to seek some me-time more often.

It was the end of the day for most of the staff and it was almost time for dinner. I had hoped that Gigi was feeling better and was keeping Specs and Brit down to Earth, but before I got back to the red room, I ran into Patty, who called me into her office, with a smile on her face.

"Come here for a second, it won't take long," she said. I strolled in with no expectations. Patty looked as if she was all packed up and ready to go home. She rummaged in a box under her desk and tossed me a rolled-up cloth. When I unrolled it, I stared at it for a few moments and even held it up. My mind wouldn't compute that I was holding a green sweatshirt, but when I saw the look on Patty's face, I could finally put two and two together. My eyes lit up.

"Welcome to the Gems, Eve," Patty said with a wink. I was speechless. I guess Brit was right after all and what she heard wasn't just talk.

"Come see me first thing tomorrow morning before class. We need to go over the details of your new program." I nodded so fast I nearly gave myself a headache and raced out of the door, fighting everything within me to let out a loud cheer for myself. All that worry and all that pity for myself was for nothing. I stopped for a second because I had let my old self come back; the girl who wanted everything her way and in her own time, not even realizing that I was well on my way up the pipeline to where I wanted to be. I held the sweatshirt close and hugged it tight.

"From this day forward, I *will* be better," I told myself before skipping down the hallway. The first person I saw was CO Rivers, who was escorting another girl to Patty's office.

"Rivers, look!" I exclaimed, holding up the sweatshirt. He flashed his beautiful, wide smile and gave me a high five.

"Hey, great job! I'm proud of you!" he commended. I could see he was busy, so I rushed off, both of us assuring each other we'd cross paths again and I hightailed it back to the red room where the first thing everyone gravitated towards was the sweater.

"See! I told you!" Brit said jumping up and swinging me around. Specs and some other girls jumped up and gave me high-fives, fist bumps, and back pats. I was so giddy and high on the news, but when I saw Gigi, who would now be the only one of us in our group not in the Gems, my smile faded and I felt like I needed to acknowledge her. When our eyes locked, she gave me a half smile and a head nod which told me she was happy for me in her own little way. Once the rest of the girls went back to what they were doing, I bounced to my bunk and stuffed the sweatshirt in my drawer. It didn't make sense for me to flaunt it in front of Gigi, especially since I didn't like the way Specs and Brit had been moving that day. Gigi was so on edge and I didn't want to contribute to her stress.

"Hey, cheer up," I told her. "Your birthday is coming up soon, isn't it?" Gigi nodded.

"Yep. On the 10th," she said dryly. I knew not to test my limits with Gigi because she could throw a punch and when she became short with anyone, I knew it was time to back away. Gigi grabbed her journal and began writing, so I got up to leave so she could have more time to herself before dinner.

"Congrats though," she said with a little more enthusiasm.

"Thanks, that means a lot coming from you," I responded before catching up with Brit and Specs who began giving me a rundown of the Gems, what they were working on, and the sorts of things I could expect.

The next morning, I arose bright and early. After becoming friends with the girls, I became less of an early bird and got more comfortable showering when others were around, but since I had a meeting with Patty, I freshened up before most of the other girls woke up. When I popped up at Patty's door, she already had my file handy and was ready to begin the meeting.

"What do you know about the Gems?" she asked me.

"Mmmm, not much aside from you get early release if you get in and that you get to do things the rest of the girls don't," I joked. I don't think Patty caught my sarcasm because she raised an eyebrow and her smile faded.

"Not exactly. The Gems is your gateway to release, but early release is reserved for a special few. Most girls go all the way up until their release date... who told you that you get early release?"

I flashed back to the day when Brit and Specs first mentioned the Gems and how they claimed early release was a perk. I felt a large lump in my throat form because I thought I was a giant step closer to getting out and going back to my life, but I was still only taking baby steps.

"Uh, I think I just heard some girls talking about it... but what you're saying is, I shouldn't expect to get out before May?" I responded. We stared at each other for a second and I watched as her eyes narrowed and then softened a little.

She nodded and with a calm voice, she replied, "Yes, you shouldn't expect to get early release. As I said, early release is circumstantial and rarely happens. We don't tell the girls about that possibility because it's highly unlikely." I sighed deeply and sat back in my chair, disappointed. Patty gave me a few seconds to gather my thoughts before she continued.

"I'm sorry I busted your bubble but being in the Gems is very rewarding by itself. Trust me, you'll enjoy it and your release date will be here before you know it. She opened her side drawer and brought out a yellow paper and a pen. Upon reading the bold title, I noted that it was a declaration of my participation in the program and that I promised to be an upstanding member of the Gems. I signed it without reading too far into the document and handed it back to her with a fake smile plastered on my face. I was getting good at hiding my contempt because she genuinely smiled back at me and began her spiel about the group and what it *really* meant to be in the Gems.

She mentioned the incentives that both Specs and Brit explained to me the day before, but she heavily focused on the hard work it took to be in the Gems. I knew I could do it, and I wanted to, especially if it would keep me busy and make the time go faster. She gave me another notebook specifically for the Gems assignments and notes and a packet that had mental health improvement exercises. I flipped through it as she grabbed another sheet from behind her and slid it my way. At first glance, it looked less important than the other stuff, but she directed my attention to it and asked me to read it out loud. I looked at it once more, raised an eyebrow, and then glanced back at her. She nodded towards it, telling me to look at it, so I reluctantly grabbed the paper and read it aloud:

> *We are the gems.*
> *We are the light in the darkest of nights.*
> *We are the twinkle in the caves riddled with gold.*
> *We are the diamonds in the rough.*
> *We are the treasure beneath the sea.*
>
> *How do we know this?*
> *Because you must search to find us.*

I let the words digest in my system, as I figured that's what Patty wanted me to do.

"That's the Gems' mantra. We say it every day before we begin our group sessions and classes. I not only want you to memorize it, but I want you to think deep about what it means and how it relates to you." I nodded and placed the paper on top of the other items she gave me.

She smiled and asked, "So, any questions?"

I looked at the papers in my hands and recounted all the information she just told me. I shook my head no, but then quickly interjected before losing my thought.

"Actually, yeah... will Gigi be in soon?" Patty's gaze quickly found mine. Her eyes narrowed again and this time they stayed sharp.

"I want to remind you that you are here for you. You need to stay focused on improving yourself. But, to put your mind at ease, Gigi will be welcomed into the Gems soon enough." I realized based on Patty's serious tone that I might had overstepped my bounds just a bit by advocating for Gigi, but I got an answer I felt good enough about and went ahead with the rest of my day, casually awaiting my first meeting as a Gem.

The day sort of inched by, probably because I was thinking more about the meeting than I was about anything else. The others could tell I was distracted by my thoughts, but they brought my focus back to my schoolwork when I was too far gone. Before I knew it, it was almost 7 o'clock and time for my first Gems meeting. I didn't want to admit it, but I was excited. I wanted to see what Specs and Brit were experiencing and I wanted to look my friends and family in the eyes and for them to see a different person-a *better* person.

"Come on Eve, we're going to be late!" Specs called to me from the door as she and Brit watched me scramble around trying to find the stuff Patty gave me earlier that day. The last thing I wanted to do was make a horrible impression on my first day in the group, but I finally found what I was looking for after Gigi pointed out the pile of papers sitting right on my side table, practically right in front of my face.

"Relax," Gigi said, handing me the packet. I guess the worry on my face matched how frantic I was feeling.

"You're fine, now go," she said turning her back on me, grabbing a book she had been reading and plopping down on her bunk.

"Hey, are you cool?" I asked her. She glanced over at me with a smirk.

"I should be asking you that question. Now go before you're late." She brought her attention back to her book and continued to read, completely unfazed that Specs, Brit, and I were heading out for an hour, leaving her alone. Gigi was hard to understand, but if there was one thing I knew to be absolutely true about her, it was that she was a master at hiding how she felt. I looked back at her one more time, watching her as she flipped the page, and I let the thought of her not coming with us go. I was about to step into the first night of the rest of my time at Bennings and I needed to remain focused.

I raced through the hallway after realizing that I only had a minute to spare before being late. The clock struck 7 p.m. and I jumped through the doorway as if I were jumping through some portal that would close right as the minute hand touched 12. I let out a deep breath and scanned the room, looking at everyone staring at me. I became uncomfortable with the attention I was getting, so I quickly walked to the empty seat next to Specs.

"As I was saying," Patty continued. "We have two new members with us. Everyone welcome Eve and Tatiana to the Gems." The group erupted with applause. I looked over at Tati, whose smile was beaming from ear to ear. She was so proud of her accomplishment and honestly, I was proud of her too. We both had come a long way, but I knew her journey was way longer than mine, so I think it meant even more to her. I joined in on the applause and when I caught Tati's gaze, she nodded and smiled in my direction. Even after all the hell she gave me when I first got to the center, she turned out to be cool after all.

We started off reciting the Gems mantra. I didn't know it by heart yet, so I was a bit sloppy with my execution, but the other girls said it with pride and confidence, as if they felt every word in their bones. We spent only a minute going around the circle introducing ourselves and then we jumped right into business, with Ms. Jenkins leading the group today.

"As we discussed last group session, we will talk about our

strengths, weaknesses, and things that are weighing heavily on us. Most of you are getting out soon and though you all have so much to be proud of, we need to tackle some potential triggers that could land you back in trouble and in a worse place than this," she explained with a concerned tone. She looked each one of us in the eyes when she spoke, which made me feel like she really cared.

"Let's start with the ones getting out in a few weeks," Patty insisted, gesturing to both Specs and Brit. Both girls stood up and took bows, gave each other high-fives, and danced around a little while the rest of us laughed and praised them. Once we all settled down, Brit went first.

"Well," she hesitated. "My main weakness is tall, dark, handsome, older men, emphasis on the older," Brit said playfully nudging Specs. Specs rolled her eyes because the thought of being with anyone older than her disgusted her and she never understood the appeal. The rest of the girls chuckled at Brit mocking herself, but Patty and Ms. Jenkins kept serious, hoping Brit would get serious too. Brit quickly straightened up after seeing Ms. Jenkins give her the stink eye and reworded her response.

"My weakness is that I'm always looking for something I won't find in men I shouldn't have." We all stared at Brit in amazement, including Patty and Ms. Jenkins. I don't think any of us expected that straight-forward of an answer from Brit, but then again, she always expressed that she knew her attraction to grown men was not healthy.

"That's a very thoughtful answer," Ms. Jenkin's said. "You've been doing some reflecting and it shows. Good for you, Brittany."

A smile slowly spread across Brit's face and she even blushed a little while she got a round of applause. It really did seem like she thought deep about that, but she explained it so simply, it almost seemed too easy of an answer. I thought back to that day when she explained why she ended up at Bennings and I realized I didn't know much about her. Why was she the way she was? What was it about older men that made her think she could get whatever she needed from them? The mere idea of young girls flocking to grown men because they were "missing something at home" seemed like such an overused cop-out excuse, but then I reminded myself that I shamelessly fell into the same pool as Brit, just like many other girls at Bennings, and none of it was our fault. I jolted in my seat, which caught Patty's attention, who narrowed her eyes at me and mouthed, "Are you okay?" to which I nodded and mouthed back, "I'm fine."

"So, what about your strengths you plan to keep working on when you get out? You have many of them, believe it or not," Ms.

Jenkins pried. Brit smiled again and nodded.

"Oh, I know," she said, brushing the compliment away. The circle giggled again, and Brit got serious once more.

"I'm strong and I get whatever I want no matter what comes my way. So, like, I persevere? Is that the right word?" Brit asked Specs, who then nodded. Patty and Ms. Jenkins both commended her for her expanded vocabulary and the fact that she recognized her power to overcome all obstacles that stood in her way.

"Brittany, you are such a strong girl. You can get through anything, and that also means that you can get rid of the negative influences that are holding you back. That'll be something to think about and work on while you're here," Patty concluded. Brit nodded and thanked everyone for the support, and then the attention shifted to Specs, who seemed jittery. I couldn't understand why she was so nervous. She was low risk, and not only that, what she did actually opened doors for her in a big way. Specs fiddled with her sweatpants pockets before Ms. Jenkins cleared her throat and asked Specs to speak up.

"I'm smart! That's a plus," Specs admitted, which prompted head nods from every single person in the group. When she went to talk about her weaknesses and what she was most worried about, she froze.

"Um, I don't know... I'm excited to be back at school, but I'm afraid that I won't have friends when I get out," Specs proclaimed.

"Why do you think that, Roz?" Ms. Jenkins asked. Specs shrugged and continued to keep her hands busy, this time messing with the hem of her sweatshirt.

"I guess because they've all been going on without me. I feel like they won't know me anymore."

Brit took Specs into her arms and Specs hid herself from the rest of the group. She was ashamed, but she didn't need to be. Specs was such a good person and deserved the world. In fact, the world didn't even deserve her. Patty walked over and knelt in front of Specs, holding her hand.

"Roz, sweetie. You have one of the most vibrant souls. You are so sweet, kind, and generous. If your old friends can't see that you've only gotten better, then you can make new ones." Specs slowly pulled away from Brit and revealed reddening eyes and a couple streams of tears. I couldn't help myself. I got up and hugged Specs from behind as the rest of the girls began telling Specs how amazing she was. She felt the love and I could feel her body release its tension. Her shoulders dropped, and she breathed slower and deeper. Patty assured her that she would do her best to make the transition back into school seamless for her so she wouldn't have anything to worry about, and then her eyes shifted to me. I quickly reverted my eyes back to Specs, hoping that Patty would catch the hint, but she called my name and then suddenly all eyes were on me once more, which made me break a sweat.

I stared up at the ceiling, thinking, pondering *hard*. When I thought of strengths, I couldn't name any off hand, but when I thought about my weaknesses, I created a laundry list. I mentally shuffled through my list of failures and issues and couldn't even stop on one because so many popped out at me all at once.

"Eve?" Patty asked again. My attention snapped to her and without having to say anything else, I knew what was going on in her head. This was a test. Now was my time to prove that I deserved my spot in the Gems and that I was ready to put in the work, but when I opened my mouth, I said the opposite of what I was thinking. Patty, Ms. Jenkins, and the rest of the girls just stared at me as I stared at them. The displeasure in Patty's eyes screamed at me.

"You have nothing to share?" She asked, giving me one more time to redeem myself. I shook my head even though my thoughts were raging. I wanted to participate, but something held me back. Even if I tried to explain that to Patty, she wouldn't buy it, but it was the truth. I guess I just wasn't ready to be that vulnerable yet. She raised an eyebrow and then moved on to the next girl. I sunk in my chair and zoned out for the rest of the session.

My first day in the Gems was officially a fail. At the end of the meeting, I knew Patty would want to speak to me, so I hung around while the rest of the girls shuffled out of the room. Specs and Brit offered to stay with me, but I told them to go on back because it could be awhile.

"You don't even have to say it," I told Patty as she stood in front of me and stared me down with her light brown eyes.

"Yes, I do. Being a Gem is about growth. You can't grow if you're not willing to admit some things about yourself," Patty reprimanded me. I refused to look up at her because her energy was intense, and I knew she was aggravated at me.

"I know, I messed up. It's just hard for me. I'm not used to talking about this type of stuff," I admitted. Patty's eyes softened, and I knew she understood.

"It may take a little time," Patty told me. "But you have to try. That's the key." She patted my back and gathered up her supplies so she could head home.

"I'll be better, I promise."

Patty looked at me with confident eyes and nodded in my

direction before leaving me to myself for a moment. I was disappointed in myself. I tried everything in me to say something, but I got choked up. Part of me didn't want to admit to anyone that I was more than afraid. From the outside looking in, no one could understand how I ended up the way I was. Everyone at the center knew where I came from, who my family was, and they secretly judged me for it. They thought I was some entitled brat who had it all and threw it away for some no-good dude, but that wasn't it. That wasn't it at all. The problem was, I couldn't really say what it was—not eloquently, anyway. I wrangled with the idea of just laying it all on the table for the sake of getting through the program versus staying in my comfort zone and I had a hard time reconciling that I could only do one or the other.

"Hey, you all right in here?" I heard a voice ask. I perked up when I saw that it was CO Rivers standing at the doorway of the meeting room. "It's time to head back to your bunk." I nodded, took a deep breath, and followed him out.

"So, what's eating you?" he asked me as I made baby steps to the red room. I played around with my words before spilling my guts to him. I may have rambled for a good few minutes before realizing that I said a lot and yet nothing at all.

"So, basically, I feel a little abandoned. Actually, *completely* abandoned. I know things will be so different when I get out and today's meeting made me realize that I'm not sure I want to face what's next for me." Rivers scoffed at my worry and I couldn't help but feel offended by his lack of empathy. I glanced up at his handsome profile and didn't stay mad long, but I was still a little agitated.

"I have absolutely no doubt that you will be just fine. Trust me, every girl on her way out feels the same way you do now. When the time comes, you'll be ready. That's what Bennings is preparing you for."

He was right. I was being set up to transition back into society and I hadn't acknowledged that being in the Gems was catapulting me forward. Though I still felt like I had a long way to go, Rivers definitely put me at ease.

"Besides that, you've made so much progress already. You've seen the worst of this place, but you're starting to see the best too, and I think once you see just how much you're worth, no one will stop you. You're powerful and strong, and you've proven that you can do whatever you want to do, and even if it's not the best choice, you still get it done and that's something to build on. You got this in the bag, so worry less and work harder on yourself."

His words regenerated into song notes that floated around me as we walked side by side. I could feel myself lift off the ground as he serenaded me with his compliments. The music I could hear in my head went perfectly with his lyrics and just as I stepped on cloud nine, I could smell his amazing cologne. His arm wrapped around my shoulder and he brought me in close to him. The music in my head got louder the closer I got to him and as I rested my head on his chest for that split second, I felt them–the butterflies. The powerful thud of my heart against my chest. The hard lump forming in my throat rose with every second that passed. I looked up at his clean-shaven face. He looked so young without the scruff he usually had. He looked down at me in slow motion and just as his eyes met mine, I propped myself up on my tip toes. I closed my eyes and when our lips touched, I was on fire. If only for a second, I felt passion, lust, and love.

I was in love with him.

Then suddenly the music in my head stopped. The cloud we were both on disappeared from underneath us and the song I thought he was singing to me vanished. I stood still, mortified, as he quickly pushed me away from him. His hands stayed connected to my shoulders as if he wanted to keep me up, but the force he used to pull me away from him was strong–so strong it whipped me right out of the fantasy I was in.

"Don't do that," he said to me and suddenly I was surrounded by darkness. There was only one light overhead that outlined his magnificent face, but then suddenly he was gone. When I blinked, I was back in the hallway, but I was in my own presence. I stood frozen in place as I watched Rivers dart away from me. My heart slowly sank and broke all at the same time.

What did I just do? I asked myself. My brain sent a message to my legs to move, but nothing else was working. My eyes stayed trained on the floor and my mouth gaped open. I don't even think I blinked until I got back to my bunk.

"Hey, Eve, what took ya' so long? You tryin' to get whooped in a game of 21?" Brit asked, shuffling the deck of cards with a devious smile on her face. I zipped past her, Specs, and Gigi without a word and slammed myself on my hard mattress, placing my pillow over my head as if to suffocate myself. Unlike the last time I ignored the girls, they didn't bother me after that, and I appreciated them for it.

sixteen.

*P**assion.*** I tossed and turned all night. When I finally got to sleep, I stayed knocked out for as long as I could. I skipped my usual morning shower and breakfast and went straight to class. Specs asked if I was all right, and I lied and told her I was, but she knew better. After she pried a bit, I promised her I would tell her at lunch, but I just needed some time to gather my thoughts. As we transitioned from class to class, I kept my head down to the ground. Rivers was usually just getting to the center around my second class period and I knew I'd see him around, so I did my best to avoid crossing paths.

I dreaded every step I took to lunch. Rivers alternated lunch duty with a couple other COs throughout the week so if I had to see him today, then would be the time. I poked my head in the cafeteria to see if there was any sign of him. CO Bates and Jones stood next to each other whispering as they watched everyone eat. I let out a sigh and strolled into the lunchroom happy that I was being spared at least another 30 minutes without seeing Rivers. I quickly grabbed my lunch and scurried to our usual table where Specs, Brit, and Gigi all waited patiently for me to get situated.

"What?" I asked them, taking my first bite of my sandwich.

"Specs said you were going to tell us what was wrong with you last night," Gigi said. I eyeballed Specs, who innocently shrugged and smiled.

"Was it something with Patty?" Brit asked. I shook my head.

"Did you find out something about your parents?" Specs asked. I shook my head again.

"Girl, if you don't tell us what happened!" Gigi snarled, balling up a napkin and throwing it at me.

"Okay, okay!" I licked the peanut butter off my thumb and took my time to get my words just right. There really wasn't a "right" way to tell the girls that I kissed Rivers, so I just blurted it out. They sat in complete shock for a moment, they all looked at each other, and then busted out laughing. They punched each other's shoulders and slapped the table like it was funny, meanwhile, I sat horrified at the whole ordeal.

"Oh my God! Was it good?" asked Brit.

"His lips look so soft," Gigi joked as the rest of the girls cackled and laughed.

"It was an accident. I mean, I don't know what happened, it just... happened." When they saw just how disturbed I was, they settled down and lowered their voices.

"Well, what happened next?" Specs asked.

Just as I was about to answer, Gigi chimed in with, "That could be why he's not here today." All our gazes shifted to her.

"How do you know that?" I asked her.

"I was in Patty's office this morning and she and CO Fillman were talking about how he called out today."

A blast of relief rushed throughout my body so quickly that I let out a loud moan.

"Oh, thank God!" I sighed. Brit chuckled and shook her head while Specs patted my hand, giving me a little comfort. I shook the stress from my body and quickly changed the subject.

"So, why were you in Patty's office?" I asked Gigi. She was mid bite when she paused and looked over at me and the other girls.

She cleared her throat and said, "My case worker's coming next week. We just talked about what would happen when she comes, you know, getting prepared I guess."

"Prepared for what?" I asked, not realizing that I was digging too far until Brit quickly nudged me. She shook her head, and I took that as my cue to exit the conversation. Gigi played around with the rest of her food and there was an awkward silence, but thankfully Brit reverted the conversation to a different topic.

"Word in the cell is two of the girls have been writing love notes to each other in a stall in one of the bathrooms, and one of the COs found out about it."

"What? Who? I bet it was Tabitha and Bethany. They're always holding hands and rubbing each other's knees. It's weird," Specs replied, sparking laughter amongst our group, including Gigi.

After classes were over, I led the girls to the library, my new haven, so we could work on our journal entries for that night's Gem meeting. This time Gigi tagged along. She wanted to keep busy, so she browsed the miniscule selection of books and sparked up a conversation with the librarian on duty, who also agreed that the library could use a major upgrade. I didn't know why I couldn't focus, but every little thing distracted me. Specs and Brit were scribbling away, while I had no clue what to write.

What are you passionate about?

I sat, completely stumped and irritated that my brain couldn't bring itself to recall *anything* that I liked. I thought back to when I was with my friends back home and all the things we'd do together. Like clockwork, we would alternate doing homework at each other's houses, music blasting and crumbs from snacks getting stuck on our papers. Most of the time, we wouldn't even get it all done because we were so busy gossiping or making plans for the weekend. If we weren't doing that, we'd be on Instagram clowning our classmates and stalking our crushes or watching our shows on Netflix. For some reason, I couldn't pinpoint one thing I loved, but I could name Rachel and Mackie's hobbies with ease.

Mackie loved design and building things. She was the only girl in the shop class, and she nailed every single project. She'd even stay after school sometimes to create structures and plans with Mr. Finch. Rachel was a theater geek, and though she couldn't act to save her life, she knew aesthetic when she saw it. She was quickly promoted from stagehand, to stage manager, to assistant director. They'd often invite me to do things with them, but I would always decline–I always "had something else to do," but the fact was, I had nothing to do and that was my problem. I didn't do anything worthwhile, and I felt so crappy about it. I wasn't prepared at all for what would have been life after high school, and now I was being faced with answering a question that, had I had the answer to, I may have been more busy doing that instead of getting into trouble. I banged on the table and buried my head into my folded arms.

"Whoa, Eve, you good?" Brit asked me. I shook my head no.

"I can't do this," I told them, slamming my book shut.

"Oh, come on, yes you can," Specs said, grabbing my book to see what I wrote. She glanced down at the empty page and looked up at me, slowly closing the journal and sliding it back over to me.

"It's okay, Evie. We're all passionate about something. You're just having writer's block. It'll come to you." It was just like Specs to be so optimistic and positive. I couldn't stand it sometimes.

For the rest of the afternoon, I remained only half-focused. I couldn't keep my mind off of the journal prompt or how ill-equip I was for life outside of Bennings' walls. I couldn't even name a passion I had. Not one thing interested me or made me happy enough. I was setting myself up to fail, forever doomed to be reliant on a family that would forsake me in a second. I had to stop myself from tearing up as I was coming to realize that the ship towards success was sailing without me on it. I was going to be some has-been that peaked in high school without a thing to her name but a criminal record. The thought of that scared me more than getting out of here and not having anywhere to go.

I sat quietly as Brit and Specs yammered about random things. I insisted that we be the first ones to arrive at the meeting because I figured if I couldn't do the assignment, the least I could do was be early.

"Hi girls," Patty said, surprised that we beat her to the meeting room. "You're early."

"Yeah, we're good noodles," Specs said as she and Brit snickered with each other and I sat unamused.

"Yo, you all right?" Brit nudged me. I shook my head no but lied and said I was fine. Soon enough, the rest of the girls trickled in and right at 7 p.m., we began another session. Everyone knew to take out their journals because we were going to start out discussing our journal entries first. Though I was completely dreading it, I followed suit, hoping not to let on that I had nothing to show for all the serious thinking I was doing.

"Eve. You'll start us off. What are you passionate about?" Patty addressed me. Her cat-like eyes zeroed in on me and so did the rest of the group. It was so quiet; I was certain that they could all hear my heart pounding, and I was shook. I didn't want to disappoint Patty again, and I genuinely tried to do the assignment, but I failed. I did my best to stall, claiming that my so-called passion was stupid and that no one wanted to hear about it, but Ms. Jenkins assured me that no passion is stupid, that we were in a judgment-free zone, and that I should feel free to tell everyone what kept me going.

"I don't know..." I told her, looking down at the ground.

"Let me see your notebook," Patty demanded, reaching her hand out for it. I twitched a little, hoping that she was just joking, but she kept her arm extended and her eyes trained on me. I slowly walked my book over to her and when she flipped to the empty page that should have had words on it, she stared at it for a second, calmly shut the book, handed it back to me, and told me to go have a seat. I did what she said, only I felt like an even bigger failure than I did coming into the meeting.

"What are you passionate about, Eve?" Patty asked me again. Confused, I looked down at my notebook and then back at her.

"You saw my answer," I told her, hoping she would ease up and let me off just one more time. Instead, she shook her head, scooted to the edge of her chair, and placed her elbows on her knees.

"Dig deep," she told me. "What is something that you love?" It was as if Patty was squaring off with me and everyone else in the room were spectators. I became a bit uncomfortable at how much attention I was getting versus the other girls, but I could tell by the way Patty planted herself that she wasn't going to let up until I gave her an answer she believed. I inhaled and exhaled deeply, closing my eyes while I attempted to gather my thoughts. I took my time in concocting an honest enough answer, but I was just as stumped as I was earlier that day. There was nothing in the tank, and that was the truth.

"I–I'm not good at anything and I never had hobbies," I finally admitted. I felt so ashamed and like I didn't deserve to be there. The girls continued to watch, unsure of how to respond to this showdown between me and Patty, but I for one was ready for it to end.

"Can we move on, please?" I asked in desperation, but Patty shook her head.

"Though your passion can be something you're good at, it isn't fueled by skill level. It has to do with what you genuinely love and what motivates you. What motivated you before coming to Bennings?" Patty inquired.

"Nothing important. I just wanted to leave home."

"Dig deeper, Eve. Do the work."

On the verge of tears, I closed my eyes and covered them with my sleeves so the rest of the girls wouldn't see me get upset, though I'm sure they already saw how frustrated I was becoming.

"Okay, let's do this. What did you want to be when you were a kid?"

I let her question settle in before exposing my face again. I was a bit flushed, but I was willing to have another go. I hadn't thought about anything regarding my childhood in a while, but recalling little Eve came easier than I thought. As soon as I closed my eyes again, I saw five-year-old me. I was so bright-eyed, I looked like an anime character. Everything was exciting to me and I couldn't wait to get my hands dirty. I was in love with the world.

I saw myself with a gigantic smile on my face and I was a mess; blends of red, blues and yellows coalesced with greens, purples, and oranges on my face and t-shirt and then suddenly I was back in my five-year-old bedroom. My smile beamed because I had just created, what I thought, was the most magnificent painting known to man. It was supposed to be a bunch of different animals herding together, but it became more than that; it was about friendship, love, and the respect each animal had for another. It was random, but I was so proud of myself and could feel my heart dancing for joy as I admired every color and every stroke that my hand and my paintbrush were responsible for.

"Eve!" My mom screamed, yanking my paintbrush out of my hand. The force behind her pull was jarring, and I remembered almost losing my balance, but she caught me, only because she didn't want my wet clothes to touch the clean parts of the carpet. Soon, my dad came rushing in, already boiling and ready to burst. When he saw what I did, he went off, per usual.

"He was so mad that I turned my room into an art studio," I explained, chuckling with my eyes still closed. "They had to replace everything. I think... I think that was one of the first times I pissed my parents off that bad. I didn't mean to, though, I just-" I paused for a second, remembering how proud I felt of that painting.

"I loved how all the colors mixed together and created other beautiful colors, the smoothness of the brush strokes across a clean canvas. Oh! And the smell of the paint! It was like smelling a freshly cleaned kitchen to me. I felt so calm, so in control, so in love. I just wanted to be an artist. I wanted to create." I opened my eyes and was a little disturbed at the smiling faces gleaming back at me.

"What are you guys smiling about?" I asked. Patty and Ms. Jenkins glinted at each other and then back at me.

"So, art is your passion," Ms. Jenkins concluded. I nodded, but then backtracked.

"Well, was."

Ms. Jenkins shook her head and said, "It sounds like it still is. I can tell by the way you just described your experience that it's deeply rooted within you." Patty and the rest of the girls nodded in agreement, and Brit even patted me on my back.

"Did you ever explore art beyond that growing up?" Patty asked. My smile faded as I shook my head. I once told my parents that I wanted to paint ceilings like Michelangelo. We had been learning about some of the most famous works in history and that particular day, we talked about the infamous Sistine Chapel. I was amazed at the detail and so desperately wanted to see it in person. It looked so grand and wondrous. It inspired me to do the same, but when I explained it to my parents, they shot me down.

"That's a waste of time and you'll never make real money doing that," my dad told me. "How about we find something more practical? How about business?" he insisted. I was eight.

"I never brought it up again," I told the group. I refrained from looking up as the pain of reliving those moments was too hard to deal with without bursting into tears. I hadn't even realized that I lost something so dear to me that day and that it changed my life.

"How did your parents' response make you feel?" Patty asked.

"Rejected. Like, what I wanted didn't matter at all." As I lowered my head, Specs grabbed my hand and caressed it, giving me a great deal of relief. I had never admitted that to anyone, not even Mackie or Rachel, and here I was pouring my heart out about a dream I was told wasn't plausible to people I just met.

"It's no big deal, though," I brushed it off. "My parents were right, anyway. There was no way I would have been able to take care of myself selling paintings."

"Well, how do you know that if you don't try?" Brit asked me. I went to respond, but a few of the other girls signed off on Brit's sentiment. Seeing the smile on Patty's face mixed with the emerging feeling I had in my stomach every time I thought about splashing colors on a canvas was all I needed to feel like I might just be on a new path.

"You know, art can be therapeutic," Ms. Jenkins interjected. "No matter the medium, it gets people through their toughest times and you should explore it more, not just for yourself, but for others." Though I agreed with her, I had no idea where to begin. I tucked that dream away for years and now that it was reemerging, I felt myself getting overwhelmed at the idea of trying to figure everything out.

"I haven't even drawn so much as a stick figure since I was a little girl. How can I get back into that groove?" I posed. I and the rest of the girls seemed stumped, but Patty and Ms. Jenkins seemed fairly confident.

With a smirk, Patty said, "We will think of something."

Standing in front of a paintbrush and an easel, imagining my first masterpiece was all I could think about. I couldn't get painting out of my head, and I was okay with that, but I also couldn't keep my parents' words from replaying either. Just as the image of me tossing buckets of paint on a wall was becoming clearer to me, so was their ridicule of my decision to not be some money-craved zombie lawyer or business owner. My heart wrenched when I thought about little me being mocked for simply wanting to express myself on a canvas. I remembered looking in the mirror after my parents told me my dream was a bust and how pitiful I looked and how pathetic I felt for thinking that my dream was actually within reach.

A couple days after that Gem meeting, I was called into Patty's office to discuss a "major development" in my program.

"What's up?" I asked her as Ms. Jenkins stood to her side. They both seemed chipper and eager to tell me what was on their mind, and judging by their huge smiles on their faces, it was certainly good news.

"First of all, we are happy that you are participating in the Gems," Ms. Jenkins began. I thanked them both, as Patty's approving look told me she shared the sentiment.

"We were thinking about how you could tap into your artistic side and use your talents here. Simply talking about art made you happy–that was clear–so we figured we'd go out on a limb and see if we could spark that creativity that is no doubt still in you and in other girls too."

Ms. Jenkins' words were clear, but they weren't registering to me. I blankly stared at them, waiting for the "major development" they were talking about. Patty saw that I wasn't quite catching Ms. Jenkins' drift, so she interjected and broke things down a bit more.

"That large wall in the cafeteria is a bit bland, don't you think?" she asked me. I took a second to recall the wall she was talking about and it was the wall with the high windows, the wall that me and the girl gang sat right in front of every day during meals. I never paid any attention to it, so I agreed with her observation of it being bland.

"We got permission from Marie Trumbull to allow you and a few of the other girls to create a positivity mural. You'll be supervised, but it should be a fun project for you."

I stared at them in disbelief. I suddenly felt like a thunderbolt shocked me awake and I jumped up, screaming, "No way! This can't be true!" When both Patty and Ms. Jenkins confirmed that it was not only true, but that they wanted me to lead the project, my head nearly exploded. I paced quickly back and forth, holding my head, trying to process all of what they were saying. The irony of the project being a wall mural wasn't lost on me, but the beautiful part of it all was that I was being encouraged to do it.

After catching my breath and letting the idea settle in my head, I looked at them, both of them grinning from ear to ear, and gave each of them a tight hug. I was so grateful for them having my back.

"I can't believe this!" I yelled swinging Patty's office door open and running down the hallway making a ruckus.

"Hey, stop running in the halls!" CO Bates called out to me as I whizzed past him.

I stopped myself, nearly toppling over and yelled, "Sorry!" back at him before continuing to do a jig. I looked over my shoulder and saw that he was still staring at me, so I kept myself contained. When I rounded the corner and Bates was out of sight, I re-upped my cheering session and even proceeded to dance backwards. I then thought, *I have to tell the girls,* but just as I turned around, I was face to face with Rivers, who I had managed to forget existed. I gasped dramatically to the point where I had to hold my chest because I was so startled. Somehow, I had forgotten how good he looked and although he looked well-rested and unfazed by my presence, I was still in avoid mode. I stammered about, trying to find the right words to say to him. Sorry was a good start, but I felt like he deserved an explanation.

"How are you?" he asked with a sweet smile. I melted at the sound of his voice and wished I could be wrapped in his beautiful milk chocolate arms as he stared at me with those shimmering eyes waiting for my response.

"Oh, um, I'm fine... how are you?" I asked him, trying to avoid eye contact.

"I'm pretty good..."

With each second that passed, I held my breath and dared myself to just come out with it, but it was hard. Apologizing to him meant that I was sorry for what I did and honestly, I wasn't. I wanted to kiss him for a long time–hell, I wanted to do a lot of things to him, but when I looked at his roaming eyes, I saw how good of a person Rivers was. He could have taken advantage of that moment and me. If he would have lingered, even just for a second longer, it could have been a *thing*. He did what was right, and it wasn't just to save his own job, but because he was just good.

Coming to that conclusion made me realize that I was doing it again–forcing myself onto people and into situations that were bad for me, despite knowing the repercussions of things going wrong. I thought back to the breakthrough Brit had when she admitted to everyone in the Gems that she knew she had a problem with dealing with older men and that she wanted to reign herself in. In an instant, I became a little more self-aware of my own faults in that department.

"I'm so sorry for the other day," I finally said. He had stopped fidgeting with his hands and looked dead at me. We shared a brief moment where he understood me, and I understood him.

He nodded his head and said, "I accept your apology." I felt as if a massive rock had been rolled off my body. It seemed as though our bodies were in tune because we both took a deep breath and then chuckled at the dissipating awkwardness between us.

"So, what are you all happy about?" he asked me, swiftly changing the subject. I instantly perked up, remembering the news Patty and Ms. Jenkins shared with me about the project. As he walked me back to the bunk, I told him about the meeting and about the approved art project.

"Wow, congratulations!" he said giving me a high five. I could see a knee-jerk reaction to hug me, but he used his better judgment and pulled away before he thought I could tell. I didn't mind though. As much as I could've used the hug, I understood the boundaries of our relationship and that it was probably too soon for that.

"Yeah, I'm *so* excited!" I exclaimed. "It's weird. I had totally forgotten about it. In fact, if it weren't for Patty pushing me to 'dig deeper', as she said, I would have never thought about it again."

We made small talk for the rest of the walk and when we got to my room, he congratulated me again and quickly scurried off because he got called to mediate a rising situation in the blue room with the low risk girls. I entered the red room like I owned the entire building and the girls could see it.

"What's up wit' you?" Tatiana pried. "Why you so cheery right now?"

With a big smile, I announced the news.

"Your girl just got put in charge of an art project for the cafeteria wall and some of the Gems can help me!" Brit and Specs both jumped for joy and I assured them that they'd be on the team.

"Now Bennings will never be able to forget about me," Brit smirked, patting her chest. A couple of other girls from the Gems walked over and congratulated me, also hoping they could be a part of the team. I told them I'd seriously consider them as I winked at Specs and Brit, who were giggling to themselves. It felt great that everyone was just as excited about the project as I was, but when I saw Gigi and how off she looked, my happiness faded a little. She sat on her bed and looked like she was so deep in thought that no amount of distractions could pull her away. I walked over to her, and she snapped out of her daydream and gave me a sincere smile, though her eyes looked very distant and sad.

"Are you cool?" I asked her. I knew the answer, but I had hoped she would be open with me and tell me what was eating at her so bad. She shook her head no and admitted that she was a little stressed.

"Okay, I'm *very* stressed. I have a lot on my mind right now, so I'm sorry if I'm coming off some type of way," she said. I brushed off her apology because it wasn't needed. I knew what she was up against within the next few days and I empathized with her 100 percent. Brit and Specs soon walked up to us and joined in the conversation.

"I can't even be excited for my birthday because my case worker is bringing some news the day before and it's not looking good," Gigi explained.

Brit took Gigi's face into her hands and leaving only an inch between their faces, Brit said, "Gigi, you got this. That judge knows what happened, and you did what *anyone* would have done in that situation. Give yourself a break, chica." Brit finished her pep talk with a kiss to Gigi's forehead and for some reason, it made me and Specs giggle, though it wasn't a laughing matter. Whatever Gigi was up against was serious and it was getting very real for her. Gigi smiled through her clear pain and it was sweet seeing Brit be the cheerleader and friend Gigi needed.

"Besides that, you've made so much progress here. You've stayed out of trouble and you have Patty," I explained to her. "I know she's rooting for you and willing to do whatever she can to help." Gigi rolled her eyes and shook her head, seeming to doubt every word I said.

"I don't know, y'all," she began. "Patty has been talking to my case worker, but she won't tell me what's happening and it's pissing me off."

I got why Gigi was mad. Her life was hanging in the balance and no one was throwing her a limb. It seemed like she was being left out to dry until the very last minute when she wouldn't have time to prepare herself for what was to come. What was even more surprising was that Patty was in this mix and not being much of a help, but then again, there was always a method to her madness. Maybe it was better for Gigi not to know everything. I kept my mouth shut and let Specs and Brit continue to spew compliments and good vibes towards Gigi.

I guess she got tired of hearing it, because she quickly turned her attention to me and said, "But hey, congrats on the project! I'm sure it'll look amazing." I hugged her tight, hoping she would feel my love for her and just as I pulled away, Brit and Specs jumped on us, creating a dog pile that ended up on the ground.

"Y'all are so annoying!" Gigi cackled loudly.

"Oh, shut it! You love us!" Brit yelled, holding us all together like the glue she was.

seventeen.

*F*ebruary 9th. **Gigi's Day of Reckoning.** My heart raced from the moment I woke up, so I couldn't imagine how Gigi was feeling. She kept herself away from most of us and when she was forced to be amongst the rest of the girls, she was silent. Specs, Brit, and I all took turns checking in on her, making sure she was okay, and that she wasn't going insane.

We kept the conversation light during breakfast, talking about my ideas for the wall mural and what we wished they would serve us for our meals, but the energy was so off, we eventually stopped pretending that the moment we were in wasn't as intense as it was.

"Maybe we should leave her alone," Specs observed as we lined up to go to our first classes. Gigi and Brit were in the same class, so Brit insisted that she'd do her best to keep Gigi's spirits high. Knowing Brit, she would be the one to crack Gigi and get her to at least smile, but knowing what she was dealing with, I didn't blame her one bit for going mute.

I couldn't stop thinking about Gigi throughout math and language arts. I hoped that the judge would spare her, but because I still didn't know what she had done, it was hard to say what the outcome could even be. Specs and Brit remained mum on what it was Gigi did. They continued to claim that it wasn't their business to tell, but they both asserted that if it were them in that situation, they don't know that they would have done anything differently. Still confused, it did give me a little comfort knowing that whatever happened was something that people somehow understood.

I went back and forth, trying to figure out what she could have possibly done, but eventually I gave up guessing. If I was meant to know, I'd know. Prying into Gigi's personal life just wasn't as important as her being able to go home instead of being transferred to an adult prison.

We knew we'd miss Gigi at lunch once Brit told us that she was called out of their last class to meet with the case worker.

"It can't take that long, right?" I asked Specs and Brit as we slurped on our chicken noodle soup. They both shrugged. According to Brit, her meetings usually only lasted about 30 minutes max, so we were hoping that we would see her right after lunch and she could update us if she was feeling up to it.

Two hours passed and there was still no sign of Gigi.

"This is either a really good thing or a really bad thing," I noted. Brit smacked her lips and rolled her eyes.

"Thank you for that unneeded commentary," she said as she shuffled her playing cards and dealt them out. We did everything we could to keep ourselves busy, but the girl gang wasn't the girl gang if we weren't all together. When dinner finally rolled around, we hung back for a few moments, hoping that Gigi would turn up, but CO Bates barked at us to get in line or miss dinner. We scurried to the back of the line and kept our eyes peeled for any sign of Gigi as we headed towards the cafeteria in a single-file line. Just as we rounded the corner, Specs gasped, which caused Brit and I to see what was up. Just a second later, all three of us stopped and stood frozen in place as Gigi trailed Patty. We quickly jumped out of line and rushed to our friend. Just as we reached her, we made eye contact, and we stopped again. Her eyes were bloodshot red, and her face was flushed except for her rosy nose and cheeks. She had been crying a lot, that was obvious, but *why* was the question we all wanted the answer to.

Before any of us could even say hi, Gigi shook her head, raised her hand, and gestured for us to stop, so we did.

"I'll explain later," she said, continuing to follow Patty.

"Will you be at dinner?" Specs asked, concerned.

Gigi looked back and nodded and then said, "In a little bit." We watched them walk and chat down the hall until they were no longer in sight. We stared at each other for a few moments and silently agreed that no matter the news, we would be there for her and get her through her transition.

"Ladies, let's go! I'm not going to talk to you again!" Bates called down the hall to us. We rushed into the cafeteria so we wouldn't have to hear his mouth. After our little debacle where I ended up in max hall, Bates became a little different, but just a little. I wouldn't say he was nicer, but he did more talking than punishing. He seemed more willing to shell out warnings and actually talk to us like we were people and not criminals unworthy of human decency. Now, I didn't want to take credit for it, but I was happy that our crazy moment created a shift that made him slightly more approachable and a little less scary.

We secured our usual table in front of the big, empty wall that would soon be covered by the art that I created. I stared into space and suddenly saw myself covered in paint and laughing with the girls as we carefully painted within the outlines. The smile on my face was so foreign, I didn't even recognize it. I hadn't genuinely smiled that wide in a while, but before I snapped out of my dream world, I promised myself that I would take my time and have as much fun as I could with the project.

"Look!" Brit motioned to Gigi and Patty walking into the cafeteria. The rest of the room remained busy with their own cares and conversations, but we stopped everything. I couldn't tell by the way Patty spoke to Gigi if the news was good or bad and we couldn't see Gigi's face well, but she nodded a few times before finally saying her goodbye to Patty with a lackadaisical wave. Gigi instantly looked dead at us but didn't even flinch. She made her way down the line to grab her lasagna and casually strolled to the table in a concentrated state that made it even more difficult for us to read her.

We gave her a minute to get herself settled, but we practically sat on top of her when she seemingly ignored our concerned stares and began eating her food as if her missing in action for half the day was nothing.

"So.... What did they say?!" Specs asked, starting off the rapid-fire questions. After letting us get all our questions and concerns out of our system, she stared at us for a few moments, wiped her eyes, and then took a deep breath, as did we.

"Well, it turns out that my brother and sisters will stay in different group homes."

We all felt the air get tight around our table, and as every moment passed, it became more suffocating. I felt horrible for her because I knew how much she worried for her siblings, her brother especially. The little she did tell me about her life back at home mostly involved talking about her siblings and how close they were. She felt especially protective of her brother though because he was often made fun of for being too "girly."

"He's sensitive," Gigi once told me. "He's a sweet boy and people just don't understand that. They always want boys to be rough and tough, but then demonize them when they actually are or humiliate them when they're not."

After a few conversations, Gigi confided in me that, though she wasn't sure, she believed her brother might like other boys and wanted to protect him at all costs.

"He's too good of a kid to be lost in this world, wondering around, hoping that someone would love him despite that," she spilled. My respect for Gigi grew tremendously that day. I couldn't say that I was some social justice warrior who allied against all disenfranchised people because I wasn't, but the love she had for her siblings outweighed everything else and I thought that if I had someone who fought for me like Gigi did Ronnie, I might not have ended up at Bennings.

"Damn, I'm sorry girl," Brit comforted Gigi.

"But the good news is it's only temporary. My case worker said that she'd been talking with my aunt on my dad's side and she agreed to take them. The only problem is she has to prove she has the accommodations, so it's going to take a little time, but they'll be together again." A faint, but optimistic smile inched across Gigi's face and it caused us all to light up. Overall, there was some positive movement and Gigi could breathe a little easier knowing in the very least that her siblings were going to be okay. Then I thought back to how anxious she looked the days leading up to this moment and couldn't help but wonder, *what about her?*

"So, how about you?" I asked, tearing through the happiness that we all felt. Specs and Brit stopped mid affirmation and looked at me and then back at Gigi, realizing that we couldn't rejoice just yet. She looked every single one of us in the eyes, and though she looked so exhausted, I could see a glimmer of something in them that gave me a little hope.

"So, the judge looked at all my case files and had some questions," she explained. "The case for my release was strong thanks to my brother and sisters' testimonies and stuff, but there were some inconsistencies with my program. Me having to switch centers so often didn't look great at all. Not to mention, I would get on a great track and then I would get set back a few times, so Patty and the judge had to have a *long* conversation."

I immediately thought back to the part I played in the fluctuation of her progress and felt ill knowing that if she wasn't granted freedom, that it would partially be my fault.

"I don't know what Patty said," she continued. "... but it saved me."

It took a few seconds to process what Gigi was actually trying to tell us, but once her faint smile turned into a cheesy grin, we all got it and we couldn't contain ourselves. Our energy quickly built in each of our bodies and we awaited Gigi to say the words so we could finally release what was being riled up.

"I'm getting out, y'all. I'm going home."

The moment we squealed, the cafeteria fell silent. The sounds of just the four of us celebrating overtook the sounds of 50 other girls in their own worlds. We all ended up on our feet in a group hug with Gigi in the middle, and though everyone gave us the strangest looks, we didn't care because our friend was getting out. Suddenly, what she did didn't even matter. What mattered in that moment was that Gigi was going to get a second chance at life and that she was the happiest I had ever seen her.

eighteen.

February 10th. Gigi's Birthday. Now, we had more to celebrate. In Bennings fashion, when it was a girl's birthday, she would get a personal cake made by the cafeteria staff and an extra privilege. Most of the time, girls requested more TV time or extra time in the rec room, but Gigi asked for more time to sleep in. She didn't have to tell anyone that she was drained, her eyes said it for her. The staff granted her request and told her she could have an extra hour to sleep in and that they'd have a packaged breakfast for her to take to her first class since she'd be missing our breakfast time.

The rest of us woke up normal time and quickly planned out the best wake-up call she could get. We watched the clock as we put together our cards and gifts to Gigi and when she started rustling around, we put everything in place.

"We seem like creepers," Tatiana whispered as we watched Gigi slowly wake up from her much-needed sleep. The room fell quiet, and we all stared as she stretched out a couple times and took a few moments to recognize her surroundings. The hair bun that sat neatly on her head the night before was now halfway out of the hair tie and the imprint from her pillow made deep creases in her skin.

"Oh, she slept *good*," Brit said, causing us to snicker. Gigi immediately propped up when she heard the growing pandemonium and the jig was up.

We yelled, "Happy birthday!" and a wide smile crept across her face. When she pulled back the covers and went to set foot on the floor, her eyes widened as she glanced over all the cards we placed around her bed. She picked up the card that Specs made and read it silently. Line by line, she took in the love that Specs expressed for her and by the time she was done, we were all shocked at the tears welling up in her eyes.

"I'm a G, so I ain't gon' cry, but I love this," she said as she walked over to Specs and gave her a hug.

"Thank you guys so much. It means a lot." The bell rang, letting us know it was time to start the day. "All right, now get to class!" she demanded. We all chuckled and trickled out of the room, each one wishing Gigi a happy birthday personally before disappearing into the hallway. Brit, Specs, and I stayed after everyone left, just to see how Gigi was feeling.

"18?! What are you going to do with yourself old woman?" I asked, lightly punching Gigi in her arm.

With a smile, she rolled her eyes and replied, "I'm gettin' out of here, that's what I'm doin'!" before punching me way harder in my arm, causing me to cower behind Brit.

"I'm glad you're feeling good, Gi. It's not a real birthday if you aren't happy," Brit said as she went through Gigi's drawer and threw her a red sweatshirt and a pair of gray sweatpants. As we gushed over Gigi's glow, CO Fillman walked in and broke up our girl gang meeting, telling us to head to class.

"I'll see y'all later," Gigi said with a smile as she slipped on her sweatshirt. We all nodded and said goodbye for the moment and went on about our day.

I was really beginning to get the hang of being in the Gems. I didn't think I'd feel different as quickly as I did, but the work I was putting in was real and so were the results. Within the couple weeks that I had been in the Gems, Rachel and Mackie could hear a change in me. They weren't able to come see me because Mackie's brother hated driving in snow, but they called up often to check on me and update me on life outside Bennings' walls. I still heard nothing from my parents, but I eventually stopped hoping they'd reach out because my friends gave me enough love and support.

"Girl, you even sound different! You been doing yoga or something?" Mackie quipped.

Though I couldn't see them, I just knew Rachel had nudged her or was giving her a stupid look because Mackie then said, "What? I hear that calms you down." I laughed because I hadn't noticed the change myself, but if they could hear it, I just knew people around me could see it. I paid Patty daily visits, and we just talked things out—whatever I was feeling, she helped me conceptualize it, see if from other points of view, and apply solutions to derail negative thoughts, emotions, and actions.

Every day, I broke down a level of the walls I had up around my inner self and I got to the point where I could talk about what was going on inside, not be afraid of judgment, and be open to advice. Patty warned us that the next session would be hard for some of us because we would discuss the chain of events that led us to Bennings, but that we needed to do our best to fight through it. I mentally prepared myself all day, practicing how I'd tell the story, what facts I'd tell and what I'd leave out. I did some serious self-checking and even made notes in my journal to hold myself accountable.

"All right ladies, today we will go deep. As I mentioned in the last meeting, you will address how you ended up at Bennings and analyze what you could have done differently. We will wait for the last person and we'll get started." We all looked around confused because everyone who was usually in the group was already there. Just then, the door closed, and we all looked back to see who it was. My eyes grew wide, and the room filled with gasps.

"What?! Why didn't you tell us?!" Specs asked Gigi, as she walked towards the group, now wearing a green sweatshirt. With a sly smirk, she sat next to me in the empty seat I somehow disregarded until now.

"I wanted to surprise you," Gigi remarked. I stared at Gigi in complete awe. I guess the reason why she wasn't put in the Gems before was because they were waiting for her case to get settled. If she would have been sent to prison, none of the stuff we were dealing with would have applied to her because they would have transferred her. I looked over at Patty, who also had a beaming smile, and when our eyes met, she shrugged. She knew this was the plan all along and all the times I spent in her office annoying her about putting Gigi in the Gems was pretty much just me blowing smoke. I didn't mind though. I was just happy that Gigi was finally in the Gems and that the girl gang was all together.

"Let's officially welcome Gigi into the Gems," Ms. Jenkins said as she started a round of applause that instantly spread across the room. Once we settled down, Patty told us that Gigi was set to leave in early April, as long as she finished school, had no bad marks, and stayed out of trouble. Gigi's smile radiated so much light and hope into the room, it caused us to go crazy for her once again. Gigi was already a different person, but she would be unstoppable by the time she got out.

"Don't worry. I will be the best-behaved person in this center," she said, prompting laughs from the group. Patty and Ms. Jenkins gave us some room to calm down and get back into the mindset of the day because in a few moments, we would be feeling much different.

Ms. Jenkins began with a girl named Taylor. She was a Black and Korean girl who acted like she spent time around nothing but hood rats all her life, but she was cool. She explained that she fought a lot in school and that was why she was at Bennings.

"I guess they got tired of moving me around. They couldn't handle me," she said, referencing the various detention centers she was at before Bennings.

"Why did you feel the need to fight all the time?" Patty asked her.

"Well when you look like I do, you have no choice." She was short and petite–definitely not the kind of girl you'd expect to land a punch, let alone throw one. Apparently, her rap sheet was extensive too. Despite only being 4' 11", she was out there fighting girls and guys at least a foot taller than her and winning on a daily basis. She was fearless and didn't care what anybody thought of her. It didn't matter anyway because she was going to show you what to think of her.

"People underestimated me. They treated me like dirt until I dragged them. Then they became afraid of me, which was the best feeling ever, I ain't gon' lie," she admitted, prompting head nods from a few of the girls.

"I guess it was finally nice to have people back off me. I might have went on a power trip or two. I beat up a girl so bad, she ended up in the hospital with a concussion."

"You know what you should do," Brit chimed in. "MMA. You could rip those girls to shreds and what's better is no one would even expect it. Not only that, those women make big money." It was as if a lightbulb went off in Taylor's head. She had never thought about fighting professionally, not that most people do, but she seemed to like the idea because she got up in the middle of the circle and started fighting the air, pretending to be in a ring. Brit began cheering her on, while the rest of the girls laughed. I laughed too, but then saw Patty shaking her head, disturbed that the conversation went left so quickly, so I held myself back from engaging. Patty finally got the rest of the girls to settle down and got Taylor back on track.

"Now, I want you to think about where that anger stems from. It may not come from one instance, it could be many things that happened over time, but how do you think this all started?" Patty asked. Taylor got quiet and put on her thinking face. She thought long and hard. She prepared herself to talk a couple times but then stopped herself.

"I–I think seeing my dad throw my mom down the stairs a lot did it." The mood in the room suddenly got grim.

"It used to scare me–had my heart pumpin' fast and everything," she admitted. "I guess I figured that if I could fight and hold my own, no one could ever treat me like I wasn't worth a damn."

Ms. Jenkins and Patty both let out a quick, "Mmm," before Patty finally asked, "What would you do differently?" Taylor didn't have to think about that answer. She quickly inserted that she'd hold back from fighting and walk away.

"The girl didn't deserve what I did to her," she concluded. We clapped for her enlightenment and Patty praised Taylor for being willing to tell us about her family and for thinking of an alternative way to handle confrontational situations.

"I expect that you'll take that mindset with you and avoid fighting. You can walk away and be the bigger person, keep your dignity, and your freedom," Patty said, before turning her attention to Becky, the leader of the "white trash mob" at the center. She thought she was cute because she was skinny and blonde, but the girl looked 15 years older than she was and sounded like an old man who smoked a pack a day. She walked around the center with at least four other girls behind her like everyone should bow down to her, but she got no respect from anyone but her little posse.

"Becky, why are you at Bennings?" Patty asked. Becky joined the group not too long after I did, and though she did the work, she always acted like everything was a joke. It wasn't a shock that she had a crooked grin on her face as she told us about her serious drug use problem.

"When I was high, I used to get into all sorts of trouble-robbin', stealin', and partyin' even more. Y'all know I once stabbed my mamaw when I was high on coke?" She continued to rave about her misadventures as a meth, coke, and pot head and all the while, everyone else showed various levels of disgust and aggravation. In the midst of it all, Gigi nudged me and when she got my attention, her eyes rolled so hard I wasn't sure they'd reconfigure correctly. I did my best to hold back a chuckle, but Patty shot me and Gigi a glare which made us straighten up.

As I listened to Becky, I realized that she and I had a little more in common than I originally suspected. She admitted to turning to drugs because she also couldn't stand being at home, and though her home life was the complete opposite of mine-I was rich and my parents paid no attention to me and she was poor and her parents breathed down her neck every second-our motives for getting into things we shouldn't have were the same. I couldn't relate to the checklist of drugs she had tried, though. I took ecstasy a couple times, but other than that, I damaged my brain with good old-fashioned weed. Johnny offered me bumps of new crap he was pushing here and there, but truth be told, I was way too scared to try any of it. The last time I took X, I spent half the night dancing my butt off and staring into bright lights and then the other half of the night in front of a toilet and almost passing out from dehydration.

"I ain't even gon' lie, I miss doing some of them," Becky admitted, talking about the drugs. Patty and Ms. Jenkins both perked up at the same time and just as Ms. Jenkins prepared herself to respond, Patty cut in.

"You can't say things like that in the Gems. Your mind has to be stronger than your body in this case."

Becky, looking confused, said, "I don't even know what that means, but I can't help it, Patty. I'm shocked I even made it these five months without any meth or a line." For the first time, we all saw Becky take things seriously. Her smile faded, and she looked like she was thinking deeply about her actions.

"It means that you can't hold on to the mindset you had before you got in here. You're a Gem, honey. That not only means that you are on the path to being ready to get back into the world, but it means you are becoming a better, greater version of yourself. I understand how addiction works, but the mind is a strong vessel and your survival depends on keeping your mind on track. That means that whenever you have an urge to use, you must fight it. It won't be easy. You'll need some help, and we will help you get it," Patty explained. The whole group understood Patty's words, including me. *Will power.* I guess our success in the world all boiled down to our willingness to aim for the gold, which might mean turning our backs on people and things we knew we were going to miss but weren't helpful in our growth.

"So, what would you do differently?" asked Patty.

Becky thought to herself for a moment and then replied, "Well, I definitely wouldn't have tried coke in the first place." With a smile inching across her face, she quickly added in, "Meth, maybe, but not coke." A couple of girls giggled, but the rest of us were so over her, so we just groaned and waited for Patty to move on to the next person. Patty scanned the circle, trying to decide who should go next. I had half a mind to volunteer so I could get it over with, but before I could raise my hand, Patty zeroed in on Gigi and pounced. Gigi was shocked and very taken aback by being called on so early into the session.

"Just throwing me into the lion's den early, huh Patty?" she asked with a light chuckle.

Patty flashed her a half smile and said, "Now is as good of a time as any. You can explain as much or as little as you want, but bring us into your world. Why are you here?" I glanced over at Gigi who appeared to be preparing to give us a rundown of what happened. My initial thought was *Finally!* but as I watched her take herself back to that moment, I slowly began to regret caring so much. She began to shrink, and her face scrunched up. She sniffled a little, trying to hold herself together, and the moment she opened her mouth I knew that whatever she was going to say would be a lot worse than I expected. Gigi took a few deep breaths and began.

"I know there's been a lot of talk about what people *think* happened. I've heard some really crazy theories, but I can tell you that none of them are true. I've been fighting this case for a year and I've been in and out of centers wondering if I'd ever be free, but now that I'm officially getting out, I feel okay to talk about it." I watched Gigi's hands tremble as she fought to keep going. She began fidgeting with them, doing her best to hide her anxiety, so hoping to give her a little comfort and support, I grabbed a hold of one of her hands and rubbed her back with my free hand. I felt the tightness in her body slowly ease as she breathed in and out, keeping herself contained. She looked over at me with glossy eyes and I nodded in support of her continuing when she was ready.

"A lot of y'all know how having a single parent can be. Either your mom does her best to make ends meet on her own or she finds someone who can help or do it all. My mom preferred the latter, and I get it; there are four of us-me being the oldest, my sister Vera, my brother Ronnie, and my baby sis, Cara. I'll admit, we didn't always make things easy for her. When you got four constantly hungry and growing kids, it's easy to get overwhelmed.

Mom dated around a bit, some dudes were cool and some were absolute trash, but we never really had problems. She'd just come home with bags of groceries or new coats and clothes or even a new handbag or two. She was pretty happy with how things were, and we finally had everything we needed so I guess she figured why stop there? She realized she could con money out of these suckers, but once their money ran out, so did she. That's where Vern came in. Dude was a well-known drug dealer, and he promised to take care of us, and he did for a while. When they were starting out-him and Mom-he was the coolest guy. He used to bring each of us a gift whenever he dropped mom off after what we thought was a date. He buttered us up real good and once mom announced that Vern was movin' in, we were actually pretty happy. I knew he was a gangster, but I can't lie, I felt more secure with him being around, but I should have known that all of it was an act. He switched up real fast.

The day after he moved in, he started getting real loud. He'd cuss us out in English and then in Spanish. He'd march through the apartment punching and kicking holes in the walls when certain things weren't done his way. He hit our mom in front of us every day and she just took it. I won't even mention how much of an ass he was to me and the kids. He pretty much ignored me for the most part and I did my best to stay gone, but when I was around, I couldn't stomach him. He'd make Vera fix him food, and he'd call Ronnie a sissy and a bitch because he liked to play dress up with the girls. The only one he wasn't rotten to was Cara. She was four at the time and I think he had a genuine soft spot for her. I once heard him say that she reminded him of his daughter back in D.R. Anyway. The day everything went down was supposed to be normal. I was supposed to get the kids up and ready for school. Mom started making early drops for Vern, so she'd never be home by the time we woke up. I was supposed to fix everyone breakfast-the girls loved their Fruit Loops, and it wasn't breakfast for Ronnie if he didn't have a warm bagel with jelly. I would have then gotten everyone out of the house by 7:15 so Vera and Ronnie could catch the same bus to their school, and I could walk Cara down the street to the day care. It was supposed to be normal... It was supposed to be normal..."

The room was quiet as Gigi quietly repeated herself. She had since let go of my hand and was now using both of hers to shield herself from the world. After a few more deep breaths, she regained her composure and soldiered on.

"I woke up that morning feeling so off, and I couldn't explain why." Gigi looked up at the ceiling to avoid eye contact with anyone else. We watched her as she dabbed escaped tears from her eyes before they could fall and then when she regained her strength, she kept going.

"Vern said he wanted to be more helpful with us and that it wasn't fair that I was stuck being a mom to the kids when I was a kid myself. So, he offered to get them ready for school for me. I didn't think anything of it, and actually, I was happy to be getting a break. I usually made it to school right on time, so now that I was going to have that extra 20 or 30 minutes, I figured I'd treat myself to some food and meet up with my friends before classes.

As I gathered my stuff, I sensed that the kids were a little scared, but all I could think about was myself. I remember looking into Vera's eyes as I said goodbye to her and the other kids. She didn't say a word, but her eyes-they were screaming for me to stay, but I didn't. I closed the door on them and rushed out to meet up with my girls. I guess I thought that if there was a problem, one of them would immediately tell me. Vera and Ronnie had phones, so if Vern was acting up, I could rush back home and grab them. I didn't hear anything from them, so I assumed the drop off went okay. I went through the whole day of school fighting this feeling of something being wrong, but just didn't know what it could have been.

When I got home, it was quiet, as I figured it would be. Vera and Ronnie's school let out not too long after mine and Ma normally picked up Cara from daycare. I went into the room I shared with Vera and Cara expecting to be alone, but no. Vera was actually home, and she was snuggled under the blankets. She looked so peaceful, and I didn't want to wake her, but the fact that she was home and Ronnie wasn't was so odd to me. She would have texted me and told me she came home early. I would have grabbed her a snack or something if I knew she wasn't feeling well.

Before I went to leave out the room, I looked at her one more time and noticed how tight she was gripping her pillow. Her eyes were shut real tight, like she was having a bad dream, and when I looked a little closer, I saw that her pillow was soaked and her face was wet. She did this sort of whimper thing when she was having nightmares, so I quietly walked over to her and tried to comfort her, but instead of soothing her, I guess I only scared her more. I finally woke her up and let her know it was just me, and when I tell you, her eyes-they were so big and scared. They were different. *She* was different, and I knew it. It wasn't a dream she was having, it was something else.

I held her in my arms and she just shook like she was cold, but she was also sweating so bad. I went to pull the blankets off her so she could feel some cool air, but she freaked out and snatched them away from me. I held her close, rocked her, and asked what was wrong and why she was home early from school and she just burst into tears. Her sobs were unreal. They came from deep within. I grabbed the covers again so I could get her out of bed, but she refused to let them go. After we fought over them for a little bit, I finally yanked them back and there she was, sitting in a little puddle of blood. I was relieved because it all made sense. She wasn't feeling well because she started her period and was embarrassed that she messed up the bed. But that look in her eyes. It was... pure fear.

So, I asked her, 'Did you start your period?' When she shook her head no, a rush of so many things came to me at once. I felt my heart rip because if it wasn't her period, then something was seriously wrong with her or something happened to her.

I looked her straight in her eyes and asked, 'Did Vern do something to you?' She didn't respond, but she stared back into mine and I could see that she was trying to tell me something without saying it, but I had to hear it.

'It's okay, you can tell me,' I told her. She finally looked away from me and as she told me what happened, everything I was feeling-all those emotions I felt went away. The only thing I felt was rage,"

Gigi continued, wiping sweat from her forehead and tears from her eyes.

"She said Vern claimed he had something to show her and told her to stay home and he'd take her to school a little later. He took Ronnie to school and Cara to daycare and when he came back, he..." I watched as Gigi finally broke down. She finally let go of what she kept pinned up for so long. Her big tears fell freely as she tried to keep telling the story. Patty told her she didn't have to say anymore, but Gigi insisted on finishing the story. Sharing the story out loud was like therapy for her.

Vern brutally raped Vera multiple times that day. She was only 12.

"She said all she could do was lay there," Gigi sobbed. "She laid there while he did unspeakable things to her and I-I wasn't there. I couldn't save her," Gigi cried.

"You know what she said to me? She said, 'Gigi, it hurt so bad I could feel my insides break.' That's what she said to me. And then- all I could see was black."

Not a single eye in that room was dry. Ms. Jenkins grabbed a box of tissues and passed it around the circle, each of us grabbing a few. After I grabbed mine, I buried my face into my hands. I couldn't bear to see Gigi this way, but even more so, I couldn't bear to hear this story any longer.

"When Vern came home that day, he turned the TV on and took a nap on the couch like nothing happened. I didn't have a plan. I didn't know what I was going to do. All I know is that when I saw that he was asleep, I spared no mercy. I don't even remember grabbing the knife, but I remember the blood and his body after. I remember my siblings' cries as the cops took me away. I'll never forget that. It wasn't my intention to kill him. But then again, maybe it was."

We sat silently, watching Gigi as she graciously wiped her tears away and sat up in her chair. She looked around the room at all of us and when she stopped at me, she held her stare a few seconds longer. I didn't know what to think or what to say. I just knew I wanted to give Gigi the biggest hug. In my eyes, she did the Lord's work, but in the eyes of the law, she took a man's life, even if the reason was noble to many.

"So, the question is, what would I do differently?" Gigi said breaking the silence in the room. She stared at Patty, who was dabbing her face with her clump of tissues.

"Not a damn thing." Gigi scooted her chair out of the circle and strolled out of the room, leaving us in her dust.

nineteen.

Family Over Everything. It took me a while to process what I heard. When Gigi left the group, we didn't see her until it was time for bed. Specs, Brit, and I looked all over the place for her, but apparently, she was hiding out in the library between bookshelves. She needed her time, and we understood that, so we didn't bother her, but I had *so* many questions.

Gigi went mute, avoiding us and everyone else through the next day until I finally dug up the courage to ask if she was okay. Based on how she responded when I first met her, I wasn't sure how she'd take the prying.

"I'm cool, why wouldn't I be?" she replied, looking genuinely confused at my concern.

"Well, yesterday was intense..."

"Don't worry about it. I feel better than ever now that I finally got all of that off my chest," Gigi said with a shrug. She continued to eat, but Specs, Brit, and I were seriously concerned about her and hoped that she wasn't just burying her emotions to avoid the conversation.

"Are you sure? Because-"

"I'm good," Gigi said slowly. "I don't need anyone to baby me, all right?" She didn't give me any time to apologize. She quickly swiped her tray, dumped the rest of her food, and rushed out of the cafeteria.

"Am I doing too much?" I asked the other girls, who acted like nothing happened. Specs avoided my question, but Brit proudly nodded.

"I told you not to mention it," she said, casually eating her mashed potatoes and then stuffing her face with her chicken patty sandwich. I rolled my eyes.

"Well I wouldn't have so many questions if you two would have just told me what happened. I wouldn't be shocked at this point."

"Like I said before, it wasn't our story to tell," Brit interjected.

"And if it makes you feel any better, she never told us any details, just that she killed a man for hurting her sister." I stared at the both of them as they continued to eat their food. I was shocked that I seemed to be the only one even remotely haunted by this.

"That's all she said? And you just believed her and didn't ask questions?" Specs and Brit both gave me the same look you give when someone asks a stupid question.

"Of course we asked, but she said not to worry about it, so we didn't," Specs mentioned.

"Besides, the last thing I'd want to do in juvie is mess around and make a murderer angry," Brit added. They both got quiet again, and that was my cue to leave. The conversation was going nowhere and although there were still so many thoughts running through my head, I couldn't let any of them overshadow the fact that Gigi did in fact overcome all the odds and was actually going home. I rerouted my curiosity and went to our bunks where I figured Gigi would be.

Just like I thought, Gigi was sitting in the red room alone on her bed. She glanced over at me and then continued looking at what looked like a photograph. I had hoped she didn't think I was coming to be nosey. I just wanted to be a friend to her. If I were in her position, I knew I'd want someone to check on me, even if I didn't feel like being bothered. Intention matters, and I wanted her to see that mine was only good.

"I come in peace," I said with a smile. She rolled her eyes, and a smile inched across her face, signaling to me that it was cool to engage with her.

"You know I meant no harm, right? I just want to make sure you're okay."

Gigi nodded. "I know you were just being cool. But now that you know everything, I don't want to hear anything else about it. I'm good now. Vern's gone, I'm getting out, and I'll get to be with my brother and sisters again." When she said that, I finally understood. Yesterday was something she wanted to do, but it wasn't productive to dwell on the past since she was going to be able to start fresh.

"I gotcha," I told her. We both took deep breaths and sat in silence for a moment. Gigi then handed me the photo of her and her siblings at a beach. They all looked so much alike, and her siblings were gorgeous. Ronnie had dark curls that hung freely just around his face. Vera held Cara on her hip and they both looked like twins in the face, both smiling through the cutest, chubby cheeks. And Gigi-she stood not too much taller than them, holding them all together in her arms. The smile on her face was so big, you couldn't even see her light brown eyes. She looked so happy-they all did. The happiness that they exuded in that photo shined and caused me to smile just looking at them.

"When was this?" I asked her.

"Eh, a few years ago. Well before everything happened. We were really happy." To avoid any more talk about the "situation", I reverted the conversation to how cute Ronnie was and how I wished I had Cara and Vera's long hair. Gigi kept her locks shoulder length, but they were thick and wavy.

"I used to have long hair like that, but boys used to pull it at school. I would have to shove their faces in dirt to show them who was boss, but I got tired of doing that, so I just kept it short." We laughed and continued to share our moment together.

"When was the last time you saw your siblings?" I asked, hoping it wasn't too personal of a question. She paused for a second, and I wasn't sure if she was thinking or if I hit a nerve and needed to take back my question.

"It's been a minute," she finally said. "My mom brought them a couple times when I first got here, but after she abandoned the kids, I didn't see them again. It's been like six months and I miss those faces..." she said, staring deeply at the photo.

"But, I'll be seeing them really soon, so, I'm excited." The confidence in her eyes and the optimism in her smile gave me so much hope for her. She once seemed so angry and bitter, but now that the light at the end of the tunnel was coming at her quickly, she brightened up.

"Now that I'm 18, I can get us an apartment and take care of them myself. I'll get a nice job and we'll be all right." Gigi's certainty was very unsettling to me. Though I felt happy for her, she seemed a little too confident that things would be that easy. I didn't want to crap on her new ideal life, but I hoped she knew it would be difficult and I didn't want her to deal with that. I was glad that I didn't have to say anything though; I think she saw how worried I was, and she assured me that she already had a back-up plan in case things didn't work out.

"Don't worry about me. Patty said she'd help me with whatever I needed, and I'll see if I can qualify for food stamps or WIC or something."

I sighed. My friend was about to get out and be on her own after being locked up for a long time, and her first recourse was going to be government assistance. I then realized just how lucky I was. I knew I was privileged, but I never really had context. I was always around other privileged kids and we just moved like we didn't have a care in the world. I knew my parents would bail me out every time

I got into trouble. That might have been why I kept finding my way in some. I knew that, if I wanted or needed something, that they'd get it for me, even if I didn't deserve it, and maybe that was why I never thought about that when I thought about them. It just came so easy for me.

Hearing Gigi talk about her independence in accordance with getting help from the government not only put some things in perspective for me, but it made me sick. I hated that Gigi, a girl who would have probably never ended up here if it weren't for this situation, was going to be confined to what the government believed she deserved and would be forced to hustle for the rest to make ends meet. Then there was me–a bratty, entitled rich kid who'd be all right regardless of where I ended up just because of my last name.

"I want to help," I blurted out. Gigi glared at me with some sneaking suspicion that I was being funny or disingenuous. "I'm serious." Her eyes continued to narrow until something clicked in her head.

"Oh yeah, you are rich," she said with a chuckle.

I rolled my eyes. "Well, my parents are, but-"

"Yeah, okay," Gigi brushed me off. It was clear by her facial expression that she didn't believe I'd follow through, but I had a stash that even my parents didn't know about and I was going to help her. I kept my mouth shut though because Gigi then suddenly felt comfortable enough to rant about her mom, who had dropped her brother and sisters off at a community center to "play" and never came back to get them.

"I know she did it because of me," Gigi claimed. "When she found out I might be going to prison for what happened, she just said 'forget them kids' and dumped us."

Why and how could she do that!? I thought to myself. I couldn't believe it.

"She didn't believe Vern did it, you know," Gigi explained. Shock translated clear across my face and through my body as I jumped back, feeling like I was being dealt blow after blow with this story.

"Yeah," Gigi said, feeling my reaction. "I think she just didn't want to believe it. I think she knew he was after Vera, but she didn't want the money to stop coming in." I sat in silence, not knowing what else to say as she looked at the picture again.

"I'll tell you one thing; I'll *always* believe my kids. It's family over everything."

twenty.

February 28th. The Day Before Brit Left. The mood was so off, it wasn't even funny. I couldn't tell you how Specs, Gigi, and Brit got on before I came, but once the girl gang became a foursome, we were thick as thieves and we couldn't be a gang without all of us together. We had been with each other day in and day out for months, so for us to trickle out, it was tough to process, and it was throwing us all off balance. The silver lining to this was that none of us would have too much longer to wait until our day came when we could walk out those gates and hopefully never look back.

It was the eve of the first center graduation that I'd get to see and both Brit and Specs were graduating. Graduation was big because many of the girls probably would have never finished high school if it weren't for this program. The schooling set-up in the center was different than what I expected. They were preparing us for our GED, a test that we could take at any point in time with a little or a lot of studying. If they believed that a student was ready to take the test, they would administer it, and if they passed, they'd graduate. Moving along well in school went hand-in-hand with getting released on time or even early. Because girls came in every day who were on different levels, there was no real structure to how classes were taught or what was taught, unlike normal school.

They broke us up into two groups; one was more "advanced" or closer to being GED-ready, while the other needed a little more time or attention. When we were admitted to Bennings, the center received our latest school records, and based on our grades and what level classes we were taking, they placed us in a group, and our program would merge our education plan with our mental health and rehabilitation plans. It was tactful how they made everything come together while still keeping track of individual programs.

Specs was ready to take the test shortly after coming to Bennings, but Patty and Ms. Jenkins decided against it because they didn't want Specs to be idle for long. They couldn't be sure what sort of trouble she would get into if she became "bored" and though she was low risk, they didn't want to chance it. They put her in the advanced classes, hoping it would keep her in the very least entertained for a while, but Specs was already light years ahead of what the advanced class was learning, so she was still bored, just in a controlled setting.

Brit, on the other hand, was a bit more like me-though not quite, because when I skipped school, I easily made up for it with good test scores. Brit would just not show up, and when she did, she would have no idea what was going on. She never mentioned how and why she got involved with her teacher, but I was willing to bet that getting her grades up was part of the exchange. Regardless, I was so proud of the both of them for getting their GEDs and getting out of Bennings.

When we weren't in class, Brit spent her free time cleaning up her bunk, which was surprising because she almost never kept it neat. I think what she was really doing was keeping herself busy. She looked deep in thought every time anyone approached her, so I knew she was thinking about what would happen when she got out.

This wasn't customary, but since everyone loved Brit, us girls from the red room gathered with the girls from the blue room and created what we called "Brit Day". We wanted her to know that we loved her and she would be deeply missed, so when we caught her taking a break from tidying up, we all approached her with the perfect idea for her last day.

"Today is your day, Brit! You get to decide what we all do!" Specs exclaimed as the rest of us gathered around. Brit was speechless. She didn't know what to say, but she gave it a little thought and finally came back with some ideas including us going outside to enjoy the unusually warm winter day, have a karaoke session at dinner, and then ending the night with a giant braid circle. Brit was obsessed with braiding hair and I'm pretty sure she braided everyone's hair at some point or another.

After lunch, the COs agreed to let us have a longer recess. We usually got outside time for about 30 minutes every day, but since it was colder, we hadn't been able to go outside. It was the perfect day to spend a little more time out, enjoy the fresh air, and celebrate Brit moving on to bigger and better things. We played a massive game of four square, which was harder than we thought with all 50 girls participating, but it was so fun. We then had a basketball game, where Brit was a team captain and Tatiana was another. Me and Specs cheered for Brit's team on the sideline while she and Gigi's team annihilated Tatiana's team. Finally, we played a huge game of tag, which surprisingly was the most fun we had the entire time. We were dodging each other, falling on the ground, and carrying on like we were on a schoolyard.

Most of us still had a couple more classes left, so for dinner, we met up with Brit and she led the dinner crowd into the cafeteria. The karaoke session proved to be the absolute best thing I had ever seen. A few of the girls made beats using their fists, utensils, and trays. Some girls got up and showed us dances from where they were from, and Brit pretended to have a fake mic and started singing and rapping into it, prompting the rest of us to sing along to all the songs we heard and remembered before we came to Bennings. I half expected the guards on duty to stop the noise, but when I saw that it was Rivers and Jones, two of the most laid-back guards, I knew they'd let us have this moment.

A couple hours before lights out, Brit called everyone into the rec room for the braiding party. We made a giant circle and turned to our left, so each of us would braid the next girl's hair. Brit had me and I had Specs. I wasn't that great at braiding, but neither were half the girls, so I didn't feel too bad. We waited for everyone to finish their braids and then just as Brit adjourned the party, Specs stopped her and brought her to the middle of the circle.

"Since it's your last night, we just have to do it," Specs stated, causing a bright smile to spread across Brit's face. As tradition had it, when a girl was about to leave the center, she'd be sent off with compliments and well wishes during her last Gem meeting. We were supposed to meet today, but when Patty heard about "Brit Day", she canceled it and let us all hang out. So, instead of the Gems praising Brit, the entire center would commend her.

One by one, each girl told a story about a time that Brit was there for them, helped them, or cheered them on. When it was Gigi's turn, she talked about how their vibe was off the charts as soon as they met. She knew they'd be friends, but she didn't know they'd be best friends. When it got to me, I told her how I was initially afraid of her because she had just come out of max hall. She looked tough, but I soon learned how soft and caring she really was.

Brit hung on to every word and we all knew that she was fighting back tears. She never cried, but when it was Specs turn, she lost it. Specs didn't get a word out before they both wept and held each other tight. Specs and Brit were the best of friends. Gigi grabbed my hand and when I looked over, Gigi's pout only triggered the emotions in me and then I couldn't contain myself. Sniffles filled the air as Specs did her best to articulate just how much Brit meant to her.

"The moment I got here, I had you. You were always so good to me. You stuck up for me, you cheered for me. You're my best friend and I'm going to miss you. I just hope you won't forget about me once you're gone," Specs said as she let her tears flow freely. Brit wiped both hers and Specs' tears away and hugged her tight again.

"I'll never forget you Specs and I'm going to miss you more than you know. We have to stay in touch, and we will," she told Specs, still holding her close.

"I'll miss all of you. Thank you for this." Everyone clapped and cheered for Brit, including CO Fillman, CO Jones, and Patty and Ms. Jenkins, who snuck in on the love fest. We all followed Brit out of the meeting room and the girls dispersed to their designated bunks.

"I don't want you to go," Specs whimpered, as she stood outside the red room. Lights out was in about 30 minutes and we had to be in our own bunks. Brit hugged Specs one more time and assured her it wouldn't be the last time they'd see each other. After their moments long hug, we all went our separate ways and chilled at our bunks until the lights switched off. Brit looked distant and checked out. Perhaps that compliment circle was too much for her.

"You good up here?" Gigi asked, poking her head up to Brit's bunk, using mine as a lift. Brit nodded, but her face said otherwise. "No seriously though, what's up?"

Brit kept her eyes trained on the wall in front of her and her voice was dry.

"I'm not sure I can do it, guys." Gigi glanced at me and I'm sure I looked just as confused as she was.

"What do you mean? Now's not the time to second guess yourself," said Gigi.

"I know, I know and I'm probably overthinking all of this, but what if I get out there and do the same stupid stuff I did to get in here? What if I really didn't change?" she posed. I then propped myself up using my bunk so I could see if Brit was serious and she was.

"You don't really believe that, do you? You made so much progress. Look at you; you had every single girl in this hell hole telling *you* how awesome of a person you are," I remind her. Despite the effort Gigi and I put in to make Brit see how ridiculous she was being, nothing worked. She was finally getting out, and she didn't believe she'd stay out.

"I don't know... maybe I'm being crazy..."

"Uh, yeah," Gigi and I both said together causing all of us to laugh. For the rest of the night, Gigi and I tag teamed in making sure that Brit felt as good as she always made us feel and by the time she went to sleep, her attitude completely changed.

The next morning was heavy for everyone. This was the first time in a long time that we had more than a couple girls graduating and all leaving not too long after that. Brit woke up singing a different tune than she had been earlier the night before; she literally woke up singing and twirling around the room like a fairy princess in some cheesy musical. Admittedly, I was jealous, but I kept in mind that my time was coming up and that I had a lot to look forward to when I got out.

It was great to see Brit feeling good on her official release date, but it seemed like whatever was up with Brit latched on to Specs. We only saw Specs briefly because the graduation was scheduled around 10 in the morning, but she didn't say much, and she looked exhausted. Her eyes, which usually sparkled, were so dull and for a lack of a better word, dead. We wished her and Brit luck before they were called to get ready for the ceremony and for the rest of the morning, Gigi and I sat in our respective classes, bored out of our minds and ready to get the graduation over with.

I watched the clock like a hawk, eyeing it every other minute. I had wished that we could have phones because Gigi and I would have been texting to keep each other company or maybe in "old me" fashion, we would have agreed to skip out on classes and meet up somewhere just to get away. The 9:30 morning bell rang, Mr. Kole lined us up, and led us to the auditorium where the graduations took place. I quickly scanned the room trying to locate Gigi and once I spotted her and she spotted me, she pointed at the empty seat right next to her. I rushed over to claim my spot, and as I walked over, I saw Brit and Specs in their caps and gowns. I stopped in my tracks and took in the sight of my two friends gleaming with enormous smiles on their faces. Brit sat next to Specs and whispered something in her ear causing her to giggle and I became emotional. They were leaving me–that part sucked–but more than anything, I was proud of them. They were going back out into the world new, better people and it pained me to know that my experience with them was most likely going to be confined to this place. I was glad to say I knew them, though.

"Eve, hurry up!" Gigi waved me over. I snapped out of my sappy moment with myself and scurried over to my seat just as Ms. Jenkins was beginning the ceremony.

"You good?" Gigi asked me. She must've saw how misty-eyed I got, but I nodded to her and we listened to Ms. Jenkins introduce the next graduating class before handing the mic over to Patty so she could say a few words and recognize each of the four girls individually. She opened the floor for any of them to speak, but none of them took the chance; they were just ready to be done, and I didn't blame them.

"Ladies, you are official graduates of the Bennings Detention Center for Young Women's Rehabilitation Program. You did it!" Ms. Jenkins announced. Pandemonium erupted in the audience and we all clapped, screamed, and cheered for our friends' success and their bright futures ahead of them.

Once Ms. Jenkins dismissed us, she allowed us to mingle a little before lunchtime. Gigi and I rushed over to Specs and Brit who were hugging and sharing a moment neither of us wanted to interrupt.

"This is it," I said to myself.

"Mhm," Gigi agreed.

As they continued to hug, a boy and a girl who looked very similar, bolted down the aisle and were followed by an older, limping woman who had a bright smile on her face.

"Roz!" The kids yelled together. When Specs turned around, she shrieked. She embraced her brother and sister in one huge bear hug, and despite her own small frame, she harnessed all her might, picked them up, and swung them around.

"Oh my goodness! I didn't know you'd be here!" Roz said to them, then eyeing her grandmother who seemed to pick up her step when she locked eyes with Specs. I could see through her glasses that Specs was overwhelmed with joy. A few tears fell as her grandma engulfed her in a warm hug.

"I wasn't expecting to see you for another week!" Specs exclaimed, hugging her brother and sister once more.

"Yeah, well, we couldn't miss your big day. We're so proud of you, baby. You know you got a lot of people waiting to see you," her grandma mentioned. Specs' eyes lit up once more, and she squealed and spun around in typical, excited Specs fashion. When she got a hold of herself, she noticed me, Gigi, and Brit waiting patiently while she had her moment and her smile got brighter as she brought us together and introduced us.

"Mama, these are my best friends! That's Gigi, that's Brit, and that's Eve!" She said pointing us all out. Her grandmother smiled widely at all of us and waved. She congratulated Brit on graduating as well and then gave us a few words of wisdom.

"Now, I'm gon' tell y'all what I told my baby, Roz, when she first came here. We all make mistakes, but they don't have to define you. I don't know why you're here, but I believe God put you all here at the same time to meet each other, to learn from each other, and grow and learn for yourself. This is a setback, yes, but setbacks are also set ups for what the Man upstairs has in store for you girls. I can see from your faces that you aren't bad. I can tell that you're intelligent, thoughtful young ladies who only want to be seen. Well, I see you and I want you to know that God sees you and loves you. It might seem like he's forgotten about you, but he hasn't. He's preparing you for breakthroughs you don't even know you need yet. Just wait on it. In the meantime, stay encouraged and keep working hard. It pays off."

I stood hand in hand with Brit and Gigi, all of us on the verge of tears. Those words–they were just what I needed. I wished that they came from my own parents, but Mama was on to something. Things happen for a reason, and though we don't always understand why, everything makes sense eventually. I looked at both the girls to the side of me and then at Specs, thinking about what Mama said. Out of all the girls we could have linked up with, we hit it off best with each other. We had each other's backs from the start, and we learned to trust each other. The only other people I felt that way about were Rachel and Mackie, but I had known them since elementary school. We grew up together in the same neighborhood, living the same way, and liking the same things.

I wondered if I would have given any of these girls a chance had we not met like this and I concluded that no, I wouldn't have. I would have looked down on them, judged them, and dismissed them. Then a bell rang in my head. This was a lesson for all of us, but probably more so for me. Once I got knocked off my high horse, I learned to *see* other people. I learned to do the one thing that I so desperately wanted my family to do for me. I *saw* these girls for who they were and learned to love and cherish them, and I accepted the fact that one reason for me being here was to learn that very lesson.

"Hey Brit," Gigi spoke up. "I don't know, I might be seeing things, but that lady over there looks just like you." We all looked to our right, and just as Gigi described, a tall, fit woman who looked like a slightly older version of Brit stood, waiting for her turn to talk to her graduate.

"Mom?!" Brit said. She ran over to her and jumped into her arms. "I thought you were coming later?!" she exclaimed.

"I wanted to surprise you! They said I could take you home earlier than originally scheduled, so I made sure to be here," Brit's mom explained. Her voice was soft and smooth like melted milk chocolate. I couldn't believe that this woman was actually Brit's mom; she could have passed for an older sister, but definitely not a mom.

"Y'all! This is my mom!" Brit exclaimed, now bringing her mom into the mix. We all made introductions and reminisced about the many times we had together. The lunch bell rang, which meant that the graduation was officially over, and it was back to business as usual. The rest of the girls and staff trickled out of the auditorium, but we stayed because we just wanted to remain in that moment for as long as we could.

"No, I don't want you to leave me," Specs whimpered, hugging her grandma and siblings tight. Mama reminded Specs that she was coming back in less than two weeks and that she needed to stay strong. Specs agreed and hugged them one last time.

"You ready to head out?" Brit's mom asked her. With an enormous smile on her face, Brit nodded her head.

"Yeah, I've been ready."

Patty and Ms. Jenkins waited for Brit and her mom at the door to guide them back to the front, where Brit would get her stuff, change, and be on her way.

"Wait, can we see Brit off?" I asked Patty. We were hungry, but this was important enough to hold out for a little longer. Patty looked at Ms. Jenkins and they both agreed that we could follow them, but we couldn't go outside. With each step we took, reality set in deeper and deeper. The girl gang wasn't going to be the same. All four of us squeezed through the hallways, walking hand in hand until we reached the changing room where Brit's mom gave her some clothes she brought her to change into. When Brit came out, she looked crispy in a bright orange Nike T-shirt with some fitted jeans and white sneakers. We pretended to catcall her as she walked out of the room and she took the bait and pretended to model for us. We all laughed, but then the mood quickly changed. Brit, who was always so stable, seemed a little unhinged. Specs hurried over to Brit, giving her a big hug, and Gigi and I quickly followed suit. We held on for a while, all of us wishing the moment would last forever. When we finally let go, we held each other's hands.

"I'm going to miss you guys," Brit said, quickly wiping away her tears.

"We're going to miss you too," Specs said, now whimpering. She collapsed into Mama's arms, while Gigi and I comforted each other.

Brit grabbed her box from CO Jones and headed out with Patty and Ms. Jenkins followed them. Just before she went out the doors, Brit turned to us and said with a smile, "I love you guys and I'll never forget you!"

Without hesitation, Gigi called back to her, "You won't have to forget us because we're all staying in touch, bitch!" We all laughed, even Brit's mom, but Patty shot Gigi a disapproving look, which caused Gigi to look around, notice Specs' little brother and sister, and she sheepishly apologized for her language.

"I was just in the moment," Gigi admitted before we quickly turned our attention back to Brit and watched her as she giddily jumped in her mom's car. They slowly drove down the path separating us degenerates from the rest of the world and soon there was nothing else to see.

"See you later, Brit," I said under my breath as Ms. Jenkins directed Specs' grandma and siblings towards the exit and Patty escorted me, Gigi, and Specs to the cafeteria where we would have our first lunch as a threesome.

twenty-one.

*T**he Mural Committee.** I should have known that once Brit left, Specs would change. The poor girl moped around the center for a few days and acted like she wasn't about to get out herself. Like with Brit, Gigi and I did our best to keep Specs' spirits high, but she didn't bite. She spent a lot of her free time, which was *most* of the time, in Patty's office getting talked down because she was so anxious. This version of Specs was so new to me, it almost didn't seem real.

After what seemed like weeks of waiting to hear back about the mural, Patty confirmed that the supplies had finally arrived after a major delay in shipping. She said we couldn't use Gem time to plan the mural, but she suggested I get together with some girls who expressed interest during lunch or our free times. Though the only people I cared to hang out with were Gigi and Specs, I agreed to lead the project, so I had to be a big girl and bridge some gaps.

After getting the news that we could officially start the mural, I rushed back to the red room to tell Gigi and Specs.

"So, are you guys in?" I asked them. Gigi agreed without hesitation, but Specs' remained silent. I stared at her for a few more seconds, thinking she was just quiet for dramatic effect, but when I called her name again, she still had the same blank stare on her face from before.

"I don't think so," she stated dryly. Gigi looked at me and shook her head slightly, motioning for me not to push the issue, so I didn't.

"It's cool. You don't have to. I get it." Specs looked up at me with her big eyes and smiled a little. I was happy to see a little bit of old Specs back after feeling like she completely disappeared.

"Thank you," Specs' murmured. "I just- I can't think straight. There's a lot on my mind, as you can imagine." It became clearer that her lack of participation and energy was about more than not having her closest friend around; she was afraid to jump back into a world that was different when she left it. This reaction was not foreign to girls in places like this. So much can change in an instant and then when it's time to jump back into society, we all feel unprepared. Perhaps my anxiety hadn't kicked in yet because I still had some time, but I was slowly starting to understand the rationale behind their delayed excitement about getting out and decided to just be a friend.

I left Specs and Gigi alone and envisioned my team and the mural. The team could only include Gems, and after scanning the room, I saw I had slim pickings. Gigi was official, but I figured I needed at least three or four more girls to make sure we got it done in good time. After all, a lot of us were leaving within a couple months. I remembered a couple of the girls who approached me when I first announced the project–a girl named Trina and another named Joegina, Joe for short, so I asked them if they were still interested and their smiles glimmered as they nodded their heads in unison. Trina and Joe were locked at the hip like the girl gang was, so it couldn't be one without the other. I spotted Tati skimming through an old comic book and smiled. We had already squashed our little beef, if that's what you want to call it, but this was my official olive branch to her.

"Hey, you want to help me do the mural?" I asked her. Her gaze stayed focused on the comic as she examined each page intensely.

"Sure," she muttered.

"Cool. I'll check back with you later," I told her and trotted off. The team now had five girls, but an even six would be perfect. I didn't want to leave any of the other girls out in case they actually wanted to help, so I went into the blue room where all the low risk girls stayed and spotted a few more who could be potential candidates.

"Any of you guys want to be a part of creating the mural in the cafeteria? I have a spot for one more girl," I asked the girls in green. The low risk Gem girls sat in a circle playing war and seemed disturbed that I interrupted their little game. They all looked at me with varying degrees of annoyance and as I turned to leave without an answer, I spotted Becky, who was actually high risk, but often hung out in the blue room with her weirdo friends. She was certainly the *last* person I would have thought to ask and had hoped that someone would step up to the plate before I was forced to ask her, but I had no other choice.

She sat in the middle of her clique, the white trash mob, appearing to speak some weird white power declaration into existence. As I processed what she was saying, I decided that being inclusive was not worth the drama that would come with having someone like Becky, the daughter of a supposed KKK member, in a group full of Black and Latina girls. Just as I turned around to walk away and settle with the five girls I had, Becky's raspy voice pierced my ears.

"Oh wow, look who's in our neck of the woods. You lost, Black Barbie?" she asked, prompting her followers to all turn their heads and scowl at me. They all stood up from their Nazi youth meeting and faced me head on. If we weren't in a controlled environment with guards all around, it would have been on. I refused to show that I was slightly entertained at the Barbie comment and kept a straight face. I was in it now, and there was no turning back.

"I was going to ask if you'd like to be a part of the mural committee," I said, looking around at all the peering eyes staring back at me. "But I see you're busy, so I won't bother you about it." I swiftly made my exit, and I almost got away too, but Becky responded with an answer I wasn't expecting.

"Yeah, sure. Thanks for thinking of me, princess." I cringed, and for a second, I hated myself for trying to be nice. I would have never been this nice in any other setting, in fact, I would have told Becky and her crew to kick rocks and that nobody liked her, but I was changing and part of being a better person was trying to affiliate with people I would have otherwise ignored. Maybe trying to make things work with an overt racist was a bit much, but one thing was for sure; one racist remark from her and I would not hold anyone back from beating her ass.

I called a meeting for the next day during free time. It was a bit cold that day, so we were confined to the rec room, which was perfect. Before I started the meeting, I couldn't help but look at them and wonder how this would work. No one liked Becky, Tatiana became a bit of a lone wolf, Trina and Joe were always in their own little world, and me and Gigi were in our own too. If there was any chance that we could work together, it would be a miracle.

"Okay, so did anyone give some thought about what they want to see in the mural? Patty and Ms. Jenkins have to approve it, so obviously it has to be appropriate," I explained. The group was silent for a little bit until Trina slowly raised her hand.

"So, me and Joe were talking, and we think it might be cool to have, like, different color girls holding hands or something. Like, showing a- what did you say yesterday, Joe?"

"A sisterhood," Joe responded.

"Right! Like a sisterhood," Trina finished. I was pretty impressed with the idea, and though it seemed a tad bit surface and maybe even overdone, I applauded them for thinking of it. Besides, it was an idea that Patty would approve and that was the first hurdle we had to get over.

"Anyone else?" I asked the group. Crickets. Either no one else had an idea, or no one wanted to speak up. I took a deep breath and jumped into leader mode.

"Look, there are no bad ideas. Just throw out what you think would look good. Girls holding hands is a great start, but let's build on that!" I pumped them up. I stood firm and used my "power voice," something I learned in speech class back in school. They seemed to eat it up, even Becky. After giving it a little more thought, they began throwing out so many ideas, I had to grab a piece of paper and write them all down.

We ended up with a list of 20 things, but only about half of them were relevant and would most likely get approved. I scrapped the ones I didn't think we could do, and we brainstormed how we could enhance the ideas we had left. Just like I figured, everyone wanted to do their own ideas, and no one wanted to budge. I could feel an argument coming on, so I nipped it in the bud and suggested that we incorporate as much as we could into the mural.

"The mural doesn't have to be one thing. It can be many things all wrapped into one piece, so let's decide what we like the best and focus on how we can put it all together." The other girls agreed, and we ended up with a short list of the kumbaya circle of different girls, colorful flowers, rainbows with gem raindrops, unicorns, and inspirational quotes.

This is a mess. I thought to myself as I stared intensely at the list. I didn't know how we would pull this off, but I would do my best to keep everyone happy.

The next plan of action was to draft the actual mural. With the help of the other girls, we fleshed out a sketch that didn't look half bad. We hadn't decided on a quote yet, that was something we would have to request computer time to find, but everything else looked pretty darn good.

"I'm actually excited for this," Gigi expressed. I glanced at her, admiring the sweet smirk on her face, and agreed.

"I'll meet with Patty tomorrow morning and see what she thinks. She said she got a batch of colors and paint brushes, so we could start painting as soon as we finish outlining the mural." The girls seemed excited enough and after dismissing them for the day, I sat next to Gigi, who had a bit of a devious look in her eyes.

"What are you thinking?" I asked her.

With a raised eyebrow and a smirk, she said, "I'm thinking either this will be really good or really bad." I nodded in agreement. This planning stage wasn't as much of a struggle as I thought it would be, but I couldn't be sure that tensions wouldn't rage once we started getting down and dirty. We chatted a little more about the project before I saw Specs, moseying about like she was new. Gigi and I walked over to her to see what her deal was.

"Hey Specs, you doing okay?" I asked. Specs had been quiet since I asked her to join the mural team. She nodded.

"You sure?" Gigi chimed in. "Because you've been ignoring us, and we only want to be here for you." Specs looked at the both of us and bowed her head. She felt guilty. We could see it on her face, but I don't think she could move any other way.

"I'm sorry, I really don't mean to," she said. "I've just been doing a lot of thinking."

"Look, we get it," I said, wrapping my arm around Specs' shoulder. "But we're your friends and we want to help you out any way that we can." I stared at Specs, who was avoiding eye contact with the both of us and then at Gigi. Gigi was at a loss for words too. I guess she was just as exhausted with chasing after Specs as Specs was of dealing with her issues.

"What do you say you be on the mural team? It'll lift your spirits and will give you something to do," I suggested. I just knew she'd stand firm and say no, but I had to try again. Specs stood in silence for a while, appearing to be deep in thought.

Finally, she said, "I'm not the artistic type," to which Gigi then said, "None of us are! Well, except Eve." Just to add some icing on the cake, I showed Specs the mock-up I drew combining all the best ideas and with only a split-second pause, she cracked up laughing. I glared at Gigi, completely confused about her sudden mood change as Specs keeled over, holding her stomach.

"That drawing is horrible!" she said pointing out the wide-eyed unicorn with big teeth and stick figure girls connected by stick figure arms. "What is that?!" she asked. I looked at it closer and pulled back, now annoyed at Specs' poking.

"It's a rainbow sitting on clouds," I explained as Specs sat down to catch her breath. I didn't see what was so funny about it; it was good for it being a quick sketch, but as I looked over the picture, I saw how bad it was, and it was *bad*. I swallowed my pride and did my best to suppress my ridicule of my drawing but succumbed to it after Gigi started laughing too. We continued our little fit until we all calmed down, finally just staring at the strange sketch in front of us.

"Fine. I'll do it," Specs said. Gigi and I high-fived and then took Specs into a bear hug.

Now the team felt complete. The meeting with Patty and Ms. Jenkins went well and despite the sketch being horrendous, I sold them on the vision. They ate it up but suggested that the best quote would be the Gem mantra and I agreed. We discussed a designated time to work on the mural and we set a deadline for the end of March. Though I had wished that we had a choice in the colors we got to use, I assured Patty that we'd make do with what we had. Luckily, she got a can of all the basic colors of the rainbow which was more than enough to work with.

"So, it's agreed. You girls will get an hour every other day between dinner and the Gems meetings to work on the mural. A CO will chaperone you and once you're done for the day, we'll cover it up with a tarp so we can have a grand reveal. It'll be great," Patty said. I loved the idea of a grand reveal, but now the pressure was officially on and there wasn't any room for mess ups.

Our first mural session was that night. During Mr. Kole's class, I reworked the sketch, so it looked like something worth putting on a wall. At lunch, I shopped the sketch around, getting the team's input and the girls seemed really impressed by it, even Specs who practically ripped it apart when she saw the first mock-up. I even had CO Rivers and CO Fillman take a look and give me their thoughts and they both agreed that it looked amazing, so I felt 100 percent confident that the night's scale drawing would be nothing but productive.

•　　　•　　　•

"Yo, are you stupid?! You must want to get your face slammed in," Tati yelled as Becky cackled. We had only been together for 10 minutes and they were already going at it. CO Bates was our first chaperone, and he stood with his arms folded, ready for something to pop off. I had designated each girl to draw out a separate part of the mural, that way no one was forced to work with anyone they didn't want to, so I couldn't understand why they were starting drama. I ignored them, hoping that the fact that they were in the Gems and couldn't afford any setbacks would sink in and they'd simmer down on their own, but when I saw Becky still poking fun at Tati, I stepped up.

"Okay, what is happening?" I asked them. Becky didn't say anything, she just laughed and pointed at the unicorn Tati was working on.

"She said my unicorn is fat and I'm about to give her a fat lip," Tati threatened. I glanced over at Bates, who was becoming annoyed at the commotion, and I tasked myself with cooling them off before he had to get involved.

"Yeah, you'd know a lot about fat lips, wouldn't you?" Becky laughed. No one else thought it was funny, in fact, all the other girls stopped what they were doing and rallied behind Tati, who was steaming. I could see her blood boiling and it was a good thing I saw it coming because Gigi and I stopped Tati from lunging towards Becky and yoking her up like she deserved.

"Becky, back off *now.*" I demanded. I glanced over at the spot where Becky was supposed to be drawing a field of flowers and saw there was nothing there.

"You have no room to talk, you haven't even started your section! Say one more stupid thing, and it's over for you. No one will hold Tati back from mopping the floor with you and I'll back her up and tell Patty all about the problems you've been causing," I barked. Everyone was taken aback, but I didn't care. The only one who needed to take in what I said was Becky.

"Oh my God, sorry," she coward. "I was just messing around."

"Well, we don't mess around like that here," I stated. "Now you can either get with the program, or get out of here," I said shooting invisible daggers out of my eyes.

"Fine, geez," Becky said, curling back to her corner with her pencil. When I saw that Becky got back in her lane, I turned back to Tati and made sure she was okay.

"Don't let her get to you. It looks fine," I lied, staring at the overweight unicorn. I stood for a second, examining the drawing. It was weird looking, but it was nothing we couldn't fix.

"It was a good first try, but let's do this..." I erased the parts that could use some adjustments, took Tati's hand, and guided her movements.

"Here, now keep your hand steady and you'll be fine," I told her. Still visibly upset, she took her time and did as I told her. I stood behind her so she wouldn't feel pressured, and when she was done fixing the sketch, it looked so much better.

"It looks perfect, Tati! All you have to do is take your time! Keep going and if you need any help, don't get upset. Just let me know and I'll help you." Tati took a step back and inspected her drawing herself, also noting that it looked better.

"Yeah, it does look good, doesn't it?" Tati chuckled. "Thanks, Eve."

When she was good on her own, I left her to it and continued working on the Gem mantra section. It would start at the top and weave its way through the scene, so I would cross over all the girls at one point to get it done, which was the perfect way to keep an eye on them and help them out when needed. CO Bates gave us our five-minute warning, letting us know it was time to clean up and get ready for the Gem meeting. We didn't get the full sketch done, but we got a good amount of it complete and even with the mishap between Tati and Becky, I felt good about it.

The rest of the girls piled out of the room, but I stayed for a little longer to make some quick adjustments to some of the other girls' stuff that they wouldn't notice.

Bates cleared his throat and said, "I have to admit, you did pretty good earlier." I knew he was talking about Tati and Becky, but what he didn't know was that I was protecting them from his wrath.

"Eh, it was nothing," I said, shrugging him off.

"No, really. You showed you have real potential to be a good leader." I cocked my head to the side and immediately questioned his angle. After months of him grumbling around the center, acting like he couldn't stand anyone or anything, he was paying *me* a compliment? *Me*. The girl who smacked him dead in his face not too long ago. I couldn't believe it and I think he saw how surprised I was.

"Well, thanks for the compliment," I remarked, to which he said, "Don't get used to it." I could sense the sarcasm in his voice, and when I looked at his face, I swear, I saw a smile crack between his thin lips. His eyes sort of crinkled, and I finally saw him; I was impressed with how nice he looked when he did something other than frown.

"You know, you should smile more," I said in a smart tone.

His smirk quickly reverted to a frown, and he said, "Get to your meeting before I take my compliment back."

"Just consider it," I said with a wink and a finger gun. I giggled and then raced to the meeting that I was a minute late to.

"Stop running!" he yelled to me.

"Sorry!" I called back to him, changing my pace to a fast walk and preparing myself to be reamed out by Patty for being late.

twenty-two.

M*arch 8th. Two Days Before Specs Left.* I looked at the covered wall we sat next to and then around the table with a smile on my face. Before a few days ago, I would have never even associated with most of the girls around me, but somehow, we were creating a bond that no one in the center could share. Gigi and Specs sat on both sides of me, Tati sat next to Specs, Trina and Joe sat curled up next to each other on the other side of the table and even Becky seemed engaged in the conversation. Though they had their little spat a couple days before, Tati and Becky squashed their beef and agreed that working together was better than creating drama.

"So, what's the color scheme we're going for?" Joe asked me. The rest of the girls looked to me as if I was supposed to have an answer.

I simply shrugged and said, "Whatever you feel looks the best. But remember, we want bright and inviting, so stay away from the black." Becky chuckled to herself. When I looked at her, I became annoyed but then played back what I said and saw how something like that could be funny to someone like her.

"You know what I mean," I cleared up. "Once we have the colors in front of us, it might be a little easier to choose. Also, don't forget, we can mix the colors too, so think about that."

We spent the rest of lunch plotting our plan of action. Since we were fairly limited on time and we were about to lose Specs in a couple days, we wanted to make sure that whatever she didn't finish, someone else could pick up without a problem. Once the bell rang, the mural team agreed to meet back in the cafeteria at our usual table for dinner to go over final ideas and then right after dinner, we'd get started.

Time went by quickly and once dinner was over, we were ready to go. This time Rivers was our chaperone, which meant we could breathe a little easier. Earlier, he told me he had a surprise for us and when he walked in with his Bluetooth speaker and his phone, I was thankful for him. None of us had heard music in a long time, and as soon as he turned on the tunes, all the girls let the music run through their bodies. He put a top 40s station on Spotify and let it play. We jammed to all types of music while we painted and even with the singing and dancing in between brush strokes, we were getting things done.

CO Bates constantly reminded us that time was ticking, but Rivers let us go with the flow, so time was less of the essence and more on our side. Though there were moments when some of us got off task, there were many moments that Patty would have been happy to see. We were so focused, and as I stood back, watching the rest of the team work hard on their sections of the mural, I couldn't help but feel so alive and in tune with myself. I loved this and I loved that Patty and Ms. Jenkins thought enough of me to let me lead the project.

I walked by each girl, assessing their work and complimenting them on what they'd done so far. It really was coming together nicely. I worked with Tati and Joe a little more closely, as they were having a little trouble keeping the paint in the lines. I looked over at Becky and she was so in her element, I didn't even want to bother her. When I glanced over at Specs, I was ecstatic that she had made so much progress, but then instantly became frantic when she stepped back to examine her work.

"Specs, watch your step!" I yelled right before she stepped right into the can of blue paint and fell flat on her butt. Everyone stopped what they were doing and gasped. We all rushed over to her to see if she was hurt and to see if we could salvage some of the paint. Just as Gigi and Trina went to help Specs up, Specs began cracking up laughing and pulled them both down with her. All three of them sat in the expanding pile of blue paint, laughing and carrying on. I, on the other hand, was mortified at the mess and at the fact that we were now officially out of blue paint. Not only were we going to have to ask for more, but we would have to explain why we needed more.

Out of nowhere, splatters of paint started flying towards the girls who weren't already covered in it and soon enough, a full-on paint fight was underway. Rivers and I tried to get the girls under control and when I saw that they had splattered blue paint all over where the green grass was supposed to go, I got angry.

I yelled, "Stop!" and surprisingly, they did. They looked at each other, all covered in various colors of the rainbow, and looked at me and Rivers, who had not a drop of paint on us. I saw each of their eyes change and then suddenly, devious smiles crept across their faces and I knew that I was no match for them. I didn't fight it. I stood and took the thrashes of paint they threw my way and just let it happen, but Rivers was still doing his best to stop the madness.

It had gotten out of hand, but every girl was happy, having fun, and honestly, I wanted in on some of the action too. I grabbed a couple paintbrushes, scooped up some paint and started tossing it in Rivers direction, now making it seven against one. It was unfair, but it was a good time. In the midst of the fun we were having, we failed to look at the time or if anyone else was around. We were a couple minutes late for our Gems meeting and since Patty and Ms. Jenkins knew where to find us, they came looking, only I highly doubt they expected to see what they saw. No one knew how long they had been watching us terrorize Rivers, but they stopped us just as we were all about to get him with the kill shot–a dozen brushes were aimed right at him, ready to fire when Patty turned off the music and yelled, "Girls!"

We all stood wide-eyed and red, blue, and yellow-handed. We looked at each other horrified, but Patty's anger and Ms. Jenkins' shock trumped all our expressions. Patty was fuming and Ms. Jenkins could feel it, so she let Patty handle us. Patty glared at the mural, the floor, and then us, but then she zeroed in on Rivers.

"I thought you said you could handle it?" Patty barked at him. Rivers looked at us and then stuttered, trying to find the right words to get him out of trouble, but there was no digging his way out of this hole.

"I don't want to hear it!" Patty snapped. "My office, *now*." Rivers looked at us once more, bowed his head, and then sauntered out of the cafeteria. We all watched him do a walk of shame until he was out of sight, to which then Patty and Ms. Jenkins returned their laser beams back to us.

"I can't begin to explain how disappointed I am in all of you. You're Gems! You're supposed to be responsible. How could you let this happen?" We all looked at one another and silently promised not to tell on each other. Though it wasn't really anyone's fault–it just sort of happened, we should have exercised better judgment. I felt horrible that I didn't do better as the leader of the project and the group. Just as I fixed my mouth to speak, Specs glanced at me and then stepped forward.

"It's all my fault," she said with a soft voice. "I accidently fell in the paint and when a couple of the girls tried to help me up, I pulled them down. This wouldn't have happened if I was more careful." Ms. Jenkins and Patty both narrowed their eyes on Specs, who was covered in paint. Patty then looked at the paint spot on the floor and saw that the story checked out, but she was still angry. I couldn't let Specs take all the blame, though. She was leaving in a couple days and although she had already been officially granted release, I didn't want this to set her back.

"No, it wasn't Specs' fault. It was an accident, and we all got carried away. I'll take full responsibility, because as the leader of the group, I should have stopped it before it got this far," I told Patty, standing next to Specs.

Then Tatiana stepped up on the other side of Specs and said, "We are *all* to blame. We just had a moment of fun and we're sorry about the mess." The rest of the girls nodded their heads in agreement and at that moment, I could see Patty's eyes soften. She looked at Ms. Jenkins and then at the mess again.

"No one is in trouble. I appreciate you all stepping up and owning your part in this, but you will have to clean all of this up *and* make up your Gem session tomorrow," she stated. Us girls looked at each other and sighed with relief.

"But no more funny business. If something like this happens again, I will shut this project down." Patty made her point crystal clear, and we all agreed not to mess up again. Patty told us where we could find the cleaning supplies, so a few of the girls rushed to the supply closet just down the hall while the rest of us stayed behind to gather the paintbrushes and sponges, put the lids back on the remaining cans of paint, and prepare the floor to be cleaned. I walked over to Patty just as she was about to leave.

"I'm sorry about this," I said to her. "It won't happen again, I promise."

They both understood and turned to walk out when I blurted out, "CO Rivers isn't in trouble, is he? It really wasn't his fault. There was no way he could go up against seven girls with paint," I noted. Patty's face turned a little sour.

"I wouldn't worry about CO Rivers. You need to focus on getting that paint up before it dries." Just then, the other girls came back with the custodial cart, and just as I turned to help everyone clean up, Patty said to Ms. Jenkins, "I guess we'll have to keep a closer eye on these girls... and order more supplies."

twenty-
three.

arch 13th. Three Days After Specs Left. If I thought
things were different when Brit left, things became very
different when Specs left. Once she was gone, it seemed
like all the sunshine she brought to the center left with her. Everyone
missed her so much, but Specs was ecstatic to go home with her
grandma, brother, and sister. It was a gorgeous spring-like day when
she said her final goodbyes, which was fitting because she was just as
bright and warm as that day.

I sat with the rest of the mural group outside in the courtyard
during our free time. The weather was warming up for us, so we were
spending our free times outside instead of the rec room. The rest of
the girls sat, talking about random things, while Gigi and I had our
own private conversation in our own little world.

"You know, I was 100 percent sure I wasn't going to like you when
I first met you," Gigi remarked with a laugh. "You came off real boujie
and entitled." She was telling me something I already knew, but it
was still funny because we had come so far together since the
beginning.

"Yeah, I knew it was going to be a struggle, but you didn't exactly
make it easy to get to know you either, ya' know," I said nudging her.
Gigi laughed again and recounted a time, not too long after first
meeting, when both Specs and Brit told her to "go easy" on me.

"They both said you were afraid of me," Gigi said, staring at me
with a raised eyebrow and a smirk. I looked back at her trying to look
unbothered. I couldn't see how they came to that conclusion
because I didn't remember ever telling them that. Then again, I
probably didn't have to; I hadn't mastered the art of putting on my
emotional mask around the girls because everything was so new to
me.

"They said you were good people, so I figured I'd give you a chance," she elaborated. I looked at her and smiled.

"Well, I'm glad they did because you were scary." We both shared a laugh and looked out into the courtyard, watching the rest of the girls play games of basketball or four square and run around the courtyard letting the breeze flow through their hair.

"I miss them so much," Gigi finally said, cutting a knife through the quiet between us. "I hope they're okay."

"Me too," I stated. Then a recent memory of Specs popped in my head, causing me to laugh to myself.

"What?" Gigi asked.

"I was just thinking about when you smashed Specs' farewell cake in her face." I could see Gigi go back to that moment and a smile spread across her face until she was giggling with me.

"She was a good sport about it too. Oh, and what about when everyone started taking the icing off her face?" she added. I didn't think about how unsanitary that actually was at the time, but it just felt right. We laughed once more and began our journey down memory lane. We shared so many moments together that it just didn't seem right that we all couldn't be together to reminisce about them. All the talk about the girl gang made me remember that it wouldn't be long before Gigi would be gone too. And then me. Yeah, we promised that we'd stay in touch, but life has a funny way of becoming busy. I reminded Gigi that she was next in line to go and she nodded, forcing herself not to smile.

"Have you started your transition process yet?" I asked her. She nodded and let her smile show itself.

"I was going to tell you later, but my aunt is bringing my brother and sisters to see me soon," she announced, her face lighting up.

"Whoa, that's great!" I patted her on the back.

"I just know I'm going to cry or something sappy like that."

I shook my head and let her know it was okay to cry. She agreed but maintained that she had a reputation to uphold. After breaking down to us about what happened to her sister, she claimed she "used up her cry credits" and couldn't cry anymore. I laughed at the sentiment but reminded her that she could never run out of "cry credits." She quickly changed the subject, completely avoiding talk about emotions and set it back on her transition, which would include her having to report to her caseworker on a weekly basis for check-ins.

"I can handle it, no problem, but one wrong move and I could end up in jail for real," she explained. The fact was that Gigi was extremely lucky she had the judge she did. He was sympathetic to Gigi's story and I think her not having a prior record mixed with the fact that she offed a drug-dealing child rapist helped her case. Had she had someone like my judge, Judge Basin, she would have gotten death by lethal injection or something. I reminded her that she'd do the right thing and that she shouldn't add so much pressure on herself.

"You're the most level-headed person I know," I told her.

"Wow, gee, thanks," Gigi said sarcastically as she nudged me. "You know, you're all right, princess."

I looked at her and smiled. "You too."

A week later, we were back at the mural, and this time we didn't have the time or the supplies to waste. We had two weeks until the mural reveal date, but really only about 6 days to complete it because we could only meet between dinner and Gem meetings every other day.

Patty pulled out all the stops; not only was there no music allowed, but she had two COs looking after us now, and Rivers was nowhere in sight. In fact, I hadn't seen him since he was covered in paint. We were beginning to suspect that he might had gotten fired over it but didn't think it was a good idea to ask around. Since CO Bates and CO Tankard were our chaperones, we made extra sure to stay on task and get as much done as we could.

The dead silence quickly turned into a great debate about who would have the best homecoming. Gigi bragged that her aunt got the family tickets to Hershey Park and couldn't wait to get on the roller coasters and eat tons of chocolate. Becky then boasted about the huge plot of land her family owned behind her house and how she had a legit dirt bike course. The other girls threw in other, tamer plans like going swimming or even looking at colleges. I kept quiet and focused on making sure each letter of the Gems mantra was clear and legible.

There was a little more chatter amongst all the other girls, but then Tatiana asked me what I had planned, and the group got quiet. I sort of shrugged off the question and kept working, pretending like I hadn't given it much thought, but the truth was, I thought about it every night. I had over a month left, but time was going by quickly and I couldn't even say for sure if I was going to have a place to stay, which meant that I potentially wouldn't get out on time. I hadn't been told that my release date could be put on hold, so as far as I knew, I was scheduled to go back to my parents. The problem was, I *refused* to do that. I still got no call or visit from any of my family, so at that point, they were dead to me just as I was probably dead to them.

"Eve... what are your plans?" Gigi repeated. I glared down at her and she cowered, but just a little. She read my eyes and then pretended to zip her lips, realizing that this was something I didn't want to talk about.

To get the rest of the girls off my back, I simply said, "Eh, I'll probably go to the movies and catch up with my friends or something."

At the next Gem meeting, sure enough, the topic was the transition process. Gigi and two other girls already had plans lined up, but a few of us were still too far out to develop a plan yet.

"Today won't just be about the transition process as it pertains to your next move out of here," Patty began. "We will discuss how you plan to stay out of here and make major changes in your life." She rattled off various tricks we could use to keep ourselves on track and focused like taking up a solid hobby, keeping a planner, getting rid of bad influences, and sticking to a curfew.

"Not everything will work for you, so it's up to you to figure out what you can stick with. I would suggest starting out by challenging yourself with developing habits opposite of those that got you here."

Ms. Jenkins handed out a piece of paper with some common scenarios and tips on dealing with our issues. We had to study it and condition ourselves to look for ways out of triggering situations. As we looked over the guide, Patty introduced something called a "reward system."

"A reward system is an agreement with yourself. When you achieve a goal, you reward yourself with something you desire. Now, that something can't be a vice-it has to be something that will add value to your life," she explained.

"Let me give you an example. I treat myself by buying something nice whenever I accomplish a set goal within a set time." She dangled her Pandora bracelet in front of us, showing off its many charms. "I love collecting charms for my bracelets. They genuinely make me happy and they give me something to look forward to as I work hard."

"Why don't you just buy it when you feel like it?" Becky asked.

"That's a good question. I conditioned my mind to see the charm as a prize to be earned. Having a disciplined mindset is the only way a reward system can work," she explained.

"Let's look at it from some of your perspectives. We'll use Gigi as an example for a second, since she's leaving soon. Let's say Gigi sets a goal to secure an above minimum wage job once she gets out. She decides that she wants to treat her and her family to a nice meal at a nice restaurant once she gets her first paycheck to celebrate her achievement. The dinner is the reward. Then let's say she wants to get a promotion in two years, and she gets promoted in one. She may decide to treat herself to another dinner or she may even decide to change it up and reserve a spa day for herself. Those are the sort of things you can consider when mapping out your reward system. Now, though most of your rewards will require money, I also want to mention that the rewards you choose don't have to be things you buy. Your reward can be a mental health day, where you take off from work or school and just relax. Maybe your reward can be a movie night in. It can be very simple." As Patty coached us, all our wheels were turning. I could name a dozen things I could reward myself with when I accomplished a goal, and by the looks on the other girls' faces, they also had some fun ideas in mind too.

"When you find yourself craving or going back to bad habits like drinking, smoking, or partying way too hard, figure out an alternative. Those things are not rewards for your good deeds and believe it or not, you *can* have fun without being under the influence of any substances." Patty looked around the room, trying to zero in on who to call out first.

"Becky, what brings you joy? What can you do besides turn to drugs?" Becky thought long and hard about her answer, so much that I could see a vein in the side of her head bulging. She never *really* did much besides that and though her physical appearance said it all, it was sort of sad that she couldn't readily think of anything else she could do with her time. Although she was a complete racist and had a nasty attitude, she had a lot to offer.

"I think I'll treat myself to a fishin' trip. I'll go out to my favorite spot and spend the day out there. I feel good when I'm on the water," Becky said. Both Patty and Ms. Jenkins were astonished. I'm pretty sure they weren't expecting her to go that far left field. I don't think anyone, except maybe her little crew, even knew she was into fishing like that, so we all were a little shocked.

"That's a fantastic alternative, Becky!" Ms. Jenkins admitted. "That sounds like a good plan." Becky's answer sparked Patty to ask the entire group what we were considering, so we all went around the circle sharing our ideas. I said I'd take a weekend trip to New York City. Gigi said she'd bake something nice because she loves to cook. Other girls said they'd buy themselves new clothes or a new item for their collections. We only scratched the surface, but Patty and Ms. Jenkins were thoroughly impressed with our answers and we were proud of ourselves for seeing that we could do so much more than we had been doing.

As the days came and went, I became more and more excited, not just for the completion of the mural project, but for our Gems meetings. I was doing more than turning over a new leaf; I was becoming a whole flower and so were the other girls. Because we were hard on time, the mural team stayed focused on getting the project done and that we did. We completed the mural by the deadline and Patty planned an entire reveal to the rest of the center, staff, and even a couple outsiders for that following Saturday.

I looked down the line at the mural team as Patty introduced the project to the attendees of the event and couldn't help but smile. This was *my* team, and I was so proud of them.

"I want to give a special introduction to the leader of the project, Eve Johnson," Patty projected to the crowd. The cramped cafeteria that barely held about 50 of us comfortably was filled with upward of 70 people and it was practically standing room only. All eyes were on me as the crowd clapped and cheered.

"Eve happily took on this project, hand-picked her team, remarkably led the group, and now we're here. This mural is a visual story of companionship, hard work, and the joys of life."

When the crowd simmered down, she looked to me and the rest of the group and asked, "Will you girls do the honors?" We all nodded, and each grabbed a hold of the tarp shielding the mural from the rest of the world.

We counted together, "One... two... three!" and ripped it away from the wall, exposing our masterpiece. Mouths dropped open and even we were astonished at how good it looked, even though we saw it before everyone else.

It all became real. Applause and more cheers echoed throughout the entire cafeteria and soon enough, we were asked to take a couple pictures, shake hands with random strangers, and fraternize with everyone. All the girls from the center bombarded us with compliments and questions about how we got it done and how we got it to look so good.

"Congratulations, Eve," a soft-spoken voice said behind me. When I turned around, I was a little shocked at how high she towered over me and then I looked at her face; it was sweet, and she gave me serious "aunty who doesn't have kids, so she spoils her nieces and nephews" vibes. She extended her hand out to shake mine and usually I would have just stared at it and backed away slowly, but her smile was so inviting, I felt like she meant no harm. Our hands met and we shook as her dark brown eyes stared into mine.

"Thank you so much!" I said. She smiled again and then glanced at the mural, nodding her head. Right next to her was a shorter, pale white girl with darker hair. The woman whispered something to her and while they chatted amongst themselves, I slipped away. I searched the crowd to see if I could find CO Rivers. I still hadn't seen him since the painting incident, and I was worried that he really was gone for good. I at least wanted to know if he was okay, but I didn't see him. I scanned the crowd one more time for good measure, but Patty quickly got my attention.

"Eve, once everyone leaves, can you come to my office?" I nodded and floated around the room for the rest of the time the crowd was gathered. Once the last girl left, I said I'd catch up with the rest of the team later and headed to Patty's office. She sat plunking away at her computer like always and was very focused. I sat right down and waited for her to finish doing whatever she was doing.

"You have a little more than a month left, so now's the time to talk about your transition plan. Do you know what you want to do once you leave here?" she asked. I stared at my fidgeting hands. I had a few things in mind, but nothing set in stone. I would be getting out before the rest of my classmates graduated, which was a good thing because it meant I wasn't behind, but since I'd be getting out in May, I would have missed many deadlines for college application submissions. I thought about getting a job too, but I was afraid that my record would keep me from getting anything good. Eventually, I shook my head no. I glanced up at Patty who had a somewhat disappointed but understanding look on her face.

"Don't worry, I will help you figure it out. In the meantime, we need to discuss your living arrangements." I rolled my eyes hard so she could see that I was not interested in talking about that.

"I've been in contact with your parents for the last couple months. They're thrilled about your progress and are more than happy to welcome you home." I stared at Patty and as the last word left her mouth, I scoffed at the idea.

"Not a chance," I told her.

"You don't have much of a choice, Eve. Although you will be 18 when you leave, you have to be turned over to a trusted adult in your life. That's just how these things go," she explained. I threw my head back and let out a groan as I pondered how I could get out of this. My so-called parents *still* hadn't visited me and never even left a message for me. Now Patty was telling me that they had a change of heart and wanted to welcome me with open arms? Yeah, okay.

"My friends will be 18 and I trust them. Boom, I'm good to go," I proposed. Patty shook her head.

"No can do. You have to have a place to go and I'm pretty sure your friends don't have their own place."

"I can find a place to go, that won't be a problem," I maintained, but Patty continued to push the issue.

"Your parents seem sorry."

I just stared at her. It was like everything I had ever said about how my parents operated just went in one ear and out the other. They didn't really care about me and I didn't know how else to say that.

"Just because they *seem* doesn't mean they *are*," I said scooting right out of my chair and out of the room. I was startled and happy all at the same time when I saw none other than Rivers standing right outside the door and he appeared to be just hanging out. Without thinking, I pulled him close to me in a tight hold which caused him to have to gasp for air.

"Nice to see you too," he said. I looked up at him, searching for the words to express how happy I was to see him without seeming too eager.

"I thought you got fired!" I told him. He shrugged it off and began walking in the direction towards the red room.

"Yeah, I definitely didn't get fired, but I was put on max hall duty for a couple weeks and then I had to run the main gate after that. I'm just now getting back in the building."

That explained why he was MIA. I felt so much relief rush throughout my body because on top of hating the idea that my irresponsibility would have caused someone to get fired, I couldn't stand the idea of Rivers no longer being there to help me make sense of my drama and give me clarity when I needed to hear the truth. He was a part of the foundation I needed here, so losing him could have sent me backwards in my progress.

"I'm *so* sorry about the paint thing. We all felt bad that you got in trouble," I told him.

"Don't worry about it, it's okay." It really wasn't okay, but that was just like Rivers to not dwell on the past.

"Do you have time to talk right now?" I asked him. He nodded his head, and we sat at our usual table in the rec room. I told him about me having to go back home to my parents in order to get out on time and of course, in his typical "devil's advocate" fashion, he asked me why it was such a bad thing.

"Because, as I've told you and everyone else around here, they don't want me. This has got to be a stunt to help them save face. What will they look like taking back their screw-up of a daughter after she spent her entire Senior year in juvie? Like a pair of forgiving, good parents–that's what, but that's not the truth."

"How do you know that? I mean, how do you *really* know that they haven't changed? You haven't even been around them." I clapped my hands together and threw my hands in the air dramatically.

"That's *exactly* why! They haven't even seen me since I've been here. My friends from school even came to visit for a while, but have my own parents come and visit? No. They haven't. They made it clear that they weren't interested in that and they've kept their promise."

I folded my arms on the table and nestled my head into the space between them. The more I thought about this transition and my parents, the more frustrated I got and the more I wanted to explode. The only one I could give a pass to was my sister because she was in school out of state. I didn't expect her to make a genuine effort or even my brother, who stayed swamped in cases, but I would never forgive my no-backbone having mom and vindictive dad for what they did to me.

"This sucks," I mumbled.

"Need I remind you that you are here because of you and you alone?" Rivers dryly commented. I pulled my head up to make direct eye contact with him to see if he really was being serious, and he was. He raised an eyebrow and waited for me to respond, and though I knew I was there because of my actions, I wasn't going to admit that without the other players in this game taking some blame too.

"Whose side are you on, Rivers?" I asked him, matching his energy.

"I'm on yours believe it or not, but sometimes that means calling you out when you're wrong. It's sort of my job," He said, pointing to his patch that read "Corrections Officer." I sneered at him and remained quiet because I knew he was gearing up to lecture me.

"You still seem to think you're in here because your parents didn't give you any mercy, but a judge made this decision based on *your* file, not your parents, and you're going to have to accept that."

"Yeah, but if they would have gotten me out like they usually did, I would have changed. I wasn't even a part of that stupid robbery, I really wasn't! I'm in here on a fluke."

"No, you're in here because you needed to be." I stared at him, completely blindsided by his candidness. His voice was harsh and demanded that I hear him out, but his eyes were so soft and caring and though I hated to admit it, I knew that he was speaking from a clear place.

"Look, I understand what I did, but had certain things been done–had my parents proved they cared about me, I wouldn't have ended up this way," I maintained. I was proud of all the work I had done on myself up until that point, but there was no way I was wavering on that fact. My parents weren't supportive, so I looked for it in places I shouldn't have had to. End of discussion.

"So, a roof over your head, good schools, great food on your table, getting whatever you want and–oh, and let's not forget to mention bailing you out of trouble when you *were* guilty isn't caring?" I shot him a disgusted look as if he should have known better than to come at me like that. He knew what he was doing, and I was insulted that he responded that way.

"You *clearly* haven't been listening to me. None of that shit matters, Rivers. We could have been poor, without all that you mentioned, and if they would have treated me like that, I *still* would have ended up here. Us having money has nothing to do with what I'm talking about."

"Then be clear about what you mean," he told me.

"None of that stuff matters if you treat your kid like what they want and who they want to be doesn't matter. They made me feel like what I wanted wasn't good enough for them, like I wasn't on their level, and it didn't help that they were able to trick my brother and sister into believing that they really wanted to be a lawyer and an engineer. They just couldn't fool me into playing some part and *that*'s why they treated me like this. That's why they hate me," I said all in one breath. I felt a rise building up in me, so I buried my head into my arms once more to diffuse the bomb that was ticking away in my stomach.

"I can assure you, your parents don't hate you. You know something that I learned? Sometimes, parents don't know how to love a kid the way they *need* to be loved. Every single parent thinks giving their child a better life than they had is the ultimate sign of love, while the child just wants quality time, to be hugged, or even just to be told they did a good job."

"Yeah, that sounds familiar," I murmured.

"It's familiar to a lot of kids," he stated. "Don't hate your parents. Forgive them for not loving you the way you needed to be loved and appreciate them for what they *have* done for you, because from where I'm standing, they've done a lot, even if it's not all what you've wanted."

As much as I liked talking to Rivers, I hated this moment because, once again, he was right. My parents were a sore subject for me and I sort of hardened my heart to hearing out any reasoning behind how they did things, but it did dawn on me that them going about life the way they had was also them going along to get along. It was possible that they were constantly wearing masks that hid their desperation for a fruitful life and the exhaustion that came with attaining that.

"Okay," I said. "I'll do better."

"That's all you can do," he said, rising from the table.

"How did you get to be so wise about this?" I sarcastically remarked.

"I know a thing or two about the topic," Rivers said with his eyes shifting down to the ground. As I stared at him, all the pieces of the puzzle clicked together at the same time.

"I'll be right back," I told him as I shuffled back to Patty's office. She was surprised to see me, but she welcomed me back in.

"Okay, I'll go back with my parents," I told her.

Patty nodded and said, "Good. I'll let you know when everything is settled."

"Cool," I said before walking right back out, wondering if I had just made the right decision.

twenty-four.

pril 4th. The Day Gigi Left. I sat on the edge of my bed brushing through Gigi's thick, wavy brown hair for the last time. I wanted it to look perfect for her first day free after over a year of battling her case.

"Eve, you should have seen them. They're so big. I hardly recognized Cara and Ronnie, but you know what was crazy? Vera looked exactly the same. It was like she was frozen in time or something." I stopped brushing her hair as I thought about the story Gigi told her first Gem session and it sent shivers down my spine.

"I flashed back to the day everything happened and all I could do was hug her and cry," Gigi said. "She even apologized to me... can you believe that? She said had it not been for her, I wouldn't have had to do what I did, and I wouldn't be in here."

"Oh my God," I said, horrified. The poor girl. She blamed herself.

"Yeah," Gigi scoffed. "I let her know it wasn't her fault at all. If mom wouldn't have let that sicko freak into our lives, none of it would have happened." We sat in silence for a little while, both Gigi and I wondering how to follow up the conversation after discussing something so dark. Luckily, Gigi had a lot of good to look forward to, so she quickly rerouted the conversation towards the future.

"But girl, there's so much out there for me, I can hardly wait to get into it," she spoke.

"I'm so proud of you, Gigi," I said with a smile creeping across my face. She looked up at me and then rolled her eyes.

"Oh, stop being such a sap," she laughed, nudging me in the leg. "But I'm proud of you too."

I finished up her ballerina bun quickly because I was on the verge of being late for class. It sucked that she was leaving so early and that I wasn't going to be able to hang out a little more, but that's how these things went. She examined her bun in the mirror, gave her stamp of approval, and then offered to walk me to class. I looked back one last time at her packed-up bunk and my heart sank. I was genuinely happy for Gigi, but I wished that I was following her out. I still had a month and a few days left and I wasn't sure how I was going to make it without my last real friend at the center with me.

Soon enough, we were in front of Mr. Kole's class, but Ms. Jenkins was sitting at Mr. Kole's desk. I peeked up at the clock in the hallway and noted that I still had another minute before I had to be in class, so I savored every second I had with Gigi. She pulled me into a hug, and we rocked back and forth, absorbing each other's energies.

"Stay cool, kid," Gigi told me.

"You too... kid," I said.

"I really hope that we can see each other again," Gigi said.

I nodded and replied, "I think we can make it happen."

"Eve!" Ms. Jenkins called from inside the classroom. She then waved her hand for me to come in and I nodded, letting her know I was on my way.

"Be good!" I called to Gigi as she strutted down the hallway back to the red room.

She laughed and looked back at me saying, "Oh, I will!" and then she disappeared around the corner.

I walked into class and went to take my usual seat in the back next to the bookshelf. The seat next to mine, the seat that Specs' sat at, had a new girl in it. I glared at her for a moment, but then remembered how good Specs was to me when I was new. I changed my glare to a smile and even threw in a wave as I made my way back towards her. She looked astonished that I even acknowledged her, but she soon smiled and crazily enough, she reminded me of Specs, except white and platinum blonde. She was short and skinny just like Specs and even had glasses like her too. Once I sat down, I introduced myself and so did she.

Katie was her name. I let her know that if she needed any help with the classwork, she could ask me, and even though I didn't have too much longer left, I made it my mission to ensure that Katie had a comfortable transition at the center, and more importantly, a friend.

I watched the clock closely in each class and once it hit 11:30, I was the first one to jump up and head to the cafeteria. I wanted to eat my food quickly so I could catch Gigi leaving. She said she was leaving around 12 since her aunt, who lived in Pittsburgh, wanted to get some work done before taking the rest of the day off to pick Gigi up. I timed it just right–if I finished eating by 11:55, I could see her once she changed, and I could say one more goodbye. I scarfed down my food, and with Rivers' approval, I ran to the meeting room to see if I could see a car in a visitor's spot. As I caught my breath, I looked closer and saw that there weren't any cars in the visitor spots, so I rushed right to the red room to see if Gigi might have still been waiting. I got there and Gigi's bed was completely bare and so was her nightstand.

"Oh, no..." I said, now rushing towards Patty's office to see if maybe she was in there getting her official clearance or something. As usual, Patty was immersed in her work and I might've even startled her because she was so engaged.

"Where's Gigi?" I asked, propping myself up on the doorpost. She looked at me with a confused look.

"Gigi left about an hour and a half ago. Her aunt came straight here, so we processed her out early."

"Oh," I said, slowly backing away.

"Are you okay? Do you need to talk?" Patty asked. I quickly shook my head and brushed her off.

"No, not at all. I just wanted to give her one more hug, that's all." I smiled at her, hoping she wouldn't sense the disappointment I felt in not catching Gigi sooner. I sauntered to my next class and kept my head down, mentally preparing myself to spend the rest of the day alone.

twenty-
five.

April 25th. Two Weeks Before My Scheduled Release. I quickly got used to being a lone wolf around the center, but I did my best to remain present and continue to make progress. I thought a lot about what I wanted to do after getting out and decided that I would pursue art. It was the only thing I could see keeping me together and I didn't care what my parents thought. Every time I passed the mural we did, I got visions of future work and started jotting down my ideas and even drawing out some plans. My journal turned into a sketchbook and though Patty and Ms. Jenkins weren't happy that I wasn't using it for what it was for, they appreciated that I kept that spark alive and that I made up for it by participating and helping around the center.

I sat up in my bed flipping through my almost filled notebook and couldn't help but smile. Instant snapshots of my best moments flashed through my mind. I had two weeks left until my release, and though I didn't like the circumstances I was being forced back into, I was proud that I made it through, even despite the fights, the tantrums, and the hard days.

When free time came around, I stayed behind to admire the mural I created. I ran my hand along the Gems' mantra that weaved its way through the scene and recited each word as my fingers grazed over them. I stood back, admiring the composition and remembering the teamwork that allowed this project to go off without a hitch.

Yeah, this is it, I thought to myself. *This is what I want to do.*

I thought back to the joy I felt from the moment I was told I'd lead the project all the way to how I felt at the unveiling. I got great satisfaction from seeing something that I envisioned up on a wall to inspire all the girls that came through Bennings. It felt more than good knowing that a piece of me and everyone who worked on it would be there forever.

In a weird way, I felt grateful that I came to Bennings. If I hadn't, I wouldn't have rediscovered my love for art. I would have been out with another Johnny-type guy, getting into more trouble and pressing my luck until I ended up here, in an adult prison, or worse. I wasn't religious, but I believe I had divine intervention to thank for this turn in my life.

"Hey, are you okay?" Rivers inquired. I turned around to see his concerned face, and I smiled at him to let him know I was just fine.

"Yeah, I'm cool. I was just doing a lot of thinking."

"About going home?" he asked. I nodded.

"How often do you see girls come back after getting out?" I turned to him. He cocked his head to the side, confused as to why I'd be asking the question. I calmed his nerves by putting my hands up and saying, "Just curious."

He took a second but then shook his head. "More than I'd like to admit. It's hard getting back out there, and most girls are going right back into the environments that got them in trouble. It seems almost impossible to have success stories in those cases, but the strongest do survive." He stepped closer and stared me right in the eyes. "And you're going to be fine."

Rivers really had seen a lot, not just at Bennings, but in his own life and everything he said was with total conviction. His faith in me was like lightening; it gave me the shock I needed to wake up and see that I didn't have as much to worry about as I thought. I was strong-willed enough and the idiots I associated myself with were all in prison, so I had no choice but to go back home and start fresh.

"I think I will too," I told him. "I just don't know how far I'll get."

"I wouldn't worry about looking too far down the line just yet," he said. "Take it day by day and once you get your groove back, everything will come." I soaked up his words like a sponge and let them marinate. I headed to the rec room to enjoy the rest of my free time when Rivers stopped me.

"Oh um, I actually came to tell you that Patty wants to talk to you." I followed him to Patty's office where she stood waiting with a smile. I could sense the fakeness a mile away. She had something up her sleeve and she was going to make me be a part of it.

"What's up?" I asked her.

"You have some visitors," she told me before walking out of her room and then gesturing me to lead the way. My eyes widened, and a smile flashed across my face.

"Ugh! Finally!" I jumped up and down, and rushed towards the meeting room. I hadn't seen Rachel and Mackie since the beginning of the year when they told me they wouldn't be able to visit again until the spring and I missed seeing their faces. The weather was so much better, and the semester was coming to a close in another month or so, so I guess they figured now was a good time to visit.

With every corner I turned, I added more pep in my step until I was about to explode with excitement. I burst through the double doors to the meeting room and shock and horror ran through my body. I turned around and tried to make a run back through the doors, but Rivers stopped me and whispered, "Go talk to them." Patty didn't say a word, but her face expressed the same sentiment, except her expression was screaming, "You better get over there."

I inched towards the table my parents sat at, acting as if one wrong move would trigger an alarm. We each played tag with our gazes, both looking at me and then one looking at the other while I shifted my eyes between the two. I didn't know what any of us expected this moment to be like, but I was shocked it was happening at all.

"Hi Eve," my mom said. Her voice was so soft and almost fragile, like if she spoke any louder, her vocal cords would get shot. She was always like that. She didn't raise her voice much, but she could be harsh with her words and very dismissive. Her demeanor towards me kept the rut between us, but dad had no problem adding boisterousness into the mix. He naturally had a strong, powerful voice, so anything he said demanded attention of others. That was the only tool he had to use to get me to cower like a puppy that just pissed on the carpet, but I learned to tune him out.

"Hi, Mom," I replied. I looked right to Dad to see what he had to say and not a word left his mouth. He remained tight lipped with a steady gaze on me.

Let's have some fun with this, the old, buried inner me said. I half smirked and shook my head, trying to shake the thought of reverting to an old version of myself for a second, but I figured there wasn't anything wrong with bringing a slightly tamer version of that girl out to play for a bit. After all, I had a right to be angry and dismissive towards them too.

"Oh, happy day, my parents came to see me!" I sarcastically jubilated. "Finally!" The faux smile that was on my face quickly shifted to a frown and I narrowed my eyes at the both of them.

"Why now though?" My mom looked to my dad to speak, but he was so busy trying to read me that, for the first time, she spoke up first.

"We wanted to see how you were doing," she said. "To see if you were in a better place." I scoffed at the thought of them *actually* caring just two weeks before I had to leave with them.

"Oh, really now? That's cute, but I needed you to check on me when I first got here. I had to fight a girl my first night and then had to sleep in a bed stained with piss and throw up for a month. I needed you to check on me when I was having full-blown breakdowns. I needed to see you on Thanksgiving and Christmas, not get some bogus card you sent to rile me up, which, by the way made me so mad that I fought a CO, one of my best friends, and ended up in max hall for a few days. But sure, come see me a couple weeks before I'm scheduled to leave, after I've already gone through hell and back. Yeah, I'm doing *great* now." I said slamming my fists on the table and then swiftly getting up to leave them. As soon as I turned around, Patty motioned for me to sit down and Rivers stood next to her with his arms crossed and an eyebrow raised.

I clenched my fists and jaw and when I released, I took a deep breath and sat back down, making direct eye contact with my parents so they could see me. I kept my head down, fighting myself to keep it together. I had worked day in and day out to keep my emotions in check and I couldn't lose it at the first sign of a major trigger. I had to show them I *was* better, and I had to prove it to myself too.

I closed my eyes and counted backwards, just like Patty told us, and I released myself to another world. The countdown rang loud in my head, but as I sat on the imaginary beach and let the breeze comb through my hair, I felt myself calming down. *Five... four... three...* I counted and suddenly stopped when I felt something. I was still in my place on the beach, but when I looked behind me, my mom stood with her hand on my shoulder. I slowly opened my eyes and stared at my mom's hand that was on my arm for a few moments. I glanced up to see if her eyes were as honest as her gesture and they seemed to be, which was surprising.

"We kept your room exactly how you left it," my dad finally muttered. My eyes shifted to his and again shock washed across my face. The first thing he said to me after cussing me out and calling me a whore was that he kept my room the same. I had to appreciate the crappy effort, but I couldn't help but poke fun a little more.

"You could have at least cleaned it up because it was a hot mess when I left," I chuckled.

"We did clean it up. I just wanted you to know that nothing changed," he coldly responded. I could see he wasn't picking up on my lighthearted sarcasm, so I toned down a little and just said, "Thank you."

I still didn't get it though. Why now? After all of that back and forth and the words exchanged, why did they even want me home? I could only imagine that they were just as annoyed with the fact that they had to take me back in as much as I was irritated I had to go back with them. There had to be something else going on.

"Is there an event coming up or something?" I stared at them, just waiting for them to wiggle their way out of admitting this was a stunt. Instead, they both shook their heads.

"No, not at the moment," Dad said.

"Shocker," I remarked. I lowered my eyes but just as I did, I saw my dad shake his head in my peripheral.

You're not being fair, one part of me said. *No, they deserve the digs,* the other part argued. Once again, I found myself in my place, but this time I wasn't counting. I was contemplating the right words to say.

You got this, Eve. Be the bigger girl.

"I'm sorry I put you both through a lot. Obviously, I was only thinking of myself. I've changed for the better, and I was hoping to show you that while I was here, but since you guys didn't come to see me, I wasn't able to. It may not seem like it today, but I really am better thanks to this place." We all stared at each other once more, each of us waiting for someone else to follow up. My mom broke the ice and with a smile, accepted my apology and even mentioned she was happy to have me home. I waited for my dad to second what my mom said, but he merely nodded and forced a smile. Since I knew that was the best I would get from him, I accepted it.

"I'll see you in two weeks," I said getting back up and proceeding to walk out of the room. I wasn't ready for hugs and kisses from them yet, but when I looked at Rivers, who seemed pleased at how I handled myself, I turned back around to say one more thing.

"And I forgive you for not loving me the way I needed to be loved." I didn't wait for a response from them; I turned on my heels and walked right out of the meeting room and back to my bunk to cry.

twenty-six.

*M**ay 2nd. A Week Before My Release.** I sat in front of the Release Board feeling confident, but humble. Patty had coached me, as she did with all the girls getting ready for release, on proper decorum and the types of questions to prepare to answer. Sitting at a table in front of me was Patty, Ms. Jenkins, a random Black woman who looked vaguely familiar, and a hearing officer from the state's Release Authority office who would grant me release. I didn't have much to worry about; aside from a few hiccups, my record looked pretty good, but this was my first time doing something like this, so I couldn't be too sure it would go in my favor.

Right at 10 a.m., the board began the proceedings. They started off with introductions and right off, the woman I thought I'd seen before, began with a sweet smile.

"Hi, Eve. My name is Marie Trumbull." My eye shot right to her as I suddenly recognized both her voice and her face. I flashed back to the mural reveal and the moment where the woman I hadn't seen before congratulated me and then began whispering to some girl, probably her assistant. A smile crept across my face as I realized I was in good graces with the owner of the center.

"Yes, I remember you," I calmly said. "Great to see you again."

"The pleasure is mine. The mural you created is wonderful. You are a very talented young woman," she said, her words floating around me.

"Thank you, but it was a team effort, really. I couldn't have done it without my group." Marie nodded and then the rest of the committee introduced themselves. We quickly got right to business with Patty beginning with a standard review of my file.

"Eve was recommended to us by Judge Cynthia Basin of Riverside, Pennsylvania after being found as an accomplice in an attempted armed robbery. The judge believed that, though she did not play a major role in the crime, she was a participating member of the crime by being present in the car and then proceeding to outrun law enforcement on foot after a long police chase ensued," she announced to the board. They all peered at their copies of my files closely and glanced up at me every once in a while. In just a flash, I saw myself, out of breath and running for my life as Johnny led me to the pits. I saw myself being pulled into that hole and being shielded by someone I thought I loved. I saw myself shivering and looking up at the stars, hoping that the cops would just let us go, but then I saw the beam of light flash right on my face and the fear in my eyes was unreal. The scene faded away, and I snapped back to my reality-the reality that I made for myself that I could have avoided if I just knew that I was worth more than that.

"It is noted that the judge's decision came after carefully reviewing Eve's somewhat extensive file. She wanted to 'teach a bright girl a hard lesson.' The judge's words, not mine," Patty explained. I raised an eyebrow at that last statement because it was quite obvious that this was a lesson wrapped in consequences, but to know that the judge specifically wrote those words gave me mixed feelings. She thought I was bright-that was a plus, but could I have been taught this "hard lesson" another way? I still had a little trouble accepting that I was there when there were other alternatives, but perhaps that was the point. Maybe I had exhausted my chances without even realizing it and this really was the only place I could come to get some sense knocked into me.

"Miss Johnson," Mr. Davenport, the release authority officer, addressed me. "Based on the progress you've made here, what would you say has been the biggest lesson for you?" he asked me dryly. I could have only imagined the types of files he'd seen in all his years of work and based on his facial expression, nothing seemed to surprise him, not even my file, which seemed to be the worst thing to everyone back home.

I thought deeply about the question because it was a good one. The truth was that I was still grappling with truly accepting my fate, but it got me thinking about all that I had been through; the fights, the "girl gang", the fun, the sadness, the progression, and the regression. I dealt with so many crazy ups and downs in the matter of seven months and I owed it to myself to see the big picture. As Rivers always told me, I was meant to be here. I just had to accept the reason why.

"There's so many," I began. "I realized while here that I actually had it pretty good considering I'd been dragged out of trouble many times before. I was clearly given many chances to straighten up, and

I seemed to find a way to cause more chaos around me. I needed to know that I wasn't bigger than anyone else. I needed to know that I couldn't be a rebel without consequences."

I looked over at Patty who was forcing back a smile and I knew that not only did she agree with my assertions, but she believed I believed them, which I did. It took me getting into those fights, having screaming matches with myself, and pretending like I wasn't devastated and extremely scared that I was here to realize that I had a problem.

"But I think the biggest lesson was understanding my why." Mr. Davenport raised his eyebrows and removed his glasses. His eyes narrowed, and I knew I had his attention.

"I never truly knew why I did those things. It all stemmed from something that I couldn't put my finger on. I realized after getting into the Gems what that something was. I didn't just want to be heard, I wanted to be *seen*. I could never understand why I always felt out of place, even within my own family. They were so different from me and when they tried to mold me to fit their standards and I wouldn't budge, I felt like they turned their backs and shunned me. I felt invisible, like, I didn't matter anymore. So, I searched for a place where I could matter and for people who made me matter, not realizing I was falling into an age-old trap. Now, I'll leave here holding myself responsible for everything I've done and everything I'll do going forward."

Mr. Davenport, Marie, Ms. Jenkins, and Patty all nodded their heads in unison. I was killing it.

"Very eloquent, Miss Johnson," Mr. Davenport commended.

I quipped, "Well, my parents are rich socialites, eloquence comes with the territory," which caused Mr. Davenport to chuckle.

"Great job, Eve," Patty said with a smile. I flashed one back, and now with an extra boost of confidence, I felt ready for all the questions they had for me.

"So, towards the end of your term here at Bennings, we collect progress reports and reviews from various staff and faculty that assess your readiness. You ready to hear?" Patty asked. I nodded, and she went down the list, reading every bit of feedback. Everyone from Mr. Kole and my other teachers, to Ms. Jenkins and Patty, and even CO Rivers *and* CO Bates reviewed me. I nailed all of them. They all expressed their faith in me and in their own ways, expressed how much of a pleasure I was to have around. I felt like I was being read my report card or something, but I wasn't mad at the comments.

They gave me everything they had, asking me about some of the marks on my record, the time I spent in max hall, and how I felt overall about adjusting back to normal life after being away for so long. I readily answered all the questions with no hesitations or stutters. I was ready, and I needed them to know that.

"Last question," Mr. Davenport inserted.

"Shoot."

"What are your plans once you get out?" he asked. For this question, I paused, only because I was juggling between saying the practical answer versus saying the answer I felt was right for me.

"I'm going to invest in me and my art. I plan to take art classes and do whatever I can to stay connected to my creative side. I don't want to lose it again," I stated proudly. A smile spread across Marie's face.

"That's a wonderful answer. The world will be a better place with your art and an even better place with *you* in it," she told me. I took her words and placed them in my mental holding cell along with the other positive affirmations I received throughout my tenure at Bennings. When I was feeling down or unsure about my potential, I was going to remind myself of everyone's words to keep me going.

"You really are a bright young lady and I have no doubt that you will be a productive member of society," Mr. Davenport spoke. My eyes grew wide, and I smiled.

"So, does that mean I'm free to go?" I asked them. They all looked at each other and then at Mr. Davenport.

"On behalf of the state of Ohio, Eve Johnson, you are granted release on May 9th of this year. So, yes, you are free to go." My arms shot up in a reach towards the heavens as I yelped and cheered for myself. The others watched on as I made a complete fool of myself, but I didn't care; in a week, I would be free. I jumped out of my chair and practically ran out of the room before Patty stopped me and busted my emotional high.

"Before you get out of here, we need to go over a few details of your release. I'll reiterate them in the coming days, but so we're clear, your parents will pick you up on the 9th. A time has not been confirmed, but they are looking at the morning sometime. I'll let you know when I get that information from them. You *will* have to report to a case worker once a week for check-ins. Failure to do so will result in a fine or jail time. We don't want that for you, so be there and be on time."

"Oh, *trust* me, I'll be there early. The last thing I want is to be sent to prison. I could barely handle this place," I casually commented, causing all of them to crack a smile.

"Congratulations on a job well done," Patty said, initiating a round of applause through the rest of the room.

"You may go. We will meet tomorrow to begin the out-processing paperwork." I nodded and then bid Mr. Davenport a good day before rushing out of the room to tell everyone that I was getting out. The first person I ran into was Tatiana, who sort of became a friend, even with our history.

"How'd it go?" she asked me. Apparently, she was also scheduled to get out within the next month and a half, so her anxiety was building much like mine was.

"I'm out of here!" I cheered. She smiled and fist bumped me, then gave me a nod of approval. I took several deep breaths and reveled in the fact that I was getting out and I felt great about myself. Just as I turned the corner, I saw Bates and Rivers, who were walking towards me and having a conversation amongst themselves. I rushed towards them, and with a huge smile on my face, I plowed into the both of them, nearly knocking all of us over. I could feel Bates tense up, like he wasn't used to hugs, but then I remembered that we weren't allowed to touch each other in any way, so I backed off and let my beaming face speak for itself. Rivers knew exactly why I was so happy, but Bates didn't understand.

"Thank you guys so much for your reviews," I said sweetly. I sounded like a different person when I spoke to them. It could have been the epic high I was on, but I was beyond jolly and it came through my voice.

"No problem. It was our pleasure, Eve," Rivers said.

"And just so you know, I don't give reviews often. Take that how you will," Bates added. Bates had slowly grown on me since our incident happened and finally, with only a week left, I was at the point where I had nothing but love for him. He still could be a pain in the ass, but I grew to accept it.

"I appreciate it so much guys. It really means a lot. And Bates, I'm sorry people around here misunderstand you. You're really not that bad after all." Bates was left speechless with the most confused look on his face and Rivers chuckled as I skipped down the halls back to my bunk.

"Walk! You still have to follow the rules!" Bates yelled to me.

Just for old times' sake, I yelled, "Sorry!" before slowing down and flashing them both a smile.

twenty-seven.

M *ay 8th. The Day Before My Release.* "Happy birthday to me," I said to myself as I smiled in the bathroom mirror. I had just gotten out of a boiling hot shower that left me refreshed and ready for my big day. The past 18 years seemed like a blur to me; I couldn't pinpoint many of my major milestones or accomplishments I had as a kid. It seemed like all of that disappeared once I got to Bennings; like I was no longer granted access to the few memories I could hold on to for faith in my moments of self-doubt.

I patted my face dry and glanced in the mirror, checking myself out and admiring how different I looked. I had no idea how it was even possible, but oddly enough, my acne breakouts stopped once I got to Bennings and my skin got a little brighter. I loved looking at the new me and better yet, I loved feeling new.

I gently combed through my coils as I detangled them from each other. There wasn't much I could do with my hair without more time and more products, so I threw it in a sleek back bun and proceeded to the cafeteria for breakfast.

I walked slow and let my mind wander, thinking about things I purposely gave little thought to after coming to Bennings. Soon, I imagined my girls, Rachel and Mackie, in front of me and in a blink of an eye, I was daydreaming that I was right back at school in the cafeteria, the day *everything* happened.

•   •   •

"Oh my God, ditch that fool. You're too good for him, Eve," Rachel slammed.

"Yeah, seriously. People been talking and Johnny isn't a good dude," Mackie added. I stared at the text as they continued to plead for me to do the right thing and finally, I groaned and sat back down at the table. I didn't even text Johnny back–I just put my phone on silent and spent the rest of the day with my girls.

Suddenly, I was at Rachel's house hanging out and out of nowhere, Rachel screamed, "Johnny just got arrested for robbery!" My eyes grew wide.

"Wait, what?!" My heart raced as Mackie and I raced over to Rachel to see what she was looking at.

"Yes! I was just scrolling through Facebook and a girl I know from Hoodside who knows Johnny's brother said he was caught racing down the damn highway after failing to rob a credit union. *A credit union!*" Rachel explained. She searched his name in Google, and low and behold, there was his mugshot and an article that was published about 10 minutes before. I looked at the time on the phone; it was almost 8 o'clock. *Those idiots!* I thought to myself.

"It's a good thing you didn't go with him today!" Mackie said almost too casually. I turned my head away from the phone and back to the show we were watching.

"Hey Mackie, what's Ramone's number?" I asked. There was a pause and then a unified squeal that came from both Rachel and Mackie and we all giggled as she scrambled to send me his number.

•   •   •

"Hey, Eve! Happy birthday!" a voice said to me. I glanced up and saw smiling faces turned to me.

I smiled back at the girls and uttered, "Thanks!" before looking down and seeing that I had eaten my entire breakfast while fantasizing about what could have been. I shook my head, trying to get myself sorted out because not only was it my birthday, but it was my graduation day too. This wasn't how I envisioned spending my 18th birthday, in fact, I had an entire party I was planning before I came to Bennings, but I had no choice but to be okay with this alternative.

I headed back to my bunk to get ready and while roaming the halls, I saw a glimpse of Ramone. He flashed his cute smile at me and in a second, the center disappeared, and I was back at school, waiting for the morning bell to ring.

He and his friends walked up to me and my girls and with no shame he asked, "You want to go out with me?"

I could feel a tug at my shirt from behind and then a nudge forward from two hands. Mackie and Rachel had been saying they thought we would make a cute couple since we were sophomores, and I finally was fulfilling their little fantasy.

"Sure, I'd love to," I responded with a flirty smirk and a quick bat of my eyes. In the midst of my imagining, I glanced over and saw Rivers, who I was still secretly in love with, talking down a new intake who seemed to be on the brink of a serious breakdown. I smiled because I remembered being in that position, hopeless and frantic. He had his hands on her shoulders and looked directly into her eyes, leveling with her. *Seeing* her. Rivers was a good guy, and he never ceased to amaze me. He wasn't just my anchor, he had a strong hold over a lot of the girls and he used his power for good.

I kept walking because I was on a time crunch. With each step, I saw a vision of what could have been; being on my first date with Ramone, him seeming nervous despite the confidence he exuded at school; my friends and I at the mall shopping for triple date outfits. Then there was our first kiss, so soft and so passionate. He must've felt as deep as I did because then he asked to make things official. Then there were the football and basketball games, all of us girls cheering on our boys on the sidelines. Whenever they'd score or do something epic, they'd blow a kiss to us in the crowd and we knew it was for us and us alone. Then there was prom; we all decided to color coordinate, so Mackie, Rachel, and I had on varying shades of blue dresses and the boys had on matching ties and bought corsages for us. The smile on my face–it was so big and real. I was happy.

"Eve, wake up," I heard echoing throughout the decorated gym as I danced with Ramone and my friends.

"Wake up!" I felt a tug and then a push and when I opened my eyes, I was almost face to face with CO Tankard. I was so startled, not only about seeing her, but how I ended up in my bed. I must have been so deep in thought that I didn't realize I had jumped in my bunk for a nap. The time read 9:50, meaning I had been asleep for a while and it was almost time for my big moment.

"You ready?" Tankard asked me. I nodded and grabbed my graduation robe hanging on the railing of Brit's old bunk. I slid it on and though I didn't feel the power that moment had yet, I knew that I'd get emotional at some point.

Tankard walked ahead, but I stopped after seeing myself in the mirror. My eyes went right to my bright green sweatshirt and again, I had a moment, but not about what my life could have been–it was about what it was. I saw Specs' smile the first day we met, I heard Brit's laugh that echoed throughout the halls, and I felt Gigi's soft curly hair as I brushed it. The fights, the makeups, the gossiping, and the growth–I saw and felt it all. I could feel Tankard's eyes on me and even sensed her annoyance with me, but I kept my arms wrapped around myself, holding on to the memories I had.

"We're going to be late," she said. I shot her a look and let the moment sink in. I was now 18, I was graduating, and I was only a day away from being free. I wished I had more time, but the world didn't revolve around me.

I paced behind Tankard, being sure to take a mental screenshot of everything I passed, the posters, the bulletin boards, even the occasional flickering light. The halls were empty, but I still saw old images of being dragged out of bed by Tatiana as we passed the intake bunk, and chatting and laughing with Brit, Specs, and Gigi as we passed the cafeteria. As we strutted closer, we passed the Gem meeting room, and I saw our circle gathering and learning.

Tankard led me right into the auditorium and the sound of cheers rang through my ears and I saw nothing but smiling faces. Everyone was already seated and ready to go, so they *really* were waiting on me to begin. I guess *some* things didn't have to change. The small sea of blue, purple, red, and green sweatshirts sprang up out of their chairs to give me applause, but my attention drifted away from their support when I saw a few familiar faces I wasn't expecting to see.

Specs, Brit, and Gigi sat together, in their normal clothes and with huge smiles on their faces. Tears immediately welled up in my eyes as they waved and blew kisses at me. I didn't have to look for the next surprise because I could hear them before I could see them.

"That's my girl! Yas, Eve!" Mackie and Rachel both yelled, prompting the rest of the audience to laugh. I was on the verge of an ugly cry as I waved to them giddily, but then I stopped. The most unexpected guests were sitting third row center. Kobi, Chelsie, my mom, and my dad sat together. They sat with smiles and approving glances, but all I could see was that court room they also sat in when the judge ordered me to come here. I stopped breathing for a second and a conflicting rush of emotions raced throughout my body, starting at my feet and heading towards my head. Anger and frustration raced elation and happiness as I continued to my seat, never taking my eyes off them. The battle was neck and neck, but a smile inched across my face and I even managed to wave back at them before I turned around and got in a zone. I was the only one graduating and leaving that month, so all eyes and attention were on me. Patty hopped on the mic and began the ceremony.

"It is a very special day for a very special young woman. Today we are not only celebrating our one and only Eve Johnson's graduation, but today is also her 18th birthday." The crowd roared and I could barely hear myself think, but one thing was sure; any doubts I had about my worthiness were being proved wrong. I blushed as I soaked in all the love and good juju I was getting from my peers and my family. I tried my hardest to listen to the speech Patty was giving, but the racing thoughts that crisscrossed in my mind made it hard to focus. I didn't have to imagine Rachel and Mackie being with me on graduation day, as they actually were, but when I closed my eyes, they were no longer sitting behind me in support, they were sitting next to me with caps and gowns of their own.

When I looked behind me, I didn't see a bunch of society's throwaways; I saw Ramone and the rest of our classmates in our school colors. We sat in a large gymnasium, waiting for our rows to be led to the stage and finally, it was my turn. As I heard my name being called, a rush of energy burst in me. The crowd was cheering, as they did for all the other graduates, and just as I got my diploma cover and took my photo, I spotted my family in the crowd of a couple thousand people. All four of them were there, and they were going crazy, even my dad.

I held back a breakdown, but I wasn't fully prepared to deal with the feelings that came with knowing I wasn't able to have a normal graduation, that I would miss prom, or that I wasn't able to do any of the things I imagined today. I sat in silence, letting it all go and when I opened my eyes, I felt lighter, I felt proud, and I felt accomplished.

"Eve, would you like to say anything?" Patty asked me. I'm sure I looked like a deer in headlights because I certainly wasn't planning on saying anything, but when I heard, "Speech! Speech! Speech! Speech!" being chanted behind me, I swallowed my nerves and decided to take a whack at it. As soon as I stepped to the podium and saw the crowd, I became heavy, not with burdens, shame, or anger, but with love and fulfillment. Seeing the smiling faces, all looking at me expressing how proud they were of me made me forget that I was in a detention center.

"Thank you," I said to the cheerful crowd as they settled down. "First, I have to thank Patty for being patient and putting up with me. Without people like you, girls like me wouldn't be able to get through something like this, or *anything* for that matter." The girls from the center all cheered for Patty as she smiled from ear to ear, blushing at the sound of her name bouncing off the walls.

"Of course, I have to thank the staff here, Ms. Jenkins, the COs, and everyone who worked with me and kept me focused. It's been a trying seven months, but I made it." More applause erupted, and I cleared my throat to begin the sappy, emotional part of the speech.

"I look out into the audience and I see so many people I'm grateful for. Rachel and Mackie-my road dogs until the end. Thank you for always being there for me and visiting, even when you didn't have to."

They both stood up and screamed together, "We love you, Evie!" and then followed up their chant with a bunch of whooping and hollering. The crowd laughed, as did I even though I was used to their dramatic antics.

"To all the girls currently here, thank you for being so great to me." I looked directly at Gigi, Brit, and Specs–my posse. My ride or dies.

"Girl gang!" I shouted into the mic with a valley girl voice. The girl gang sprang up out of their seats and shouted it back in their best valley girl impressions, causing more laughter and claps in the audience.

"Those girls right there," I said pointing to them. "They're very special to me. Thank you for being exactly what I needed. You taught me so much, and I wouldn't be who I am right now without you." My eyes immediately met Mom's, and when I saw her beaming smile, I had to take a second and tell myself that this was a real moment and that my family's presence didn't have to be fake or for show. For my own sake, I could see it as real. Instead of tearing down their attempts, I could learn to assume that they meant well.

"I want to thank my family for being here. I know I caused a lot of problems and I did a lot of damage, but I hope that I can make things better between us." I watched all four of them acknowledge me, but I paid special attention to my dad. He had remained stone-faced throughout the ceremony give or take a few smiles he tried to hide. He stared right at me and his smile, though timid, was evident.

"We love you too, Eve!" my sister yelled out, which started a chain reaction that resulted in a final standing ovation. I took my bow and proceeded to leave the stage, but not before hugging Patty.

"Thank you," I whispered in her ear.

She whispered back, "Be proud of yourself. You did it." I stood back behind the podium, hiding myself as I wiped away a tear as Patty took the mic.

"Eve Johnson, you are an official graduate of the Bennings Detention Center for Young Women's Rehabilitation Program. Well done." My ears rang and my eyes glazed over as I stopped fighting my feels. I stopped crying long enough to do the traditional hat toss and no longer felt like crying but cheering because I was transformed.

Once Patty wrapped up the graduation, she invited everyone to stay and chat for a bit and reminded the rest of the girls that they still had to go to lunch. I immediately ran to Rachel and Mackie and gripped them in the tightest hug I could. I hadn't seen them in a few months, but it felt like a year and I missed them like crazy.

"We got you something, but we couldn't bring it in, so we'll just give it to you when you come home," Rachel disclosed.

"It's a bouquet of flowers, dinner on us, and some gift cards for a shopping spree," Mackie spilled the beans, causing Rachel to give her a stink face and roll her eyes.

"I'm sorry, y'all know I get excited about stuff!" Mackie shrugged. I didn't care that she told me. All I cared about was that in less than 24 hours, I would be back home, and I would finally have some food worth savoring.

"It's okay, we have a lot to catch up on and you know I will need some new clothes!" I brought them into another group hug and then spotted my girl gang hanging back waiting for their turn to talk to me. I rushed to them and all four of us embraced. I looked each one of them up and down to get a good look at them; I was so used to seeing them in sweats and Keds, so their style choices never even crossed my mind.

"You guys look so cute in your normal people clothes!" I told them. I stared at them in disbelief as they stood in front of me; Specs in a cute floral spring dress and white Converse sneakers, Brit decked out in Nike apparel, and Gigi showing off her curves in leggings and a light blouse. I couldn't believe they showed up at my graduation. Brit explained that Patty helped them get back in contact with each other and they coordinated to come surprise me. My heart became full, and I had to hug them one more time to make sure it was real.

I turned to Rachel and Mackie and waved them over to meet the girl gang. They all hugged each other, and my heart soared seeing my two groups of friends chumming it up so naturally.

"Thanks for going easy on my girl," Mackie said pointing to me. "We *all* know how she can be." I shot Mackie a look but couldn't help but smile because she *was* right.

"Eve is one of the coolest girls I've ever met," Specs said, hugging me once more. I forgot how comforting Specs was. Once she left, I learned not to need her, but seeing her now, it made me never want to let her go.

"Yeah, she all right," Gigi smirked. We all chatted for a little bit, sharing stories, most of them at my expense, when out of the corner of my eye, I saw my mom wave me over. I excused myself from the circle and took a deep breath with every step I took towards them. The first one to hug me was Chelsie, then Kobi, and then mom and dad pulled me into one hug together. Things were still a bit awkward and weird. There was a strange air and clear tension still among us that was hard to ignore. I just stood there, smiling at them as they each congratulated me on graduating and getting out.

"We're sorry we couldn't come visit you, Eve. Work and school had us really tied up," my brother claimed. I raised my hand, letting him know he didn't have to apologize or make excuses, though in the back of my mind, I still replayed the image of all four of them sitting in that court room.

"It's okay. I don't hold it against you."

They hugged me again, and just as I was about to ask Chelsie how school was going, I heard a sniffle that drew my attention to my mom, who was patting her under eyes, trying not to mess up her makeup.

"Oh Mom," I said hugging her again.

"I'm sorry, I'm just so proud of you," she stuttered through her hiccups.

"Me too," Dad added. "We all are."

"Thank you," I said with a smile.

"So, how are you feeling now that you're done with all of this?" Kobi asked, play punching me in the shoulder.

I blocked his light jabs and responded, "I'm ready to be home, but I'm sort of sad to leave too."

Patty tapped the mic. "Ms. Jenkins just had a wonderful idea! Eve, would you like to show off your mural to everyone who hasn't seen it?" I smiled and nodded and began a brigade down the hall, leading my family and friends to the cafeteria where they'd get to see my beautiful masterpiece-the first of many.

Everyone piled into the cafeteria, all their eyes growing wide as they first laid eyes on the mural. Specs was the first to lose her mind. She jumped up and down and ran to the wall, tracing her hand over the rainbow and the field of flowers.

"Oh my gosh, it looks so good, Eve!" she exclaimed. Her excitement gave me a rush, and I felt like I was leading a group through a museum of my own art. I held my head high and presented it to everyone, detailing the thought process behind each section of the painting and the overall theme of the mural.

"It was a team effort," I said.

Tati pushed through the crowd and said, "But you were the leader, and you did ya' thing!" I graciously bowed as everyone clapped and individually walked up to the mural to feel it for themselves. Gigi helped finish it, so she stood back, but she still was in awe of how good it looked. Specs, Brit, Rachel, and Mackie all stepped closer to get a better view, Rachel even taking out her phone and snapping pictures of it.

"This is *so* good, Eve!" Rachel said. "This is definitely going on my Instagram."

"Yo, *this* is crazy!" Brit patted me on the back. "You killed this!"

"I knew my girl was good at something!" Mackie interjected. I let her back-handed compliment go and shifted my eyes to my family, who stood back staring at the mural. My sister and brother looked a bit shocked and even confused, but my parents showed a different kind of intensity on their faces.

"I didn't know you were into art, Eve," Chelsie remarked.

Kobi added, "Yeah, this is phenomenal. My office could use some sprucing up. I'll talk to the facilities team there and see if I can get you in to do something for us." I thanked Kobi for the hook up and he put me in a chokehold like old times. After getting free from his grip, I glanced over at my parents, who seemed especially entranced by the mural. I couldn't be sure what was going through their heads, but something told me they were proud of me.

"Okay everyone, gather around!" Patty called out to us. In her hands was a sheet cake with "Happy Birthday & Graduation Eve!" on it. I was shocked because at most, we only got a personal cake, but I assumed because it was my graduation and I had quite a few guests, that it was made to accommodate everyone. Everyone gathered around and sang, and soon, the melody got drowned out by the permeating thoughts of what I had hoped my birthday would have been like if I wasn't at Bennings. I closed my eyes, trying to picture my party, but oddly enough, I couldn't see a thing. All of a sudden, the singing became clear again, and I recognized that I didn't need to think about what could have been because what was here now was perfect.

"...Happy birthday to you!" everyone finished and cheered for me.

"Make a wish!" Specs yelled. I smiled at her, and then at Gigi and Brit who were smiling back. Before I blew out my candles, I took one last look at the people around me. I looked into each of their faces and saw love, empathy, and light and I could feel their energies swirling around me and protecting me and this moment.

I closed my eyes and thought to myself, *I wish this feeling would never end*, and with one blow, I sent that wish into the atmosphere, hoping it would come true.

twenty-eight.

ay 9th. The Day I Left Bennings. I couldn't sleep much, and I figured that would happen. There was way too much excitement bubbling up in me to even think about letting that feeling die down to get some rest. I managed to get a few hours of rest, but when I woke up from my nap, the clock read 7 a.m. and I jumped out of bed feeling light and ready for the day.

The rest of the girls were up, preparing to head to breakfast, but I decided that my first meal of the day had to be on the outside, so I ignored my screaming stomach. I couldn't remember what good food that wasn't rationed out like we were in the apocalypse tasted like, so I didn't mind holding out for that. I kept myself busy by doing some last-minute cleaning and tidying up. I neatly folded up my blankets and sheets, packed up my handmade cards and other random items I collected while at Bennings in a box CO Bates gave me, and began making my rounds saying goodbye to the girls. I stopped at Tatiana's bunk first and for the first time ever, she gave me a hug. She squeezed me tight and I could feel the endearment she had for me in it.

"Be good, you hear me?" I told her. She smiled sheepishly and nodded her head.

"You too, princess," she said putting her hand up for a fist bump. After I had my moment with Tatiana, I searched out the rest of the mural group and said my goodbyes, being sure to thank them for all their help and friendship.

"I'll miss you," each one of them said, even Becky, who I thought couldn't care less that I was leaving. I walked the halls for a bit, first popping in to give Ms. Jenkins one last hug and stopping each CO I saw and giving them a hug goodbye. CO Bates was as jumpy as he was the first time I gave him a hug, but I told him not to fight it and he gave in. He was warm and his embrace was soothing. When I ran into Rivers, I stopped and stared for a moment and so did he. A smile inched across his face, and he opened his arms, inviting me in for a hug. I smiled back widely as I fell right into his arms and buried my head into his chest. I wanted to savor his smell, his touch, his peace, and his aura. I didn't want this to be the last time I'd see him, but since it would be, I had to make it count.

"I'm proud of you," he whispered to me. I nodded my head and muttered back, "Thank you."

"Good luck with everything and stay well. You got this," he said to me. I nodded. I was going to miss Rivers' way of moving me with his simple language. He didn't make me feel bad about myself, but he made me see where I could be better. I had hoped that I'd meet a man like Rivers who would love me enough to support and teach me just like him.

"I will. Stay sweet," I told him, poking him in the stomach. He chuckled a little, holding his stomach as he tried to hide that he was ticklish, and he nodded.

"I'll try," he said back. "You headed to Patty's now?"

I nodded. "Yeah, my parents should be here. They got a hotel not too far from here so they could pick me up first thing this morning."

"Here, I'll walk with you."

Patty's office wasn't far from where we were, but it was sweet of him to see me off. Patty's door was wide open and as usual, her face was buried in her computer screen. I cleared my throat so she'd know I was there without barging in on her while she was in the middle of working. She looked up and a smile spread across her face.

"Good morning, Eve. How are you feeling today?"

"I'm feeling ready," I responded. She seemed pleased, and she slid a piece of paper towards me.

"All right, let's make it official." I glanced over the document asking that I certify that I was being released today. I quickly signed my name and slid the paper back over to her. She then handed me the typical transition package that every girl got on her last day. In the canvas bag was a journal, a pen, a toothbrush and toothpaste, pads, floss, and some pamphlets about resources I could use when I got back home. I glanced up at her, somewhat amused because I didn't need half the stuff in my pack, but I secured the bag on my arm, anyway.

"Thank you for putting up with me," I uttered. She sort of chuckled to herself and shook her head.

"Believe me, you were an angel compared to some of the girls that come here." I laughed too because she was right-there were some absolute terrors at the center, even now, but I kept my mouth shut.

CO Bates marched in right after that and announced, "Eve's parents are here."

Patty looked at me and asked, "Are you sure you're ready?"

I nodded and stood up, making sure my posture was tall and exuded the level of confidence I felt. Patty led the way and CO Bates and Rivers followed behind as we walked towards the front entrance. We stopped at the storage room where all the girls' outside belongings were held and CO Fillman handed me my box. I took one look at the tattered shirt and dirty jeans and shook my head.

"I-I can't wear that," I told her. She looked at Patty, who then without a word, stepped away into the meeting room just up ahead where my parents were waiting. She soon emerged with a small bag and a smile on her face.

"You're in luck. Your parents brought you some clothes." I sighed heavily and grabbed the bag, sifting through the items they brought for me to change into. As much as I thought they didn't pay attention to me, they knew to bring my favorite maxi dress; it flowed freely in the wind and made me feel like I could fly. It was very fitting, given the occasion.

Patty unlocked the door to the changing room and I quickly got dressed, but took my time admiring myself in the mirror. I finally looked like me, but I was much different. When I walked out of the changing room, I handed CO Fillman my sweatpants and t-shirt I wore, but I held on to the green sweatshirt for a little while longer. Photographs of memories flashed through my head and once I got to the last one of me in front of my cake surrounded by everyone I loved, I was able to let it go.

"It's been real," I said as I handed it over to CO Fillman. I looked right over at the box of my old stuff and said, "Please burn that whole box."

Patty laughed and responded with, "We can't burn it, but we will get rid of it." As long as I didn't have to go back home with it, I didn't care what happened to it. Patty opened the door to the meeting room and there my parents sat, seeming sort of antsy.

"You look great and well-rested," my mom said as I walked over to them.

"I feel great," I told her, initiating a hug. She held me close to her and kissed my forehead, which added to the love I already felt from her. She stepped to one side of me and my dad stepped to the other, each of them grabbing a hold of me in a secure grip. We connected and interlocked arms so that no one could let go.

I looked at the both of them with a smile and just as we walked out the door, I looked back at Patty and mouthed, "Thank you." She waved and mouthed, "Be good," and then the doors closed behind us.

We continued our walk to the car, still locked together. I began taking deep breaths and taking everything in. Seven months ago, I saw this very same scene but was coming into it. Now, I was coming out and things would be different.

"We got something for you," my dad said to me, handing me a new phone. My eyes lit up as I grabbed it.

"Thank you!" I said.

"You're welcome. I'll pay the bill until you can find a job, fair enough?" Dad asked. We locked eyes in the rearview mirror. He had never asked if anything was "fair enough" let alone ever really gave me an option. Perhaps he had changed a little too.

"Yeah, that's more than fair. I'll get one soon, I promise," I said as I began setting it up.

"Are you hungry?" Mom asked.

"I could eat just about any and everything right now," I responded. We all smiled, and I could tell that things would work out, or at least get a little better. I got my head out of my phone for a bit to revel in the moment.

I was leaving Bennings.

I rolled my window down and poked my head out, just as the gates closed thinking, *Thank you, God.* The day was so clear and beautiful. The air was warm, but not unbearable and a breeze brushed across my face and through my hair.

"I'm free," I whispered to myself. "And I'm here."

epilogue.

I couldn't have picked a more perfect time. It was early fall, and the weather hadn't turned crisp yet, but it was getting a tad bit cooler, which was the perfect work environment. I lined up my paint cans along the wall of the brownstone building I was commissioned to work on by the city, and I admired the good start I had the week before. When completed, the mural would consist of an assortment of smaller flowers that, when put together, created larger flowers, and overlapping the flowers would be the message, *Dare to Bloom.* I hadn't yet imagined the background yet, but it would be colorful and attractive. It was a bit ironic considering there wasn't much greenery or color in Hoodside, but that's what I was going for.

Concrete and brick made up the landscape of this side of town, but when I approached the city council about doing some work, they told me of this area and how they had plans of housing a small, outdoor farmer's market where the residents could get fresh produce and meats at affordable prices. I knew this was the perfect place to put it.

They gave me a deadline of four months to finish the mural so it could be unveiled right before Christmas during the first Winter festival in the area that would precede the farmer's market coming in the early spring. I figured that I'd be done well before then since I didn't have much going on; I was starting school in the spring as an art major at Riverside Art Institute, and was only working part time as a class assistant at an art studio in downtown Riverside.

I had a solid plan of how I would section off the mural and work on several parts according to color. This week I was working on the purple areas, so I began my mixing, popped in my music, and was transported into my own world where there was nothing but me and my paint. If I hadn't turned around for a split second to sneeze, I would have been scared half to death at my parents, who popped up out of nowhere. I took my headphones out and walked over to them, a bit confused by how they even found me.

They took their time getting out of their BMW and awkwardly stood in front of me for a few moments.

"You're making great progress," my mom said. I looked back at the work I had completed and nodded. I had gotten a lot done, but I could get more done if they didn't show up unannounced.

"Yeah, I should be done before the deadline for sure," I claimed. "It's kind of funny though. I'm actually getting paid to paint on walls."

Mom giggled and knew what I was getting at, but dad remained straight-faced and didn't want to acknowledge the lighthearted joke. After I left home, whenever I saw him, he always seemed like he wanted to say a lot but would never do so. In fact, he just wouldn't say anything. I wasn't about to waste precious daylight and time waiting on him to say anything remotely productive, so I went back to working on what I was there to do.

After a few more moments, he asked, "Do you need anything?"

I kept painting, but I replied, "Like what?"

"Like food, clothes, some money?" Mom jumped in. I shook my head.

"Are you positive?"

"I'm as positive as I've ever been," I said finishing a mini flower before turning my attention back to them. "How did you find me, anyway?"

"We went by your apartment and Mackie said you were here," Mom said. I rolled my eyes and vowed not to tell Mackie anything again because she couldn't keep stuff private.

When I left Bennings, things were okay. They weren't bad, but they weren't good. They were just different, mainly because I genuinely changed and my parents tried to convince me they did too, though they couldn't fool me. No, I wasn't being harsh on them. I left the center with an open mind and heart and walked back into that house hoping we really could be better together. It only took a week for me to see that their actions had no real merit behind them, so I packed a bag and my laptop and dipped. I even told them I was leaving, but they didn't believe me. It was only after being at a transition house for an entire week that they saw that I was serious. They practically begged me to come home, but I rejected their offer.

What was the point? To continue to be ignored and talked down to? It seemed like their respect level for me rose a tad bit since I was an adult, but that was about it. I was still being treated like I wasn't trustworthy and that I didn't know what was good for me, and though

I understood why, we came to an understanding that we'd all be better. I couldn't be the only one making a real effort.

I spent a few weeks in the transition house, just so I could take a break from life and then went to the bank where I had an account that my parents knew nothing about and withdrew my secret stash. It was dirty money, but I figured it was better to put it to good use. I hit up Mackie, who was staying in the area to go to the City Institute of Architecture & Design, and I asked if she would want to be my roommate. She was ecstatic because she also wasn't trying to stay at her parents' house and be bound by their rules, so she immediately moved out and we both put money down on the place.

It was humbler than we were used to and was only a couple blocks away from some of the roughest parts of Hoodside, but we loved it and it had everything we needed.

We invited Rachel to stay with us for the summer, but she passed because she got a job as a camp counselor to earn some extra cash and was going to be gone practically the entire break. She promised us that she'd link back up with us when she got back, but we weren't going to have long with her because she was going to USC soon after that to attend Freshman Week.

Things were moving for all of us in our own ways. I was happy to still have Mackie here with me, but I never stopped thinking about my girl gang. We quickly found each other on Facebook, and we exchanged numbers. We had a whole group chat, and we talked often, but most of the texts were pictures and memes we discovered after being gone for so long. I kept my promise to Gigi and sent her some money. She messaged me privately and told me she couldn't take it, but I told her it was too bad. I wasn't going to miss a few stacks, but I knew she could get herself going quicker if she had it. She thanked me and told me she'd send me something as soon as she and her siblings settled into their new place together. I was glad to know that all of them were happy and thriving, including Vera.

"Are you sure you don't need anything? Do you feel safe? Should we get someone to burglar-proof the place?" Mom asked frantically. I knew her worry came from a good place, but it was a tad misplaced. The apartment Mackie and I shared was close to a bad area of town, but we lived in a newly renovated apartment with 24-7 security and front desk operations thanks to gentrification. Not to mention, when I ran around these same streets with Johnny, I met tons of people. My parents didn't know this, but I was well-respected and looked after, even after Johnny went to jail. I was doing just fine.

"I'm good, Mom. Thanks for your concern, but please don't worry yourself to death."

"Okay, I just have to make sure. We are worried about you, Eve," my mom maintained. "Plus, your brother and sister also worry about you. At least now I can tell them that you're okay."

I thought about Chelsie and Kobi and how quickly they continued on with their wonderful lives. They were lucky to have their stuff together and therefore didn't have to deal with mom and dad on a regular basis. I missed them, and told myself I needed to call them more, but they could also do the same.

"For the last time, I'm just peachy. I got a lot of work to do today, so..." I said returning to my mural. Talking to them was draining, and I decided that when I felt my energy depleting, I would end our conversations before I bled dry. They learned to recognize when I checked out and they would go on their merry way. I watched them hop in the car, but before they drove off, the car stopped right beside me, and the driver's side window came down.

"It looks really good, Eve. I'm proud of you," Dad said. It seemed a bit forced, but I took it.

"Thanks, Dad. I'm proud of myself too."

"You're well on your way to painting ceilings."

I stopped for a second and looked at him. He gave me a head nod, slipped on his sunglasses, and then drove off. I watched the car as it sped down the road and around the corner. I didn't think there was anything my dad could say to redeem himself, but he proved me wrong. With one sentence, I knew that he got me. Though he'd never show it, or even explicitly say it, he saw me and that was all I could ask.

"You're well on your way to painting ceilings."

Yeah. I am.

the end.

about
the author.

Dominique J. Smiley is an author, publisher, entrepreneur, travel blogger, and vlogger. She graduated from Howard University in 2015 with a bachelor's degree in journalism and a minor in theater arts. She is a proponent of education, the environment, and the arts, and works to one day spend the rest of her life traveling the world, while doing what she loves – writing.

CPSIA information can be obtained
at www.ICGtesting.com
Printed in the USA
BVHW030426140820
586335BV00001B/39